PETALS AND VIOLINS
FIFTEEN UNSETTLING TALES

PETALS AND VIOLINS

FIFTEEN UNSETTLING TALES

D.P. Watt

Tartarus Press

Petals and Violins, Fifteen Unsettling Tales
by D.P. Watt
First published 2019 by Tartarus Press at
Coverley House, Carlton-in-Coverdale, Leyburn,
North Yorkshire, DL8 4AY, UK

This paperback edition published 2023

CONTENTS

For
Alfred
Euan
Watt

INTRODUCTION

THE SANITY OF MADNESS:
AN INTRODUCTION TO D.P.WATT
Peter Holman

Why do I make the things I make? The only things I have are my interests.

Jeff Koons

Dr Warren looked up at the grey sky in the forlorn hope that the heavens would answer his question. 'I don't think I'm getting anywhere at all,' he said at last. 'Thirty years on the couch and I've never met anyone quite like him.' This was a surprising admission. The British public had grown used to Warren's ability to diagnose and ameliorate if not cure many of the quirkier manifestations of disordered consciousness, and his trademark battered corduroy jackets, linen shirts and calculatedly scruffy silver hair made him a popular 'talking head' in documentaries. His particular interest was the psychology and psychopathology of collecting, but this had been vulgarised by a succession of television producers who summoned him whenever they needed intellectual ballast and sententious generalisations about hoarders for freakshows such as *Obsessive Compulsive Britain* or *Stuffed with Stuff*. It did not, however, detract from the influence of his various scholarly papers, and many of his rivals regarded him with more than a hint of jealousy as he segued casually between media appearances and his clinical work. He was experienced, perceptive and resourceful. I'd only worked with him for a few months but that was more than long enough to know that if he was puzzled, he had good reason to be.

We walked back from the cafeteria towards his office, and I noticed again how quiet and relaxing St Marsha's was. Set in attractively landscaped grounds dotted with ancient cedars, it boasted a sweeping gravel drive, an ornamental lake and a lovely late-Victorian bronze of a dancing faun which capered among the trees. Traffic noise was but an occasional intrusion. Once the home of an Edwardian textile tycoon, the main house retained much of its period charm, its modern additions being discreet and out-of-the-way. It was very different from the NHS psychiatric hospitals where I had 'cut my teeth', but that's the private sector for you. Strictly speaking, St Marsha's wasn't even a hospital but 'a therapeutic community' which occupied a slightly uncertain niche between spa, health farm, and care home. The website explained that inmates (a word not to be used under any circumstances) were 'guests' or 'residents', and staff were friendly and low-key. We weren't R.D. Laing revivalists by any means, but we liked to think that we appreciated the pressures of modern life and recognised what Warren often called *the sanity of madness*. Although we did have several nurses who could have played front row for the All Blacks and the usual arsenal of chemical coshes, no one at St Marsha's was reckoned to be dangerous, either to themselves or others. Having had a few dicey moments in other institutions, I appreciated the relaxed regime and the quiet dignity of most of the 'residents'. The sanatorium offered a 'healing space', a retreat from the world without the necessity of spiritual commitment, somewhere in which the troubled and lost could 'find' and 'be' themselves. People came of their own volition, only rarely being referred by professionals. Some stayed a weekend, some a month. Warren's enigma, Dr D.P. Watt, had so far been resident for over two years.

'In my experience,' said Warren, 'collectors tend to tip over into hoarding as a consequence of a personal trauma such as bereavement, or else they are so self-absorbed that they don't notice that their accumulation is reaching problematic proportions. One thing quite literally leads to another, and there's often no one to recognise the warning signs. They'll usually concentrate on a single item—medals, matchboxes, mustard spoons, Roman coins—but some conduct their campaigns on multiple fronts. Our friend Watt is such a fellow, but the range of his interests and knowledge is unusually idiosyncratic. He's not exactly a hoarder, but he is insatiably curious about objects, which he claims may even have some form of consciousness.'

'Wouldn't that make them subjects?'

'We've been through that,' said Warren. 'More to the point, his acquisitions seem to be increasing at a rate of knots. As a connoisseur of everything from Amarone to Airfix kits, he has all manner of obsessions to keep him company. He even claims to have a doctorate in Germanic philosophy.' Warren pointed to the main house. 'He has a suite of rooms up on the top floor, for which he's paying exorbitant rates, especially in view of all the belongings he has in storage and the meals and wine he has brought in. I don't know where the money comes from, though I can see where a lot of it goes. He's very cagey about his finances, but it's not really my business to intrude. The mind, not the wallet, is my domain.'

I was reassured by this, for there are those in the profession whose assessments are guided chiefly by the social status of their patients—the wealthy are eccentric, only the poor are bonkers (to use a technical term). I hoped Warren was not prone to such crass distinctions.

'Why did he come here in the first place?' I asked. Other staff had made passing comments, but as he was considered Warren's 'case', they had been less than forthcoming. As the senior practitioner at St Marsha's, he alone had proper access to Watt's notes and their face-to-face sessions were strictly confidential. I'd only seen Watt a couple of times, once when he was practising Tai Chi beside the lake one morning, and once when he had appeared at a window wearing a remarkable feathered mask which I later discovered to have been modelled on those worn during the worship of Quetzalcoatl. It had given me quite a shock. I couldn't recall us having spoken, though the mask episode had led to a particularly vivid and rather unsettling dream several nights later.

'Oddly enough, he says he needed a break, though I don't yet know what he was taking a break from. Was it the attritional banality of existence, or had a specific event driven him to come here? Other people might go on holiday, rent a villa in Tuscany or the Greek Islands, but not him. He checks into an expensive hosp, er, *centre*, and devotes himself to compiling what he terms "a collection". He writes, you see, but even his creative acts are governed by his central obsession with gathering and accumulation. I suspect he's been that way since childhood. He has made some intriguing comments about his schooldays.'

'What does he want from St Marsha's?'

'Oh, he isn't seeking a cure, if that's what you're wondering.' Warren took off his glasses and gave me the look he usually addressed to the television cameras before the final commercial break. 'He wants confirmation, even endorsement, of his *Weltanschauung*. There's something he wants to get off his chest, but he's obviously enjoying not telling me what it might be. He's drip-feeding me the story. I'm not his doctor or therapist, at least, not in any practical sense. I seem to be more of a sounding board. Either there is a streak of morbid secrecy in his character, or else perhaps he's just like Wilde and lives in terror of *not* being misunderstood.' He laughed. 'Perhaps I'll be able to tell you more after our afternoon meeting. I must say he makes excellent coffee.'

⁊

Client confidentiality is a curious thing. When does an honest request for a second opinion become a breach of trust? I could tell Warren was wrestling with an ethical dilemma, one which he chose not to confide in his more established colleagues or, indeed, our nominal boss, Dr Yarwood, whom we saw only rarely, her life being spent in a whirl of civic functions, charity dinners, and, it was unkindly said, a haze of opiates. The next day we met for lunch, venturing off-site to The Bluebell where we could sit in the garden and smoke undisturbed, even if the days of liquid lunches were long gone. I asked him how he'd got on with the mysterious Dr Watt. Warren rolled his eyes.

The meeting had got off to a curious start, he told me, as he had found Watt lolling in a tall, winged leather chair surrounded by the remains of a number of crab sandwiches and a bottle of Sancerre. On his lap was a complex marionette whose strings he was attempting to disentangle. Similar puppets hung from the walls, reminding Warren of the dead crows that gamekeepers leave dangling to warn others. There were sundry masks, circus posters, and small, darkly-framed photographs of what seemed the nondescript marketplace of an unnamed town. On an antique bureau was a partially completed plastic model of a Focke-Wulf FW190 'Butcher Bird' which was being painted in arctic livery for the Russian front. 'I'd just made the same one with my son,' Warren said, sheepishly. 'But Watt has a lot more pots of paint than we have.' Tiny tubs of enamel were meticulously arranged on a narrow shelf.

Much of the room was taken up with Watt's library or 'exterior brain', as he called it. Books on folklore and the occult jostled with works on European theatre, puppetry, the history of Punch and Judy, photographic folios of ossuaries and abandoned weapons installations, old picture postcards of the Hapsburg empire and silent film stars, wine guides and folios bound in calf-skin which Warren said looked like they'd been purloined from the library of a stately home. The names meant little to Warren—Aickman, Ligotti, Machen, Oliver, Schulz, 'Mr James'. Other books had Cyrillic letters along their spines, sometimes in gold or silver leaf. An ornate clock ticked slowly and heavily on the mantelpiece as if contemplating the nature of time itself.

'His rooms feel like something from the late-nineteenth century,' Warren said. 'You half expect Raffles and Bunny to drop by for a whiskey-and-soda. Sometimes, he doesn't open the curtains for a fortnight, lighting the room with those funny old-fashioned lamps that don't give any light. Other times he's up half the night, scribbling in notebooks or clicking away on his laptop. A very industrious chap. He started out by telling me all about his love of the Norfolk coast, Sheringham, Cromer, the out-of-the way places between Hunstanton and Great Yarmouth where he used to go as a child and fish for crabs in the harbours. I'm sure it has some significance for him beyond simply being a pleasant memory.'

'Always nice when someone does have pleasant memories of childhood,' I said wryly. 'Not something we're used to, is it?'

Warren smiled. 'A tough exoskeleton guards a soft body. It defends itself with sharp pincers, and always moves sideways rather than forwards. Perhaps the crab is an oblique image of the self? Jung would have him down as a Cancerian, though I think he's actually a Taurus.'

'What about this writing he's doing?'

'I've only skimmed it,' Warren said. 'He won't let me take it away, so I've had to read it *in situ*. Rather good. A bit weird at times but undeniably imaginative. He uses those Norfolk and east coast settings very evocatively. He writes all sorts of things, from off-kilter ghostly tales to theatrical . . . phantasmagoria. I'm not one for theatre myself though. I couldn't make head or tail of it.'

We sat with our sandwiches and coffee while a blackbird whistled from the birch tree at the end of the garden. 'In fact,' Warren went on, 'I can't make much sense of any of it. I can't work him out at all. His mind is so restless. One minute he's alluding to the crab shack in Sheringham, the next he's critiquing Heidegger or discoursing on the performance practices of Balinese shadow-puppeteers. Most of his mail comes from Poland, Romania, or the Czech Republic, and he steams off the stamps to use in decoupage. Just when I'm about to ask why he stays at St Marsha's rather than in a conventional hotel, he alludes to some mysterious incident and goes off into hypothetical speculations as to its significance. He seems to want me to help him explain it to himself, but at the same time, he keeps distancing us both from it, framing it as an obscure allegory.'

I brought further coffee. 'Yesterday, however, he got closer than ever before to telling me what made him come to St Marsha's. It might even be some kind of break-through.

'From what I've been able to glean over the past two years,' Warren said, 'Watt used to live in a small town somewhere in the East Midlands, or, as he puts it, "the bowels of England" or the "Ostfront". He kept himself to himself, as although it seemed friendly and welcoming at first, he soon noticed an undercurrent of hostility and, to use his word, "seething". By day, things were more-or-less fine, but at night the centre of the town was stalked by men who dressed entirely in black and congregated in the market place beneath the clock on the town hall.'

'Sounds a bit fascist to me,' I said. 'Did they have bonfires, drums and flag-waving parades?'

'Not exactly,' said Warren. 'They didn't seem to do a great deal at all, but each night Watt went out, he saw more of them. They weren't in uniforms as such, but their coats, trousers, and boots were uniformly black.' He gave me another version of his television smile. 'Gradually, the other townspeople began to avoid the marketplace at night, or else, as Watt believes, they began to dress in black too. One night he counted thirty-one men. A week later, it was fifty-four. Soon there were almost a hundred. He did not know how news of the meetings was communicated. He was thoroughly intrigued, but there was no one he dared discuss it with. There was nothing about it in the media, and he tended to avoid his neighbours, people to whom he alludes only in startled whispers.'

'Did the police get involved?'

'Watt believes a significant number of the men were police officers, though the only man he could definitely identify was one of the assistants from the town's small public library. Police involvement may account for the roads around the town being closed at night, but other aspects of the affair are more mysterious. The street lighting was turned off, and the roads began to be decorated with abstract designs in yellow and blue spray paint—Watt believes that these may have been sigils or glyphs of some sort, though he never saw who made them or ascertained their purpose.'

'And you've no idea where this happened?'

'No. At this point in his life, Watt had a job of some sort, though he is evasive as to what it may have been. I think it was something to do with theatre, or even the circus. He certainly has a flair for the dramatic, and I suspect he exaggerates his experiences for artistic effect.'

'Don't we all?'

Warren swigged his Americano. 'It's hard to tell whether what he says happened, whether he thinks it happened, or whether he's invented the entire tale as a dry run for something he's writing. Objectivity is subjective, as they say. I just hope I don't end up in one of his concoctions.'

Despite my pose of professional detachment, I was intrigued. 'These men in black he's talking about, nothing to do with Will Smith or The Stranglers, I assume? No aliens or sinister waltzes?' I hummed haplessly and doubted that Warren recognised what I essayed.

'Nothing so obvious. Watt's creative influences rarely derive from popular culture; he's naturally esoteric and prides himself on his ability to withhold information from the masses. There's a lot of Nietzsche on those bookshelves of his, and he expects me to do a lot of joining of dots during our conversations. Moreover, he never seems to be bothered about self-contradiction or implausibility. Telling the story is a powerfully affecting experience for him. He becomes wholly absorbed in what he's saying, even if it isn't true. Perhaps especially if it isn't true.'

Warren looked at his watch. 'We ought to be going. I've got an appointment at 2.15, but we can talk in the car.'

ℰꝛ

As we drove back towards St Marsha's, Warren explained how Watt had observed the gatherings growing ever larger until, one night in November, he estimated there were as many as four hundred men present. Where the women of the town might be, he had no idea, though he wondered if they held gatherings of their own, 'like maenads'. It was getting to be harder and harder for him to observe what was going on from the side-lines, and he was becoming increasingly preoccupied with notions of conspiracy and secret societies. The next night, he put on a long black coat and headed into town in search of revelations. The streets were dark and quiet; the gatherings were wordless. They were also leaderless, in that the crowd was just that, a crowd, rather than an audience listening to a speaker. At first sight, it appeared that all the men did was stare up at the clockface while standing motionless in the chilly evening air.

It was only when he became part of the crowd that Watt realised it was not silent. Instead, there was a very faint ticking, though this did not emanate from the clock. Rather it came from those watching it, who were gently clicking their tongues against their teeth in time to its movement. Each time the minute hand moved, the volume increased imperceptibly. At first, it sounded like grasshoppers or cicadas, Watt said, but slowly it changed from an aural experience to a somatic one, the ticks hitting his skin with the gently percussive effect of summer rain. He found that he was tapping his fingers against his thigh in time to the clock, and then noticed that every fifth man in the crowd was slowly revolving, seemingly without moving his black boots. He could not understand how this action might be accomplished as it seemed to violate the very laws of the body. The faces of the men were enraptured. Watt found himself hypnotised by the great white clock face covered in black veins; 'caught in that sensual music', as he said, it might have been the moon and he its moon-struck votary. 'It was clearly a powerful communal event,' Warren added, 'one to which we could attribute the preoccupation with the passing of time which is so characteristic of men of a certain age.'

'I've still got that to look forward to,' I said.

As usual, Warren disregarded my facetiousness. 'It doesn't seem to have been a formal ceremony,' he said, as a flatbed truck blared past us and nearly drove us into a ditch. 'Rather, it seems to have begun spontaneously and then been encrusted, if you will, with secondary characteristics. Watt has no idea why the men came together as they did, beyond a few lugubrious asides about us all being under the eye of the clock. If there was some sort of clandestine sodality at work, he never discovered what it was called, let alone what its aims might have been. "Such is provincial life," seems to be almost a refrain with him.

'When the clock struck midnight, the men departed. Almost immediately, the crowd dissipated into a few stragglers walking wordlessly homewards. The sense of communal energy vanished, so at a loss for anything else, Watt went home too, but found that he couldn't sleep. He says now that he felt he was reliving Freud's uncanny in his repeated forays to the same site of degraded fascination, but that's just the sort of thing he *would* say.

'The following night, the crowd had increased again, to the extent that it had begun to occupy side-streets from which the clock could not even be seen. The ticking continued, as did the slow revolving. The atmosphere was otherworldly. He said that at no point until then was he genuinely frightened, but he could not begin to understand what was happening, or what the connection was, if any, between the nocturnal activities of the townspeople and the cryptic graffiti on the roads. Occasionally, he overheard something in a pub or shop which might have had some bearing on events, but these remarks were invariably inconclusive.'

Another lorry went past, the sort that usually carries scaffolding poles and that I dread following uphill. 'Busy today, isn't it?' I said, but Warren wasn't listening.

'What happened next may be the catalyst for Watt decamping to St Marsha's,' he went on. 'He had been attending the vigils, as he called them, for three months. Numbers had continued to increase, until one Saturday shortly before Christmas, there was a very sizeable crowd which he estimated to be around two thousand. The streets were filled with black-clad men clicking their tongues against their teeth in the darkness, but the difference this time was that all of them were now revolving, slowly and inexorably, as if screwing themselves into the earth. It was, Watt realised, quite literally a *revolution.* He started to panic; he felt, very strongly, that if he began to turn, he would sink into the ground, turning and turning until he vanished from sight, heading deeper and deeper down towards the very centre of the planet. At the same time, however, he dared not break away from the gathering, not least because the other men were pressing ever closer upon him. A sense of claustrophobia began to envelop him; his heart, which had fallen into the same rhythm as the clock, began to flutter like a bird's. His spectacles fell off. He felt, he said, profound terror but also ecstasy in its true sense: he was, he said, *outside himself*, disembodied somehow, a creature of pure spirit, like a slow-motion dervish, if you can imagine such a thing. It was undoubtedly a visionary experience however he presents it, and one which has left its mark. He is, he guardedly admits, a different man since the clock chimed.'

'Is that why he keeps that clock in his rooms?'

'I know ex-smokers who still keep a packet of Marlboros with the cellophane on, just to prove to themselves they can resist its lure. That clock serves a function more complex than simply telling the time, I'm quite sure. It's an anchor of some kind, which links him to an experience he can neither repeat nor forget.'

'So was that it? Was that the last time the men met? Or simply the last time Watt was present at their gathering?'

'I haven't found out,' said Warren. He waited a moment before turning right into the drive of St Marsha's, and I saw suddenly on the road a shapeless blue and yellow squiggle about seven feet long. I don't know if Warren noticed, but he fell silent and we drove more slowly across the gravel than we usually did.

A red and white marquee like a small circus tent had been pitched on the front lawn. It had not been there when we left for The Bluebell, but we had only been gone an hour or so. Outside it, various residents were milling about under the loose control of a man dressed head-to-toe in black, wearing a shiny top hat and black riding boots. Warren swore under his breath and jumping out of the car, we all but ran across the lawn. It was Watt, who was clapping his hands and muttering into a cardboard megaphone like a film director from the 1920s. His glittering eyes met ours and he said in a voice rich with port and cigars, 'Dr Warren, Dr Rees, I'm so delighted you're here at last. Please take your seats. My performance is about to begin.' He performed a slow pirouette, like a ballerina in a music-box and lifted a flap on the side of the tent. Hesitating for the briefest of moments, I followed Warren inside.

PETALS AND VIOLINS

BLOOD AND SMOKE,
VINEGAR AND ASHES

There are many curious routes to insight; and as many, often more banal, routes to ruin. It was certainly curious to receive a call from Paul ten years after we had divorced. Not that it had been particularly bitter. We just wanted different things. He wanted kids; I did not. We went our separate ways. Such are the everyday manoeuvres of life. He had moved to New York to be with his younger partner, who duly provided him with his required progeny; three of them, all girls. I stayed in Coventry and purchased a flat, from where I managed a little online enterprise making homemade bags and jewellery. And thus a decade passed.

He had called me because his father had just died. There was no one to help. His brother was in New Zealand and was due to go out on a crew ship to Antarctica the following week for three months. His partner was seriously ill and he couldn't leave her, or the kids, with anyone, so that he could make all the necessary arrangements. He was desperate. He needed my help also to deal with the authorities in Poland, where his father had moved to eight years previously. I had studied Slavic languages as my degree, and had begun an MA in Polish Literature, before funds had run out and, on meeting Paul, I'd deferred my place for a year, and then further deferrals until they got fed up with me and terminated my studies. I had only used my Polish a few times in the intervening years, talking with some of the local immigrants and in one of the specialist Polish food shops, but I was still fairly fluent.

I don't really know why I agreed, but then again why wouldn't I? As I said we didn't part on bad terms—I had no grudge against him. He offered to pay me well enough. Perhaps I fancied a change from the routine, and a little glimpse back into the past. I had also liked his father, Dieter—he was a kind, calm and quiet man. I did it as much for him as for either Paul, or myself.

ℰℴ

A few days later I found myself stepping off a budget flight onto the frosty tarmac at Krakow airport. Paul had booked me a rental car for as long as I might need it and I slung my bags into the boot and got out the maps I'd printed off for my journey to a little village called Sobolów, some thirty kilometres south east of Krakow. I'd asked Paul why on earth his father had moved there. He didn't know, he was never one to pry—he was too self-absorbed for that. It seemed peculiarly out of the way; Dieter was hardly a recluse. It was early November and the snows would soon be coming. I needed to get everything arranged for the funeral quickly and then the house up for sale; the rest could be done from a distance.

It was lovely seeing the Polish countryside again. The area around Krakow had always called to me; the great, stunning expanses of land, punctuated here and there by copses of trees that seemed to then huddle together the further you got from the city into long sprawling woodlands and denser decaying forests. It was not simply the natural world that fascinated me about this landscape but its collision with the modern; suddenly train tracks would appear from nowhere and great yards of rusting carriages and engines. Then up would pop, miles from a town or village, an industrial estate, busy with trucks and diggers. And then there were the many isolated little houses—never lit, or with sign of any inhabitation—holiday homes perhaps, the Polish were very fond of their houses in the country. Beyond all of this, or perhaps beneath it, is the ubiquity of the little *kapliczki*, whether they be elaborate communal things on the outskirts of small villages, or the idiosyncratic wooden constructions that appeared throughout the countryside. Seeing them again reminded me of a road trip I had taken with a friend from university, Daisy Simmons, over twenty years previously. We had travelled Eastern Poland and the Ukraine, taking pictures of all the little shrines we came across. Most do not record the reason for their erection but many that stand by the roadside mark a traffic accident and are memorials for the dead. I remember being particularly affected by a very strange one near some woods a few kilometres from Przemyśl. It had pieces of long coloured twine hanging from it tied to which were numerous small dolls, each in varying states of decay. We stopped and read the dedication; it was a plea to Saint Philomena to watch over the souls of three sisters who had been murdered nearby in 1978. Daisy and I spent an hour sitting there by the roadside, first in tears and then in quiet contemplation. We ended the trip a few days later, that small shrine casting a dark shadow over the holiday.

It was weird to be thinking of Daisy Simmons again as I drove into Sobolów. Her father had been a building developer and he had been one of the first to take advantage of the fall of the Iron Curtain. He was straight into Poland, employing good tradespeople at good rates, to build countryside bungalows for the growing middle classes. The outskirts of Sobolów looked as though it could have been built by Daisy's father, all orange roof tiles and freshly-painted render. The centre of the village consisted of a great wooden church, a small shop, large restaurant, and a long cemetery that seemed to go on forever up a steep hill leading out of the village—bright with the usual offerings of plastic and real flowers, coloured glass vases with floating candles and numerous pictures of the saints; something about Polish cemeteries seemed so alive, so active, compared to the desolation of the English equivalent; private, isolated affairs, as if to say that none other than oneself might have the privilege of death.

I had got some vague directions to Dieter's house from Paul, over the phone, but these were not to be relied upon; he was never good at explaining things to other people. I thought it best just to ask at the local shop, whilst getting a few groceries to tide me over. The owner was very helpful, a Mrs Szczepanska. She had been a friend of Dieter and was pleased to hear that I had come to arrange the funeral and the estate. If I needed anything I was just to ask, and she would set up an account for me at the shop, even offering to close the shop and go with me to show me the house. I said that wouldn't be necessary; if she could just mark precisely on the map where it was and offer a few pointers to any issues on the way. She duly did and I soon found myself driving down a very steep road, heavily wooded on both sides, which opened out onto a long track through a valley. Given the amount of run-off water already across the road in the wood I guessed that it would be pretty impassable in heavy snow, or icy frost, and resolved again to get my tasks concluded as soon as possible before the real winter came.

Dieter's bungalow was not quite so modest as Paul had described. It had large metal gates that opened onto a curving drive ending with a triple garage; a summerhouse; a large wood store; a shed and the main house itself. There was an ample garden, with many well-tended beds and borders, all carefully prepared for the winter. There was an allotment area too, that had only recently been dug over, but still with a few winter vegetables now going to seed.

I unlocked the main door with the key that Paul had sent me. The house was very cold and it had that sad stillness about it that accrues after a death—a melancholy compounded by the fact that everything seems to speak of their last moments; as though the objects of the home are somehow questioning where their owner may be. I cried a little. It brought back the sudden death of both of my own parents, five years previously. They had been on their way to Heathrow to catch an early morning flight to Venice as part of a dream cruise they had been planning for years. They ended up in a five car pile-up on the M1. I remembered my first time walking back into the family home after they had died.

I sighed and set to busying myself with practical things. The house was heated by a large stove in the centre of an open plan lounge, dining room and kitchen. This also powered the hot water, Paul had told me. A pile of logs and kindling were stacked neatly beside it. I raked the ashes out from the last fire that Dieter had set, laid a new one, and soon the place was warming up.

I brought my few groceries in from the car, and my bags, and thought it best to get things arranged for sleeping that evening. Two doors led off from the dining room, one into a small bathroom area with a lovely walk-in shower. The other opened into Dieter's bedroom. Again, it looked sad; the bed still dishevelled from the last night he had slept there, a half-drunk glass of water on the bedside table, and a green hardback book open next to it. I closed it and read the spine, *Of Herbs and Spices* by Colin Clair. *A little odd*, I thought; *Dieter had never been one for cookery*. I opened it again and the title page fell open. There was a simple coloured print of a foxglove in green and pink, striking and attractive. I flicked through. There were many coloured plates of plants and even more in black and white. The whole thing was filled with Dieter's annotations, in pencil, blue and black pen, and even in places in a thick felt tip. I put the book down again and thought I'd look over his marginalia later. For now I needed to get the bedding changed and think about some supper.

There was plenty of clean bed linen and once I'd hung a few of my own clothes up on the rail it was starting to look a bit more like my room. I went through to the kitchen and put a can of soup on to simmer and cut some thick pieces of bread to go with it. There was a small utility area off to the side and I dropped the dirty bedding in there, to put on to wash later. Just beside the washing machine a small door opened into a large pantry cupboard, big enough to walk into, cooled by unplastered outer walls. As I opened the door a pungent waft of herby air rushed out. I saw above me an old clothes drying rack, tied up to the ceiling on a pulley. Hanging from it were bunches of dried herbs of every kind imaginable. The pantry had clearly been well used, the sagging wooden shelves had a good number of tins and cans—beans, fish, sauces and soups—neatly arranged in rows. There were also packs and packs of salt and many jars with spices and further dried herbs, all neatly labelled up by Dieter. Beside the salt there was bottle after bottle of every type of vinegar one could think of. More practically there were some cartons of UHT milk and various powdered products; bottles of juices and water and a few wines and bottles of beer. I spotted a row of at least six green bottles with a very distinctive shape— Becherovka! God, I hadn't had any of that in years. It was a wonderful, herbal Czech spirit that again brought back memories of Daisy Simmons. We had spent an outrageous New Year in Prague in 1998 and had got so drunk on it in a touristy restaurant, endlessly supplied with shots of the stuff by roving waiters that seemed to deposit the glasses like water at our table.

With everything that was stored in the pantry one could have easily lived for a few months without venturing from the house. At the back there was a tall metal rack on which many kilner jars were stacked, each crammed with various pickled vegetables and fruits. The whole rack had a strange air about it; as though I had walked back into another century. As my eyes scanned the jars I had an awful sense of eeriness; pickled eggs bulged against their glass prisons like dead cows' eyes; pickled cucumbers floated in brine like the fingers of drowned men, gnawed by long fronds of dill; sliced beetroot was stacked like shavings of rotting flesh submerged in blood; brown chutneys were pocked like piles of dark manure—all of it a desperate attempt to halt the inevitability of rot and the relentlessness of decay. I shivered.

In the furthest corner, beside the metal rack of preserves, there was a small wooden cabinet—more like a bedside table—with a cupboard below and a drawer above. I tried the cupboard. It was locked. The drawer opened easily enough and inside I found a green account ledger with well-thumbed pages. A darkened sticker on the front read, in Dieter's familiar script,

'Dieter Helm ~ Other Preserves ~ January 2005-May 2017'

I flicked through; neatly copied out recipes, scraps of notepaper with little recollections of old memories, a few newspaper clippings about gardening, mushrooms, foraging, and further recipes ripped from magazines and other odd bits and bobs. It looked rather intriguing so I decided to take it back through to the main house and look at it in more detail later that evening, along with the annotated book on herbs and spices.

My soup had caught in the pan but enough was salvageable to keep hunger at bay. I opened a bottle of red wine from the pantry, which was quite decent. As the silence of the dark evening wrapped about the house I realised there was one further room to check. It was on the other side of the building, beyond the lounge. It was supposed to be a second bedroom, and had a small en suite, but Dieter had used it as a study and it was crammed with his books on Marxism and Socialism and his stacks of paperwork and notes. He had been an historian and I had always found his books—he wrote only a few—to be meticulously researched and written with a passion and energy that was absolutely infectious. I looked across the shelves at all the editions of Marx and Engels; *Kapital* in German, Polish and English translation, and so many different editions of *The Communist Manifesto*. Other book spines revealed the names of the great and the good, and indeed the downright bad and wicked, of the Revolutionary Ideal; Trotsky, Lenin, Lafargue, Kautsky, Pashukanis and the wider, associated thinkers, writers and theorists; Gorky, Benjamin, Habermas, and Marcuse. I noticed a whole shelf of books by Ted Grant. I knew they had been great friends until Grant's death a few years before Dieter moved to Poland. I took out a well-worn copy of *The Unbroken Thread* and opened it up. It was inscribed, 'To my good friend Dieter, A little token of my vanity! With all best wishes, Your comrade, Ted.' The book was very dusty, as indeed were all of the books on these shelves.

The other side of the room seemed more used. On the few, low bookcases there I found many books on cookery, gardening, herbs and spices, folklore and myth. It seemed that these latter books were all fairly recently read and clearly marked something of a new departure for Dieter in his interests, and chimed with the book I had found on his bedside table. Perhaps he had given up on the project of a socialist utopia; finally realising it was impossible in a world obsessed with itself. Or maybe he had merely become absorbed in a new project for a while, before intending to return to his politics and history. I would never know now. I smiled to see a half-full bottle of Becherovka on the desk and next to it a sticky shot glass. I plucked up the bottle and took it through to the lounge to toast the memory of Dieter. I closed the door on the study; it would take a lot of sorting out.

I sat down with Dieter's book of 'Other Preserves' and looked at the first entry. It was in a green ink and was dated December 2004:

BLOOD AND SMOKE, VINEGAR AND ASHES

1. Herb and Spice Blend – For Other Preserves

Ingredients:

A whole Nutmeg, grated
One Cardamom, ground
Three inches of Cassia bark, ground
A good head of dried Yarrow flowers
Ten leaves of fresh Rosemary
Fresh Mallow root
1 tsp dried Lavender
One stem of Lovage
A spike of Plantain seeds
A drop of Oil of Sage

[Caveat: the provenance of the ingredients is of little importance, as long as they are of good quality, apart from the Oil of Sage, Mallow, Rosemary and Yarrow, which should always be picked by the one producing the blend; the latter should be dried for a minimum of thirty days, in total darkness, before use. The Oil of Sage should be made in the month of May and matured for at least six months.]

The entirety should be ground inside a mortar crafted of the rough-scraped skull of a red stag; the pestle of the base of a thick young Ash tree, taken no more than one inch from the root in one fell of an iron axe, and then, crudely, and swiftly, wrought, so that its sap may contribute to the making of the blend. For the duration of the grinding, which should take no less than one hour, but not more than two, the names of the maker's nearest deceased kin should be intoned, in a ceaseless mantra. Use only the given names, and never the family names (the latter can attract unwelcome, violent spirits!). The nature of the ancestral link is of vital import! Of most powerful application to the blend is the naming of the maker's parents, should they be departed. Beyond that proximity through the matrilineal is to be favoured. Never, under any circumstance, reverse the lineage . . . do not—DO NOT—invoke the names of departed siblings, or offspring! I cannot emphasise this last point enough!

The whole powder should be mixed to a paste with Fennel water using the same pestle and mortar and then dried again on a thin metal tray over a very smoky fire using thin sticks of well dried cedar; when the fire begins to light too much dowse with a little of the fennel water to create as much smoke as possible. Once dried, and before fully cooled, return the blend to the mortar and grind again to a fine powder in small batches. The entire blend should then be mixed together for an hour with a bone spoon (fashioned from the tibia of the same beast used for the mortar) and stored in a solid silver casket used solely for the purpose.

(Note: use precisely as directed in the recipes. If the described effects of each are not achieved it will be a result of a failure in the blend. The defective blend must be discarded, along with the silver casket, which will be forever tainted by it. A new blend must be produced in precise adherence with the above instructions.)

I put the book down, a little unnerved. It was so clearly Dieter's writing, but the subject was so strange, so oddly pagan and irrational that I could only think it was part of some fiction he was writing. He had always been an atheist, and certainly had no interest—when I knew him anyway—in anything to do with magic or mysticism. But this seemed to be like a kind of, well, *witchcraft*—I could not think of any other word for it. I flicked through the annotations in the bedside book on herbs and found little notes, again in Dieter's hand, about the efficacy of herbs in given months, for certain ailments, but I also found odd little diagrams and insignia; the kind of thing I had seen only in those tacky 1970s books on the occult—popular pulp on the supernatural. I sat, staring into the fire, topping my glass up regularly, listening to the wind howl about the house.

The following morning, nursing a rather sore head, I put all thoughts of strange preserving methods and silly superstitions from my mind. I concentrated on getting arrangements made for the funeral. It would be a simple affair, I told myself—probably just me and the priest at the graveside, a few short poems and prayers and then on to sorting out the will and the house. I gathered many of the necessary documents from Dieter's study through the morning and thought it a good idea to have a decent warm meal in the village. The restaurant was owned by a Czech man, Marek, and his Polish wife, Teresa. They welcomed me and said how much they had loved Dieter, who often dined there. A plate of steaming *pierogi* appeared for me, with a vast bowl of *barszcz czerwony*, without me even placing an order. They talked and talked as I tentatively ate, enjoying the intense evocation of memory that the food gave me. Mrs Szczepanska made an appearance as I was trying to force down the last of my *pierogi*. She was with another of Dieter's friends, a younger woman called Marta, probably in her mid-thirties, who had helped Dieter with his garden and vegetable patches. Once they all knew I was arranging the funeral they all began planning the wake, which they insisted take place there in the restaurant, and entirely at their expense. They started listing names of Dieter's friends, both locally, and in towns and cities further away, all of whom must, *they insisted*, be invited. As I began to protest Mrs Szczepanska held up a hand, as though to silence a moody child, and asserted that she would deal with it all and provide me a list of the guests the following day. All I needed to do was make the arrangements with the authorities and everything else would be dealt with. I was then presented with a large slice of excellent cheesecake, peppered with fat raisins soaked in brandy—the deal was done, apparently.

And so it proved to be. I had a couple of difficult days in Krakow, trying to deal with overzealous bureaucrats, entailing two return journeys to Dieter's house to find documents that then were deemed to be unnecessary. But finally all was in place for the funeral the following Friday. As I had no mobile reception at Dieter's house, and there was no internet connection either (Dieter and computers just never seemed to click), I spent a lot of time in the main village, making plans with Marek, or Teresa, as they offered their thoughts and opinions. I kept Paul informed as I went along. He was happy with whatever I suggested. I had chosen everything to be as basic as possible, as he had instructed—simple coffin, no flowers, and so on; just frugal and functional. The turnout though was quite overwhelming, at least fifty people, all of whom seemed to want to introduce themselves to me and just assumed that I was still married to Paul. The wake was far from austere. I think Marek and Teresa had planned to feed at least a hundred, and provided wine and vodka for nearly two hundred. It became a superb celebration of Dieter's rich life; he was clearly well respected and loved by these people. I understood now why he had moved here. If I could ever find such care and friendship I would do the same.

I left the wake while it was still in full swing, tired from all the planning, and just relieved to have seen it all go off okay. I slipped away from the crowd, a little tipsy, and drove back to Dieter's just as it was getting dark; a gentle snow was beginning to fall.

BLOOD AND SMOKE, VINEGAR AND ASHES

Back at the house things seemed even quieter than they had before. I had left the fire blazing, but it was now reduced to a few embers. I stoked it up again and realised that in all the preparations for the funeral I had neglected to get any more food in for myself. I would have to fall back on Dieter's pantry. I rummaged around to find something appetising. A can of vegetable broth would do. I also found a few hard cheeses wrapped in cloth and grabbed a pack of crackers. A jar of Dieter's homemade piccalilli would go well with them. I hadn't had piccalilli in years; it always reminded me of Christmas at my parents' house. The preserves were on the higher shelves and as I took the jar down a small key slid off the shelf and jingled on the tiled floor. I found it soon enough and realised that it should fit the cupboard door of the little cabinet unit.

As I opened it a waft of musty air escaped; vinegar and mould, damp leather and the mushroomy scent of soil. Inside there were two shelves, on the lower one very small jars were stacked, higgledy-piggledy, on top of each other. Beside them were a number of brownish muslin cloth packages, loosely bound with green twine. On the shelf above there were some very odd things indeed; a small twig all splayed and crushed at one end, where it was also blackened, as though from a fire; a thin knife—I guessed it was silver—very crudely wrought, and clearly much used as its blade was exceedingly worn. There was a hand axe, again well-used, its cracked handle held together with black electrical tape. There was also a small silver box. I recalled the ludicrous recipe I had read the night I arrived. *No, surely*, I thought, *you can't be serious, Dieter. You didn't believe this drivel, did you? You didn't actually try to make that stuff.* I opened the box. Sure enough, there was a fine brown powder within. I scoffed in disbelief. I started looking at the little jars. They were each labelled with numbers, mostly number five, and a few sevens, many had the initials D.H. on them, and two had P.H.; each was dated. One, half consumed, read '5. Marta,

13

15/05/15, A delight!' I didn't know what to think. I wondered what could be in the muslin packages. My hand was shaking a little as I reached for them, but I pulled myself together. *It's just a load of hocus-pocus*, I assured myself. I undid a couple and the stale smell became stronger. In one there were long, thin strips of meat with white, mouldy rinds, tied into bundles; small labels were tied to each strip, again numbered, initialled and dated, all with the number three and the initials D.H.; the dates were all within the last six months. My hands shook again as I unwrapped another package. Meats again, but knotted into roundish, dry sausages, almost black, but with a yellowish mould. The labels on these were stained with grease and were harder to make out. They all seemed to have the number twelve, and again the initials D.H., but with dates from 2014 to within the last three months. I looked at the contents of the cupboard, now spread before me on the pantry floor. Suddenly I had an overpowering sense of dread and scrambled to my feet and ran through to the kitchen where I poured a large glass of red wine and, in an attempt to get my composure back, busied myself getting some cheese and crackers together to eat. *It really is all just some silly nonsense to do with something Dieter was writing about*, I kept thinking. *He was such a stickler for research; he must have got rather consumed by it all and started experimenting so that he could get the details right.*

I sat down with my supper—*get a bloody grip!* I thought. The snow was really coming down now and the wind was getting up again. Against my better judgement I reached for the ridiculous book I had taken from the pantry cupboard and flicked further on.

12. To Relive a Memory from Youth – A Blood Pudding.

Ingredients:

A pint of one's own blood (or that of another requesting the sausage and who is trustworthy with the knowledge of such things.)
4 oz of hard back fat, finely diced
4 oz shallots, finely diced
1 tbsp fine oatmeal, soaked in caraway water and goat's milk overnight
1 tsp herb and spice blend (of the kind previously described)
1 tsp salt
1 tsp white pepper
1 head of coriander flowers, finely chopped
Natural casings
I buttercup, I daisy, 1 dandelion (dried together in five days of midday sun and then ground into a powder in a pestle and mortar)

Method:

Rub the required length of casings in the powder of buttercup, daisy and dandelion and set aside.

Sweat the fat, with the shallots, until they are tender, remove from the heat and spit upon it (or add the fresh spit of the one requesting it). Stir in the drained oatmeal, herb and spice blend, salt, pepper and coriander flowers.

Sieve the blood to remove clots and stir into the cooled mixture.

Fill the casings using a funnel and wooden spoon, as they are easily broken. Do not overfill as you will need to separate into smaller sausages tied with homespun twine. Leave room for the mixture to expand upon cooking, which should be for merely ten minutes in boiling water freshly taken from a free running spring. This quantity will make twenty small sausages. Under no circumstances must they be reheated, or chilled. They should be stored in a cool, dry place. They will be preserved from undue decay for up to three years by the blend, but will taste of rot when eaten. This is normal.

(Note: Should a specific memory be desired then care must be taken to recall this [as best one can] during the consumption of the sausage. A light reverie will ensue, during which one will feel as though one were present at the memory, sometimes this may involve a dislocation from it, especially if many years have passed, and one may feel as though one witnesses the event, rather than it being one's own experience.)

'Oh, you are fucking joking with me, Dieter, *"A pint of one's own blood"*,' I laughed, glancing up at the heavens. 'You silly old man! You don't think I am taking this crap seriously do you?' I urgently looked further back in the book.

5. To Dwell in Another's Dreams

Ingredients:

1 lb Apples (any variety)
2-3 ripe plums
1 large onion finely chopped
1 lb demerara sugar

16

BLOOD AND SMOKE, VINEGAR AND ASHES

½ pint white wine vinegar
A pint of spring water
A whole garlic bulb, roughly chopped (including skin)
A large stem of ginger, roughly chopped (including skin)
1 tsp herb and spice blend (as previously described)
A single strand of hair from the chosen dreamer (this may be procured from a hairbrush or anywhere really. The length of hair is immaterial.)
One long dark root of Wormwood
A larva (any species will do, but beware, maggots will invariably result in the production of a nightmare – if this is what is required then a blow fly maggot will be sure to deliver! I have found mosquito larvae particularly useful for this purpose and merely leaving a bucket of water outside within a week or two there will be ample larvae to select from.)
A handful of ashes from a Laurel Fire

Method: Rough cut the apples into 1 inch chunks. Halve the plums, retaining the stones. Taking a large pan place all the ingredients in (save for the hair, wormwood root, larva and ashes) and bring to the boil, stirring continuously, then simmer for at least two hours, stirring occasionally until the surface of the mixture retains a furrow when a wooden spoon is dragged across it. Allow to cool for half an hour before adding the live larva, hair and wormwood root. Allow to cool fully before adding the ashes and then mix thoroughly before bottling into small jars.

(Note: The finished preserve will last up to five years but must be labelled with the name of the person and the date of bottling. Do not consume beyond the point of five years as it will induce frightful hallucinations. Only a little need be consumed—say, a teaspoon—before sleep, to enable the

dreams to be reproduced. These will be in full and may come from any age of the person selected. It may take some time to become fully acquainted with these dream patterns, but once one has done so it is frequently possible to guide the dreams to a particular period in their life. Remember that childhood dreams frequently move back and forth into more nightmarish territory and care is advised in seeking out these dreams.)

'Right, then,' I said, angrily. 'Let's put you to the test, Dieter.'

I threw the book down on the sofa and stormed through to the pantry. I rifled through the little jars and found the one labelled 'Marta'.

I took it through to the kitchen and got out a small spoon. I unscrewed the sticky cap and sniffed at the gloopy brown mess inside. It had a sweet aroma to it, but the abiding smell was fungal. I scooped up a loaded spoonful and swallowed it. It was smooth, and quite sweet, but the aftertaste was woody, like damp bark.

I swigged some wine straight from the bottle to wash it down. It did not take the taste away.

'There you go, Dieter,' I shouted. 'Let's see what dreams may come, eh?'

Despite my bravado I had a sudden feeling of regret, followed by an irrational fear. What if it were poisonous? Surely it wouldn't actually work and induce dreams, but maybe the mix itself would do me some harm. The nearest other bungalow to Dieter's was nearly half a kilometre away and with the snow coming down as it was it would be unlikely that anyone would find me for days if I did get sick.

I panicked and wandered the house, desperately trying to find a place with a signal so that I could at least send a text to Paul to make him aware that I may be in danger. There was no signal anywhere. I stared at the darkness outside, watching the great flurries of snowflakes being plastered across the whitening countryside. I was alone. I would have to deal with it.

It took me many hours to get to sleep, mainly because my mind was racing with all of the connections I was making between the things I had read in Dieter's recipe book and what I had found in the small cupboard. It just couldn't be possible that this little spoon of homemade chutney would induce another's dream.

I awoke at nearly midday, feeling better than I had in years. I did dream; the clearest, most lucid dream I could ever recall; and I recalled it in great detail. There were a group of us, children, playing in an alpine landscape. We were holding hands with badgers and bears, owls and otters, all of them the same size as us, chanting nursery rhymes and singing nonsense songs. We were dancing around a single giant daisy that grew from a mound of purple soil, ringed with white rocks, almost glowing with their brightness. The sky kept changing colour, as though going through phases of sunset; dark oranges, bright reds and then an ominous mauve that darkened everything about us. We children then also became animals and we all dispersed into a wood to hunt. I seemed to be some kind of bird and flitted through the dark trees in search of insects, which appeared to my birdish sight as little glowing specks of red in the gloom. When I had had my fill I burst into a shower of glittering embers that cascaded to the woodland floor, from each erupted a huge block of grey concrete that shattered the trees around it. As my dream sight floated up into the sky, below me the whole earth was splintering into a dull block of greyness. Then all was darkness.

I shuffled through to the kitchen in my nightdress to make a coffee. The house was illuminated with the brightness of the snow outside. I looked out. It must be at least three feet deep. The sky looked dark though, heavy with another impending bout of it. I was here to stay for the next few days, at least. But I had survived the night, and chided myself for my foolish fit of terror, and impetuous risk in consuming the damned thing in the first place.

I wandered about in a daze. Had the dream been mine, or Marta's; how could I possibly know? It was certainly unlike any dream I had had before, and the sense of it too was somewhat alien, as though I did not belong there. I sat down with a pot of coffee and re-read the two recipes from the previous evening. Again I sank back with incredulity. Did this really indicate that sitting through in the pantry, in an old bedside table, there were little pots of people's dreams—that the strings of nasty looking sausages were dried up chunks of childhood memory; *preposterous*, I affirmed, but the doubt was already within me, quite literally.

By mid-afternoon the snow was back again. I had spent the previous couple of hours trying to occupy myself with anything to avoid thinking of the book and the things in that cupboard. I couldn't wait a moment longer though and suddenly rushed through and grabbed the package of small sausages. I searched for the most recent label I could find, '12. D.H., 20/03/17.' I cut a sausage into slices and crammed one in my mouth, chewing rapidly. As it described in the recipe there was a rotten taste, indeed that was the only taste; similar to the chutney, but much more intense, and without any relieving sweetness, or fruity flavour. I stood there at the kitchen sink, wondering whether I should just stick my fingers down my throat to bring the awful thing back up again. Then I began to feel very light-headed. I stumbled through to the bed to lie down, again admonishing myself for such rash behaviour.

What happened in the following hour was simply magical. I seemed to drift beside a large ship moving steadily through light, dark waves. I kept swooping in towards the deck, as though I were a gull. I was circling around a man and a small child. The man looked so much like Dieter, I was amazed. But Dieter was tall and thin and this man was short and quite heavily built. He also had a thick, brown moustache. Dieter had always been clean-shaven. On the horizon land appeared, and a city came into view, just as evening began to descend. As the ship drew closer, my sweeping, free-roaming perspective got closer and closer to the little boy, until it seemed that I was looking through his eyes. On the skyline the glimmering lights of the city came into view, and I was filled with a sense of awe and trepidation, of excitement and joy. Then there was a striking image—the Statue of Liberty. We were approaching America.

I had not been asleep during this; merely in some kind of stupor. It was as though it happened inside my mind, the way I would recall my own memories. But this, this I knew belonged to Dieter. He had talked of it at great length on any occasion we had seen him. He had travelled to America with his father, from England, in the late 1940s. His mother had died shortly after he was born and his father, a dedicated socialist, was in danger in the Germany of the late 1930s. He had fled to England in 1939, with Dieter still a baby, and had stayed somewhere in Kent, with a distant relative. Despite his clear opposition to Hitler he was interred in a holding camp for much of the war and never really forgave the British for what he saw as an unnecessary cruelty. Dieter, in those early years, had been raised by this relative but on his release Dieter's father had planned the move to America, which promised a new life for them both. This image came straight from the description Dieter had always given. Or, was it possible that I had merely projected this, given the intensity of my current emotions?

I then remembered the thin strips of meat, labelled number three. What were they intended for? I felt as though I were drunk, tottering through to the lounge to find the entry for them in Dieter's book.

3. To Recapture a Recent Moment

Ingredients:

Either 1 lb Venison Loin or fillet of Beef (venison will recall more cerebral or emotional experiences, beef the more corporeal)
30% brine solution
3 tsps herb and spice blend (as described for these purposes)
2 tsps Salt
2 tsps Pepper (coarsely ground)
The sweat of your body

Required for air drying to further preserve (see below):

3 tsps ground coriander seed
A pint of cider vinegar
Enough salt (mixed with one tbsp saltpetre) to roll the joint in and entirely cover

Method:
Soak the meat for one day and night in the brine. Remove and pat dry. Rub the meat all over your body gathering as much sweat as possible. Rub together the blend, salt and pepper and rub over the meat. Cover and allow to stand in a cool place for a further day and night.

To smoke the meat one must use a crude smoker. This can be fashioned from any wooden crate, the principal being that there must be much aeration. Choose a windy day to do this. Light a fire of alder wood and allow to smoke. Suspend the meat on hooks from the top of the crate, ensuring that there is at least a foot above the smoking wood. Leave for four hours. The meat is ready to use as soon as it is cool. See below though for notes on its consumption at this stage.

To further dry to the consistency of biltong (which is recommended) then soak the cooled meat in the cider vinegar for one day and night. Then pat dry and roll in the salt and saltpetre mixture. Leave for one hour. Rub in the ground coriander seed and then leave for a further hour.

Finely slice the entire meat joint and thread onto wooden skewers, leaving a half-inch gap between each. For the drying box one can use the same crate as for the smoking. Simply suspend the skewers from the top of the crate and leave in a cool, airy space to dry. This is best assisted by the use of a cable lamp, if the latter is used drying should take 2-3 days, if not then it will be 6-8 days.

Note: This will recapture experiences within the previous 6-12 months of the life of the producer. It is best to keep some of the first smoked cure to access those more distant memories (of 8-12 months) and the drier meat for the more recent. The former will last 2-3 weeks in a sealed container, the latter up to a year. As only one sliver need be consumed at a time this should produce enough to recall many moments. The first cure will also produce an intensity of experience that is shorter in duration—normally a few minutes. The tougher, dried meat will produce a longer recollection—even up to an hour—but one that is rather clouded, as though viewed through a slightly distorted window.

If a specific memory is required then care should be taken to begin to recall it immediately upon eating, otherwise the meat will randomly activate memories dependent upon one's mood.

I rushed through and grabbed the bundle. I took them into the kitchen and shaved slivers off of a few of them with a potato peeler. I put them on a plate and sat on the sofa, pausing a brief moment before I took the first one. It was quite chewy, and didn't have that rotten taste the other two had. A few seconds later I was experiencing a sensation of intense lust and then my eyes fogged a little before closing. I seemed transported to Dieter's bedroom. What I saw there revealed a rather deeper relationship with Marta than I had initially thought. A few minutes later I was back to myself again. It felt strange to be a voyeur into recent moments in Dieter's life, but the urge to do so was compelling. I took another sliver of meat and was walking through the woods, looking for herbs and mushrooms. I looked down to see Dieter's boots striding through emerging bluebells, and then glanced up into the trees at shards of bright sunlight. On and on I ate, binging on moments of another's existence, from the most ordinary to the most private and intimate. It appeared that Dieter had been quite the man about town; numerous recollections involved some of the women I had seen at the funeral, but there seems to have been a genuine passion for Marta.

After a few hours I stopped. The fire had burnt out entirely and a blizzard was raging outside. *What am I doing*, I thought. *What kind of madness is this*? I must stop.

I tried everything to occupy myself. Nothing worked though. All I could think about were those shards of meat and the fantastical visions they promised me; ways of knowing another person that one could never achieve otherwise.

The storm howled on, and inside its icy inferno I fell into an addict's wonderland. No drug, no drink, no physical pleasure had ever given me anything as intoxicating as this. I binged on spoonfuls of fantasy; loitered through other lives and minds in a crazy kaleidoscope of images, memories and moods. Days passed as I dozed on the bed, sipping Becherovka and nibbling shavings of the past or inducing hours of dreams, or nightmare.

I was awoken, quite when it was I cannot say, by a loud hammering at the door. I pulled on a thin dressing gown and answered the urgent knocking.

It was Mrs Szczepanska, looking distraught. She warbled on about how they had been so worried about me, with it being almost three weeks since the snows had arrived and nobody had been able to make it down to this part of the village. She hoped I had survived on the well-stocked larder that she had helped Dieter to assemble. On and on she rattled, her words jumbling together into a bizarre, hallucinatory incantation. The real world was crumbling around me, in favour of another realm.

When she had finished I stirred from my reverie.

'What do you want,' I said, curtly. 'I've got to sort through Dieter's affairs, I'm very busy.' It was true, in so many ways. All his affairs were magically arrayed before me to indulge my prurience; yet also, I was meant to be dealing with his estate. The latter could wait.

She was visibly shocked, probably as much by my appearance as by my attitude. I did not care. She left in a huff of bewilderment.

After I had seen her off I returned to those other's realities. Perhaps it was a few days later, in a rare moment of lucidity, that I recalled the other recipes in the book. Why were there only jars of a certain recipe, and the, rapidly dwindling, stocks of the two types of meat? There were other pages to explore; perhaps further stashes of even more revelatory things might be discovered.

The other numbered recipes were disappointing, and seemed to be of relatively mild effect, compared to these astounding concoctions. There were love potions, and cures for various ailments—number thirteen was for a potent poison made from simple soil. The last entry, number fifteen, tempted with something else entirely though:

15. To See Beyond the Threshold

1 lb of flesh of the departed
1 lb Saltpetre
3 tsps of herb and spice blend
Enough grave clothes, or the shroud of the same departed, to wrap the flesh to cure

Method:

The departed must have been known to the one making the cured flesh. The stronger the bond the deeper the knowledge revealed will be. The deceased must be no more than six months gone and the flesh retrieved on the first night of a waning moon. The cut of meat is of no matter, but it must be whole, rather than comprised of smaller pieces. Often a lower limb is the most convenient for this purpose.

Wash the flesh in a stream for an hour at dusk, then rub with the soil from the roots of an oak tree. Immediately rub the blend into the flesh and then rub again with more soil. Pack the saltpetre around the flesh and wrap tightly in the grave clothing, or shroud, and then bind with ivy at intervals of one inch.

The wrapped flesh must be hung in a cool, dry place to cure. The cure will take only five days.

(Note: Once the curing is complete then one must observe the following strictly! The meat must only be consumed on the first night after the cure is complete. A day beyond and

nothing will happen, a day before and you will sicken and die within three days. On that very particular night a single thin strip of the meat should be sliced, using a bone knife fashioned for the very purpose. The meat should then be left to infuse for one hour in red wine of any kind alongside root of valerian and the whole plant and flowers of Euphrasy. Upon the completion of that hour the whole strip of flesh must be consumed at once, without the aid of any liquid to assist. It will taste foul but must not be spat out, or regurgitated, or a terrible sickness will afflict you. Go to sleep immediately and the reality of the life beyond will be revealed to you. Immediately upon awakening you must take the remaining flesh and bury it beneath the root of an elder tree. The root must be as thick as the meat itself. If this final task is not done you will be forever plagued by nightmares so foul that your waking hours will be entirely lived in terror of them. Your mind will wither until your existence cannot be tolerated a moment longer and you will, if you are lucky, be able to take your own life, before being taken to the madhouse. The production, and consumption of this meat is only to be undertaken by those knowing in the craft, in the full awareness of what it is they do, and the ultimate nature of the truths that will be revealed to them – you have been warned!)

And so I sit here, Eve with the apple; what am I to do? Given the promise of such knowledge how could anyone resist? I must see! Tonight the moon begins to wane. I have a spade and shall shortly make another visit to Dieter to see what final teachings he has for me. Soon I shall know the truth of paradise or abide forever in hell.

THE MAGICIAN, OR, CRAB LINES

Doch uns ist gegeben,
Auf keiner Stätte zu ruhn,
Es schwinden, es fallen
Die leidenden Menschen
Blindlings von einer
Stunde zur andern,
Die Wasser von Klippe
Zu Klippe geworfen,
Jahr lang ins Ungewisse hinab.

Hölderlin, *Hyperion*

I watched the tide coming in, bringing its fizz of creamy foam. It was getting quite chilly now. I was in my thin trunks, knee deep in a sandcastle moat that I had just filled with water from a rock pool. I was shivering but stubbornly refused to leave the beach, or to put any of my clothes back on. Mother was fussing over me with a shirt, trying her best to catch my flailing arms as I busied myself with the final parts of my masterpiece. My father was watching the waves come in too, smoking cigarette after cigarette, mulling over some momentous worry that I had only hints of from their heated discussions late in the evening. It was, as ever, to do with money. Perhaps he hoped for a treasure chest of Spanish doubloons to wash up and solve all his problems. My concerns were more that the sea would destroy my wonderful creation. I had purchased a pack of ten paper flags glued onto thin balsa-wood poles with my pocket money and now came the time for the difficult choice as to which should finish off my fortress of sandy towers and shell walls. Mother captured me as I was distracted by my deliberations and forced the shirt on. It was a choice between a striking yellow and red flag with a dragon on it, or a powerful blue flag with a white cross—hmm! both were interesting, in different ways. It had to be the dragon, although I did like blue more than yellow.

My father stood up and said, 'Okay, we're going back to the cottage now.'

That was it. What father said happened. I had to make a choice fast. The dragon it would be. I hurried over and planted it firmly in the top. It would, surely, keep the waters at bay a little longer than without one.

He was packing up the deckchairs and mother was busying herself with the picnic basket. I knew it was best not to disturb him but this would probably be the only day of the holiday that we'd come to the beach, especially given the changeable Norfolk weather. I had to have a picture of the sandcastle.

'Er, dad,' I mumbled. 'Can I have the camera, please?' There was no answer. 'I just want one picture, just one; of my sand-castle.'

Mother held her hand out to him and said, mechanically, 'I'll do it, Brian.'

He was very particular over what he called the 'family camera'; mother and I were rarely allowed to use it, and film was strictly rationed. He didn't trust rolls with thirty-six frames, in case something should go wrong with them and all the shots were lost. He would only use rolls with twelve frames. For a week's holiday like this we had three rolls.

He rummaged in his bag and pulled out the camera and passed it to her, 'Just one shot, mind . . . just the one.'

Mother fumbled with the case and lens cap, as though she were examining some alien artefact left on a crashed spaceship.

'Now, do you want to stand by it dear,' she said, waving in an indeterminate direction.

'No, no, it's just the sandcastle I want,' I said, hating having any pictures taken of me.

'Oh, but it's a shame to waste a shot without you in it,' she said.

I was just about to voice another objection when father said in a louder voice, 'Do as your mother says.'

I could not tell whether he had raised his voice against the gathering wind, or whether he was getting annoyed. I went and stood by the sandcastle—it wasn't worth risking it.

She took the picture and then handed the camera back to him. He took it out of the case and made a point of winding the reel on. She often forgot to wind the film on and it infuriated him. We walked back to the cottage in gloomy silence.

Later that evening, after dinner and after we'd been for a stroll on the sea front, he announced that we'd take the car to Blakeney Quay the following day and do some crabbing. Mother asked if we might go out on one of the boats to look at the seals. He said that maybe we could do that on another day, which meant we wouldn't be doing it at all this holiday.

I loved our regular holiday town of Sheringham, with its interesting little shops and cafés, and the tempting lights and jittery sounds of the amusement arcade (that father wouldn't allow me in, because they were a waste of money) but I loved Blakeney more. There wasn't anything much there really; a car park, a pub and a hotel and a little shack that sold sea food. There were also a few posh antique shops that they liked to look around but never bought anything from. But we always went crabbing there and for some reason when we went crabbing my father seemed to relax and we had a happy time together. I don't know whether it was because we would always do it alone—mother liked to sit watching us from the car, reading a book.

'But, before we go we've got a bit of business to do in town first haven't we, Michael,' he said to me, with a conspiratorial wink.

'Yes, dad,' I said, happily. 'And you've got to stay here, mum.'

We all laughed. I liked it when we laughed.

It was mother's birthday on the Thursday and he had meant that we needed to go shopping for gifts for her. I also knew that meant a trip to the junk shop in town, which was always a treat every time we came away. We often found some curious things; tools or old mechanisms from objects whose purpose was difficult to guess. Father always knew everything about them though and would patiently explain each one to me, describing what it would have been used for and how it would have been assembled or employed. I loved to listen to his explanations of things; it was at those moments that he really came alive.

Tomorrow would be a good day. I went to bed early and lay awake a couple of hours imagining what fun we would have.

ဆ

We got to the shop just as it opened. A stout lady with splinters of white breaking through her black hair was putting out an A-board,

'Rose's Collectibles and Antiques
House Clearances
Gold & Silver
Bought and Sold'.

'Ah, a couple of early birds, eh?' she said cheerily.

'Well, we're after some juicy worms,' father said, grinning. 'Aren't we, son?'

'No,' I replied. 'We're looking for presents for my mother. It's her birthday this week. We're on holiday. I don't think she'd like any worms though.'

The lady laughed, 'In you go, dears. You see what you can find for her.'

The place was even more crammed than I remembered it from the previous year; china tea sets balanced precariously alongside huge stone planters; little ornaments were hidden in between old metal advertising signs and large farming equipment so that anything you touched threatened an avalanche of fragile curios and lethal metal objects. Dotted about the place were warning signs that threatened, 'All breakages must be paid for!'

'Now you keep your hands to yourself, Michael,' father warned. 'If you see something you like you tell me and I'll get it out for you.'

I nodded my agreement and headed off into the thin corridors of the shop. Things loomed from the gloom; badly stuffed animals, a cloth gollywog that was almost as big as me; rolls of maps and posters jutted into every narrow passageway between the rickety tables, traps for the clumsy browser. Umbrellas by the hundred were tucked here and there, even hanging from hooks in the rafters; most appeared broken in some way and had obviously hardly been touched for years judging by the black silt of ancient dust that coated them. Perhaps this section of the shop was 'The Umbrella Graveyard', I sniggered. I decided to head upstairs where I recalled there were three tiny rooms which had things that mum had liked to look at before. I passed by father, ferreting in a wooden box that seemed to contain a variety of chisels. He didn't notice me.

Upstairs was tidier, and most things up there were more expensive. There were shelves of old books and lots of ornate vases and plates. The walls were covered in big pictures, mostly in thick gold frames. Many of them were portraits of men in uniform from many years ago and ladies in fancy frocks. There were a few tables with what father used to call 'women's things' on them. Perfect! There were jewellery stands and lots of boxes for storing toiletries and make-up. I couldn't afford any of them though. Most of the smaller items were also quite expensive; hairbrushes with embroidery designs on the back of the handle; compact mirrors with enamel panels; loads of necklaces and rings, all of which were way beyond my means, and probably cost more than father earned in a week. In a corner of the last room, where quite a lot of mannequins stood, showing off 'vintage' pieces, there was a 'Clearance!' table with all sorts of knick-knacks; there were single earrings and damaged bracelets, reels of lace with only a few inches of material left; sunglasses with scratched lenses . . . and then I spotted it. It was a small pot, the base was pink and the top of it was a creamy colour. It had an iridescent inlay in the top, ringed by a few bright, clear jewels. A few of the latter were missing and in their cavities a grimy residue had built up. I don't know why I liked it so much. I just thought that mother would—and also it was only ten pence, so I knew I could afford it.

I went down to get father. He'd be angry if I picked it up and brought it down, especially given his earlier warning. It happened that in doing so he got irritated anyway as I seemed to be interrupting his inspection of an old water pump that sprouted like a green tree-trunk from a heap of nuts and bolts tipped into an old tin bath.

He came upstairs, huffily, to look at the pot.

'What do you think it is?' I asked.

'A bit grubby, that's what it is,' he said, turning it over in his hands with a disdainful frown.

'Can you undo it?' I said.

He unscrewed the lid. Even though the base looked quite large there wasn't much room in it, just a fairly shallow depression. It wouldn't store very much, maybe a few earrings or a locket.

'Are these diamonds on the top, dad?' I asked.

'Not for ten pence they're not,' he said matter-of-factly. 'A nice bit of mother of pearl on top though, interesting colour.'

'I think they're diamonds anyway,' I said, running my fingertips across them. They were sharp and cold. 'I'm going to get it for mum.'

Father hadn't found anything he thought she'd like so we headed off to find 'Rose' and pay. He said we'd also go by the stationers on the way back and get her some cards and wrapping paper. He said he'd try the antique shop in Blakeney and maybe find her something there later.

The till consisted of an upturned tea crate and a set of small drawers in which the day's takings were kept. The lady wrapped the pot very carefully inside a thick pink paper bag that was covered in swirly green flowers.

'You don't really even need to put any other wrapping on it with that nice bag,' father said, smiling at her.

'Well, *maybe*,' I said. 'But I'll also wrap it anyway, in the bag. That way it will be doubly nice for her.' I tucked it into the inside pocket of my bomber jacket and did the zip up to keep it safe.

I didn't want to leave it back at the cottage so I took it with me to Blakeney, against father's advice. I didn't want her to find it, so resolved to keep it on me until Thursday.

&

We got to Blakeney a little after midday and went straight to the shellfish stall, where father had six oysters and mother a pot of cockles. I hated shellfish so I just waited with my crabbing line and bucket until they'd finished. They both stank of vinegar and fishiness but it was nice to see them chatting and joking together whilst they enjoyed the food. Father had also purchased me three whelks to use as bait for my hook. The man from the stall had turned them half out of their shell with a long hook and they lay at the bottom of my bucket looking like a trail of thick brown and yellow snot. I shook the bucket and the shells knocked against each other with thick clunks. I twiddled with the orange twine of my crab line and twisted the round lead weight back and forth on the wooden frame. I kicked a few stones across the car park. I was bored.

'Right then, my boy,' father said, wiping his hands on a little napkin. 'Let's catch us a juicy crab for our supper.'

'I'll go and have a look around then,' mother said. 'Then I'll have a read in the car. See you later; you boys have fun.'

We went along the quay and set ourselves up at the furthest end, where the waters were starting to return with the tide. There was an old man already sitting there and father bid him a good afternoon. He commended us on a good choice of pitch and we sat there in a row, dangling our lines into the brown waters below. We hadn't been there very long at all when mother returned and said she'd seen something she wanted father to look at too, in a shop up the road. He started to pack up and bid me do the same. I started to protest but saw his face wrinkle in that particular way and I began to huff and puff, gathering my fishing things together.

'I'll watch over the lad, if you'll not be too long,' the old man piped up.

My parents looked at each other. I looked at them, pleadingly.

'That's very kind of you,' my mother said. 'We'll not be long at all, just to look at something in the antique shop up the hill.'

'Oh, yes,' the old chap said. 'Old Markham's. He's got some good stuff in there, but don't let him charge you Londoner prices. Tell him you know Jim Connor and he'll see you right.'

'Well, thank you on both counts,' my father said, ever keen to grab a bargain. 'We'll not be long at all. Now you be very good Michael and do as Mr Connor says.'

I nodded and sat back down to fish.

We sat there in silence for a while and then he spoke, 'Just a word of advice, lad, about your bait.'

'What's that,' I said. 'Is there something wrong with it?'

'No, not as such,' he said. 'Whelks is very fine bait. It's how you've got them on the hook that's the problem.'

I pulled my line out of the water and looked at the blob of goo on the end of the long hook.

He took out a pocket knife and clicked it open. I'd always wanted a knife but father said I was still too young.

'Now, see here, you got the whole thing on there all at once,' he said, pointing to the horrible thing. 'What you need to do is make it attractive to the crabs. They like things that flit about like strands before their stalky eyes.'

He cut into the whelk and took about half of it away with his thick fingers. He flicked that half, with a juicy squelch, into my bucket and then teased out the entrails of the half that remained on the hook. I wrinkled my face up in disgust.

'Now don't be squeamish, lad,' he said. 'They love seeing that floating about before them. And the other bit'll keep your catch occupied when you've landed them in the bucket.'

'Thanks, sir,' I said, rather hesitantly.

'Don't call me "sir", lad, call me Jim,' he said, throwing my line back into the water.

His line was very well used, and had been a bright green at one time. Now it was quite frayed and had bleached well over the years; a few knots showed where there had been a number of repairs.

'You on holiday with your mam and dad?' he said.

'Yes, I am,' I said. 'We come here most years.'

'That's good,' he said. 'I've been here most my life and wouldn't much want to be anywhere else. You done anything fun yet on your holiday, other than crabbing, of course?'

'Oh yes, we went out this morning and got presents for mother; it's her birthday this week, on Thursday,' I said, excitedly. 'I got her a little pot for putting treasures in. I've got it here, safe in my pocket. Would you like to see it?'

'I would, lad,' he said, 'if you'd like to show it to me.'

I looked around to check that my parents weren't coming back yet and then took the paper bag from my pocket. I carefully teased the Sellotape from the bag without ripping it and took out the precious pot. In the sunlight the pearly top glimmered green, silver and purple and the few remaining diamonds shone brightly. I held it up to the old man and turned it about to best show it off.

His face looked rather strange. He looked both happy and sad as he inspected it carefully.

'It's really nice isn't it?' I said, cheerily. 'She's going to love it. Would you like to hold it?'

He didn't say anything for a moment, just carried on staring at it, totally absorbed.

'It is that, lad, it's really nice indeed,' he said. 'I will have a little look of it, if you don't mind.'

I handed it to him and he turned it over and over in his hands as though it were delicate china. He ran his cracked fingers over the diamonds and the pearly lid in the same way as I had done. He almost seemed to be caressing it.

'Do you love your mother, lad?' he said, after a while. 'Do you love her very much?'

'I do, I do love her,' I said earnestly, uncertain why he might ask such a question. Every child loves their mother.

'That's good, lad,' he said, quietly. 'You should love her. You should always love her.'

We returned to our waiting for the familiar tug on the lines.

After a while I felt I had to make some conversation, 'Were you in the War at all?' The question seemed to come from nowhere but it was one I often asked of older men, although not normally so soon after meeting them.

He was quiet a moment and then spoke very deliberately, 'I was, lad. I was in the Merchant Navy.'

'My father was in the War too. He was very young then. He doesn't speak about it much,' I said. 'He was in a place called Burma. I looked at it on a map. It is a very long way away. I've never been to Burma, have you?'

'No, lad . . . Burma, eh? Poor sod.' He said. 'I was on the Atlantic ships. That was bad enough. But, Burma, *bloody hell* . . . sorry, lad.'

There was a long silence. I wanted to ask what the 'Atlantic ships' were but got the impression that he didn't want to speak about it.

'Do you want to see a magic trick?' he said after a while.

'Yes please,' I said eagerly, keen just to break the silence.

He picked up his large black bucket and showed me the small crab he had at the bottom of it. 'Now, watch this lad. Watch carefully now!' He placed his bucket on top of my small blue one, which was empty, and tapped three times. He lifted his bucket away and the crab was in my bucket and gone from his.

'That's great,' I said. 'How did you do it?'

'Ah, a good magician never explains his tricks,' he winked.

We returned to our quiet. I looked into the swirls of water as the tide increased its flow, imagining what sleight of hand had accomplished the trick. I could not fathom it. At least it meant I had a crab though.

Jim flicked his line a few times to try and get a pinch. Then a strong eddy on the surface twined his line about mine, swiftly knotting an orange and green braid. I'd tangled my lines with father on a number of occasions and they could be real devils to undo if you weren't careful. We both reached forward to stop the lines from further entanglement and as we did so his rough hand caught the back of mine. An electric tingle passed through me. It was like the kind of static shock one got occasionally from the car door, but this didn't hurt very much and it lingered a little. As I felt the prickly shock pass through me I felt giddy and my eyes blurred. As my sight returned I had the strangest sense of looking at myself from where the old man was. I looked down to see my hands—old, worn hands—struggling with a green crab line, pulling it free from an orange line that was held by . . . *by me*. I blinked and the vision was gone. I was back to myself again.

'Not much happening with these crabs today is there?' the old man stuttered nervously.

I wasn't sure whether he'd felt the same sensation. It wasn't the kind of thing I thought I could ask about.

'Not by the look of it,' I said. 'Maybe they're all having a lie in.'

He laughed.

'So how you fellows getting on then?' father said, making us jump.

'Not even a sandwich-worth,' the old man said, showing him his empty bucket.

'Me neither, dad,' I said, pointing at the tiny crab in my bucket, clawing its puzzled way round and round its plastic prison.

'Never mind,' father said. 'I guess it'll have to be gruel for supper.'

I noticed mother behind him then and also spotted that they were holding hands. I hadn't seen them holding hands in ages. She had a great beaming smile and had a package under her arm, wrapped in brown paper.

'Thanks for looking out for him,' father said. 'Now we'd better get back to Sheringham before they sell out of ice-cream.'

I tidied up my things, tipped the dizzy crab back into the waters, and thanked the old man.

℘

The next few days passed in our usual holiday fashion. There were few specific plans, each day we decided over breakfast where we might go and what we might do. With each day father's grumpiness subsided and his cares seemed to evaporate, by mid-week we were a family again. On Wednesday evening father asked mother where she'd like to go on her birthday. She didn't have any particular plans but thought it might be nice to go back to Blakeney again and have lunch in the hotel. Also, she said, I needed to catch them some crabs for supper. I was delighted. I hoped we would meet the old man again and he could do another one of his silly tricks, preferably with a larger crab this time. Even though I hated the taste of them I loved to watch father prepare them, with pliers and long needles. It wouldn't be a proper holiday without him preparing a crab.

On the Thursday morning she opened her present from me and was really emotional over it. I knew I'd done well. She said she'd only keep very special jewellery in it. Then father brought out his gift to her and she feigned surprise.

'What could it *possibly* be . . .' she said. 'I really *can't* imagine . . .'

It was wrapped in a green paisley-patterned paper but as she peeled this back I saw the brown packaging beneath and recognised the shape of it from when on the quay. She unwrapped it carefully and took out a long picture in a thin gold frame. It was of a large rowing boat, up on a pebbly shore, with great waves thrashing beyond it in a stormy sea. A figure was hunched over the boat in a mackintosh, either preparing to unload, or to set

40

out; lobster pots littered the foreground of the picture, echoed in the sky by a gathering of dark clouds. The whole thing had a greenish-yellow tinge to it, as though it were quite dirty.

'My gosh, dear, it's delightful,' she beamed. 'How could you *possibly* have known . . .'

He leant over and kissed her. It was a passionate kiss that lasted a little too long. I felt awkward, sensing something slightly strange and forbidden in the atmosphere.

After breakfast, made by father and me, we took a slow drive to Blakeney, stopping for a blustery walk on the way at Salthouse beach. It was always so bleak there. The beach curved back around in both directions so that you felt you were always out at the very limits of the land. On a calm day it was good but on a day like this whilst it was exhilarating it also felt too isolating and threatening. Father loved it and admonished me for hiding behind him from the wind.

We were soon back at Blakeney though and we ordered a special tea to celebrate mother's birthday. It came with dainty little sandwiches and lots of cakes and scones. I wanted to get down to the quay though and get crabbing and I pestered them terribly to let me go on my own. I had seen Jim there on the drive in and was almost exploding with excitement. I pointed out that they'd be able to see me from the bay window of the hotel and so they eventually assented, probably to secure a little time together on their own.

I raced down to the quay, almost falling head over heels and screeched to a stop behind Jim.

'Hello again, lad,' he called to me, without looking round. 'No need to be in such a hurry. There's plenty of them pinching today. You'll have no trouble filling a bucket—even two!'

'Hello there, Jim,' I blurted, unpacking my line and preparing the hook. 'Oh no, I've got no bait.'

'Don't worry,' he said. 'You have some of mine.'

He took a whelk from a small bucket and performed his butchery on it and then threaded the remains on my hook.

'Urgh!' I squirmed.

Plop! The hook, weight and gory half-whelk sunk into the water. In moments I had a catch—quite a big one too. Jim fetched one about the same size seconds later. It seemed that no sooner had we thrown a line in than we'd fetch out a crab.

'We're on a roll here, lad,' Jim grinned.

I was delighted. Father would be pleased; there were at least two that were eating size.

Then the gusts that were at Salthouse reached us, and they'd picked up quite a pace. The sky filled with grey clouds, looking so much like the ones in the picture mum had opened that morning. There was even a drizzle of rain in the air and everyone busied themselves packing up their rods and lines, picnics and deckchairs. Old Jim and I just sat it out; he kept saying it would pass, it would pass!—almost willing it to move on. But it didn't and it got stormier.

I heard mother's voice calling to me, and I turned to wave to her. She was struggling to put an umbrella up against the storm. Then her voice was carried away by the growing wind; her mouth opening and closing in worried silence. I felt a tug on my line and turned to see Jim struggling with our lines again; they had become entwined and something seemed to be dragging them from below the water. I reached down to help him tug them free and as I did so he leant forward and whispered to me, 'I'm so sorry, lad; I just want a second chance at it all.' He caught my wrist as I was about to fall into the water and as he did so I felt a crackle of pain ripple through my arm. It was more than the previous shock I had from him earlier in the week. This seemed to wrack my body and I stared up at him in agonised alarm. His eyes were black, like the darkest waves in night seas far from land, but then they suddenly burst into a silvery whiteness as bright as the moon reflected in a still lake;

we were all fluid, I could not tell his hand from my arm, my face from his—at one moment I gazed at him and then in another I looked at myself. Then, the deepest darkness.

∽

We docked in Oban and unloaded our cargo, mostly landing gear and transports. They're planning some offensive, that's for sure. I hope so; this has all gone on long enough. It took a full day and a half to get back to Sheringham. Beryl cried for almost an hour when I arrived. She'd dreamt I'd been torpedoed. Bloody lucky I wasn't though; we lost ten ships in the convoy, out of fifty—that's a bad run (I didn't tell her about that though, I'm back to Gourock in a week, so I don't want her worrying). I calmed her down eventually and gave her a pack of stockings I'd traded with a Yank. Also I gave her some face cream in a nice little pot; a Geordie guy had told me that all the girls are loving the stuff, so I brought her the fanciest one I could find; a pink jar with mother-of-pearl inlay and a ring of sparkling stones. She cried again when I gave it to her. It's strange to be back home again. I almost don't recognise the place. It's so different to being on ship. Then again I haven't felt quite right since we docked.

I spent time with Beryl over those few days but mostly I was down at the beach watching the sea. There's something odd going on. I barely recognise myself when I look in the mirror. I can't quite remember everything that's happened recently. Maybe the depths of the Atlantic have stolen me away. Maybe the perpetual fear on the convoys has made me different to what I should have been. I am only at peace when I watch the tide— that cascade of endless ruin—it is not a calm peace though; it is a quiet searching for a true course back to myself.

BUT THEY WITHERED ALL

Ophelia. [sings] And will 'a not come again?
And will 'a not come again?
No, no, he is dead;
Go to thy death-bed;
He never will come again.

It is nine months now since we buried father. I saw their false, sad faces, squeezing out the crocodile tears; sniffing into newly purchased handkerchiefs still fresh with the creases from the packaging. What remained of him arrived in the back of a shiny black carriage, drawn by white horses. He was in a black coffin with silver handles. The rain pissed down on their charade as he was lowered into the ground. The priest's prattlings were whipped away into oblivion by a ferocious easterly gale. The poems they mumbled fell sadly to the ground, where the grass died of shame. They had arranged for expensive caterers—an ostentatious affair that they called 'a good send-off'. They knew, if he'd been alive, he would have thrashed them with a riding crop for the waste of it all. But he is dead; he is dead and I am tired. Let me tell you a few stories from that little town that nurtured us; a town that knew so little of our family that it felt compelled, instead, to make up what they didn't know. I shall return the favour.

There's Rosemary

'There's Rosemary,' we all used to cry. She'd be shuffling along on her way to, or from, somewhere, or nowhere, and all of us kids would run along behind her, muttering and egging each other on to some cruelty or other. She wore a long blue coat with some indiscernible fur trim around the collar. Whatever the weather was she wore it. We joked that beneath it there was nothing but an old rotten skeleton, with strips of leathery flesh hanging from its bones, or rivers of black, crawling maggots feeding on her rotting carcass. An oversized brown hat was always pulled firmly down about her neck and behind her she trundled a little tartan shopping trolley, patched here and there with plastic bags and red electrical tape. Within it, obviously, were the corpses of babies she had stolen from local mothers, and her pet rats, that someone said were her 'familiars' because that's what witches had—special animal friends that were really devils in disguise, and that could work all sorts of magic with her. She could see through their eyes, someone else said, and a bite from one of them would turn you into a zombie under her command. Whenever we saw a rat, in the park or out on the long fields up to Fir Bank, we always screamed and ran away, shouting, 'Help us! Help us! It's Rosemary. I don't want to be a dead zombie!'

When we chased behind her like a spineless pack of jackals we always smelt something that makes me think now of age and death—a sort of moth-ball, urine and TCP smell, topped with a heady musk of sweat; the fusion of bodily fluids with chemicals. And in her stinking wake it was our job to goad and coax one of our pathetic band into some misdeed, more daring than the one before, until, finally, we might have some reaction from her, and solve the mystery of her perpetual wanderings, her omnipresence and strange nauseating attraction.

That day it was Thomas Barrell who was pitched forward from our malevolent throng to enact the crime. He'd probably been planning it all along anyway; he was always so loud and arrogant. He'd brought a catapult with him that he said his dad used for fishing. Quite what catapults had to do with fishing none of us could fathom. But it looked vicious—sturdy moulded plastic arms, in camouflage greens and browns, forking up to a long elastic crosspiece that had a large rubber trough at the back to hold the projectile. In this case the ammunition was a chunk of tarmac, kicked up from the road; its edges were jagged and crumbling, but it was large and we all looked on in awe at Thomas' daring. Really, could it be possible that he would fire this thing at her? We squealed in glee and hoped that finally we would see Rosemary yelping and swearing, jumping in pain and running after us. All we wanted was something to acknowledge that she was just another old lady, like all the rest. Something to reassure us that there was not really a witch in our midst—that the world was just as dull and pointless at it was revealing itself to be.

The sound alone of the catapult's elastic thwack was terrifying. The piece of tarmac whistled through the air like disturbed bees swarming. The moment hung heavily as we watched in desperate expectation, and fear, of what should come to pass. The chunk of rubble tumbled and rolled, like a great black meteor careering through the emptiness of a great, hollow vastness. All was void and silence. Time collapsed into the open mouths of us greedy torturers, and we devoured it like penny sweets. Once the world began spinning again the rock hit Rosemary's immortal coat with a dull thud, like when I had seen my grandmother beating her carpets on the washing line. Rosemary stopped. We stopped too. Everything stopped. Thomas stood forward proudly in some kind of pompous victory pose. But as the seconds went by and nothing happened his expression weakened into a guilty fear, as though he saw something that we didn't. The anticipation was unbearable. She stood there, doing nothing at all, as though she had been turned into stone by the blow. It must have been painful; it had struck full into her back, high, almost between the shoulder blades.

Then, as though nothing had happened, she began to walk on again, with that same lolloping trudge, weighed down on one side by her shopping cart. She had triumphed. We were broken.

Thomas Barrell did not, at that moment, seem to be too bothered. But we all noticed, over the following months and years, a kind of shrinkage; a quietness crept upon him, and a sort of pasty, mottled hue afflicted his skin, as though he were not eating properly. He seemed perpetually tired, and was often seen on the park bench, staring blankly into the distance, when once he would have been playing football with his friends and racing around the town, up to all manner of mischief.

Rosemary still wanders our town. I think she was here before the Romans. They may have worshipped her, and before them so too may the Celts, or whatever tribe may have lived in these parts. Her movements are as perpetual as the seasons. She will never be forgotten.

Pansies

When Thomas grew up few of us would have thought that he would ever leave our town. Fewer would have credited him with the intelligence to have gone to a University. But he did. He studied philosophy, and his parents were proud of him. But Thomas was a troubled man, and reading, and thinking, thinking and reading, were clearly not the most wholesome of pastimes for one such as him. Whatever dark places his thoughts had taken him to should have been illuminated by more enervating and physical pursuits such as hill-walking, swimming, athletics, jogging, cribbage or tennis—indeed anything would have been preferable to the dark path into a subterranean, inner world that Thomas had begun to craft for himself; he should have taken heed about gazing into that abyss.

On his return from his studies we could all see the change in him. On the few occasions that he was spotted in the streets he scuttled like some kind of beige crustacean, from shop to shop, completing his mundane tasks as rapidly as possible, before he retreated to his parents' house to resume again his monumental, contemplative work. He spoke to nobody, and nobody spoke to him. He refused to get a job. He often refused to eat, or bathe. His body was being slowly exchanged for a ruthless brain, churning and striding through history, and possibility, like a great computer. His parents worried. They consulted friends and family for advice. They visited doctors and specialists—always without him. There were no answers, often because there were no clear questions; Thomas would have brought clarity to their faulty premises, if only he had been properly consulted.

When they found the bodies of Thomas and his parents they had lain there for three days, in a vast pool of their sticky inter-mingled blood; throats slit, they had expired together into their most basic element. Why Thomas had done it none would ever know. There was no note. Somewhere, hidden in a chemical exchange in the deepest part of Thomas' brain there was an answer.

I left a bunch of yellow pansies at the door, lost amidst the vulgar bouquets with their insincere, sentimental cards. I wrote a brief message on handmade paper, 'Goodbye Thomas, I will think of you, occasionally.'

Fennel

Lady Marchment was the widow of Sir David Marchment, the wealthy haulier, who had made his fortune far too young to be of any good to him, or those around him. And with such wealth comes the dubious advantage of local celebrity. Rather than escape our little town the Marchments chose to be gargantuan fish in a very small pond, and any minor thrashing of their golden tails sent ripples through all the other dutiful fry that struggled for sustenance within their wake.

After the death of Sir Marchment, the requisite ceremonies, and mourning period, Lady Marchment was seen about the town with many different gentlemen, none of whom were recognised within the local élite; indeed many of them were clearly much younger than the good Lady Marchment; obviously they were keen to ease her woes and help her through the rocky pathways of mourning with their youthful vitalism.

Lady Marchment was soon back into the swing of her usual responsibilities; chairing local societies and clubs, bringing together small armies of volunteers for various fundraising activities, and mustering the cake-baking skills of the entire county for fêtes and celebrations that many had forgotten were even events in the calendar. Such was the force of Lady Marchment and her all-consuming grief.

The height of the annual calendar was, of course, the summer parade and fête. This event required months of preparation, not only by the grand mistress of ceremonies but also by all of her attendant vassals, competing in scone-baking, vegetable-growing and wellie-throwing competitions galore. Lady Marchment assembled her teams of judges very carefully, hand-picked from the latest coterie of sycophants that attended her famous soirées at Marchment Towers.

As the great day approached a curious thing happened. A single pink rose was delivered to Lady Marchment, with a cryptic card that read, 'Here's to a wonderful tartlet!' Lady Marchment was initially indignant at the clear insult to her character. Then the following day two pink roses arrived, with another card that read, 'Here's to two wonderful tartlets!' She was more than curious now. Each day the number of roses multiplied, as did the mention of tartlets, in equal measure until, on the twelfth day, a full bunch of a dozen roses arrived along with a well wrapped cake box, inside which were twelve small baked tartlets. They had a curious fishy aroma, with some other strange smell that Lady Marchment couldn't quite place—a sort of liquoricey scent. She paused a moment, uncertain whether some vengeful loser from the previous year's cupcake competition might be trying to poison her (it was just the sort of thing Mrs Wright would do following her strawberry icing disaster, Lady Marchment thought). But then the enticing smell of the tartlets overcame her and she gave in to her desires. She had never tasted such a delicious savoury pastry, and something in the combination of flavours and the scent of the roses sent her almost giddy. She had to find out who had made them, to set them to work producing canapés for her guests.

She did not have to wait long, for on the day of the fête she discovered the mystery baker. All of the tasting, and judging, of the produce was done in strictest anonymity, naturally. But in the 'quiches and pastries' category what should she happen upon but an entry named, 'Fish and Fennel Fancies, Contestant 134'. They were the very same little delicacies that had been sent to her a week previously. Despite the other judges favouring a stilton and leek quiche, which had won for the last five years, Lady Marchment worked her skills of persuasion upon them, seasoned with veiled threats, to secure first prize for her mystery chef. She could hardly wait for the prize giving.

The moment came and she announced the winner for that category. Opening the prize envelope she read, 'And first rosette for "quiches and pastries" goes to . . . Mr Davis of Lesser Sileby.' A small man, maybe in his early seventies, rose to claim his award. He was stooped, and walked with the support of a white stick. He was in a finely-tailored grey suit that was now far too big for him. Lady Marchment awarded him his rosette and he smiled a thin smile to her in thanks. After a further hour of awards she was free to hunt down her elderly prey.

She could not find him anywhere, despite having sent a dozen of her lackeys scouring the marquees for him. She would have to wait until the following day and make enquiries in the village of Lesser Sileby—someone was sure to know him.

All enquiries produced nothing; no Mr Davis had been heard of round there, nor any individual matching the description. The oldest man in the village with a sight-impairment stick had moved to Wiltshire to be with his daughter three years previously, and he was a Mr James, not Davis.

A week after the fête another delivery arrived—a single white rose with a sprig of yellow fennel flowers. There was no message and no tartlet. With each day, as before, the number of roses increased but always there was a single sprig of fennel flowers and no hint of the sender. All enquiries with the delivery company were fruitless—they cited data protection rules, even generous cash bribes would not budge them. By October the deliveries were becoming ridiculous, some she even refused; sixty, sixty-one, sixty-two. It was like counting out the days of the year in flowers, and always the fennel sprig; and always only one. By January the roses had taken on a faint pink, which blushed its way brighter and brighter into March and April. Full reds began to appear in June; two hundred and thirty, two hundred and thirty-one. Marchment Towers had become a rose strewn wonderland. She was mystified. It was costing Mr Davis a small fortune, surely. When would it end?

It ended the day before the next year's parade and fête. Three hundred and fifty roses arrived, red to the brink of purple, with one sprig of fennel flowers. An hour or so later the police arrived too. They arrested Lady Marchment on suspicion of keeping brothels and trafficking.

The trial lasted months, and finished just before the following year's fête. As the details emerged—to the eager ears of the local gossips—it was revealed that Sir and Lady Marchment were not the well-to-do community pillars that they were thought to be. Their deeper cravings were for something more animal and cruel; the story of the treatment of 'her girls' was astonishing but few wished to dig much further, or pass judgement too much, lest their own complicity and darker hungers be revealed.

Lady Marchment was sentenced to fourteen years; that is a lot of fêtes.

Columbines

A taxi pulled up one day at the gates of HMP Foston Hall. A stooped man, in a grey suit, struggled slowly from the back seat. He had a white stick. He asked the driver to wait for him. He gathered himself together, brushed himself down, and stared up at the gates, fixing his resolve. He strode purposefully to them and laid down three red flowers with delicate fern-like leaves, wrapped crudely in kitchen roll. There was no note. They were not addressed to anyone. He returned to the taxi, shrugged slightly and smiled a sad smile of closure, and headed off into emptiness. Later that evening the flowers were picked up by a prison officer and thrown into a bin.

Rue for you, and here's some for me

I loved you once. You knew that, of course; how silly of me. I get carried away when thinking of the past. You made me a crown of daisies when we had been drinking in the park. I smiled; an awkward smile that you did not understand. I twined yellow rue through the little garland—my gift to us both; you did not understand. You took what you wanted; I gave it as freely as I was able, thinking throughout the brief event of what a pretty maiden I must look, down there, bare arse in the cold dirt, damp beneath the rhododendrons; so innocently crowned and so bitter with sorrow; a gentle regret that bodies must so easily relent to their ceaseless yearnings.

BUT THEY WITHERED ALL

A Daisy

I kept a flower—from the crown—pressed between the pages of a thick book on Mythology that mother gave me one Christmas, when I still thought the world was all stories and perfection. I chose that book because, at the time—such a foolish, childish time—I had thought myself to be Helen, and you Paris. But no—I knew it in my black heart—I was Leda and you were Zeus; there were no heroes, no heroines. But what you never knew was that you were not my first. No, I had already been plucked. As I came of age and the blood began to flow, I blossomed and fell into dishonour. With the exponential potential of that possibility—infinite life, bounded by the finite confines of my body—what hope, what love! Thank God it came to naught and that his dead, backward seed never flourished inside the hidden spaces of his own progeny. Oh, father! Why he could not let me be cast out upon the open ground to find my own place to flourish, to flower and decay; instead the rotten paranoia of his own reflection, the obsession with a corrupt purity. And you too sowed yourself in a barren place, all for your own gratification, and some sad, pointless expression of your dominance, guile and power. I looked at the desiccated little petals often, still clinging to their faded stem, and thought of how you and father would have become good friends, had either of you time enough to look beyond the mirrored walls you had erected about yourselves.

Some Violets

So, we near the end. They sent me to the madhouse when father died; an expensive, private establishment where their money could secure my perpetual silence. I had a further springtime there though, in the old house, before they managed to sell it

53

and divide the spoils between them. I was always hated by them; the youngest, the most adored, the apple of his eye, and other such nonsense. They did not know the demon I had to live with; to care for. They did not know his anger, his hate, or his needs. No, all they saw in me was a spoilt little girl who never grew up. All they saw in him was a dwindling pot of money and a mansion, crumbling into ruin. They did not know that it was my work that set them all free; to travel and enjoy their luxury cars; to pay off their mortgages and buy holiday homes abroad. Without my final intervention they would still be waiting; their shrivelled hearts blackening with every day he hadn't died— their souls envious shadows cast long behind his still bright twilight. Those treacherous cowards; they have me to thank—but if they ever knew, my God!, if they ever knew!

As I say, I had another springtime there and got to see the violets. They thronged about the steep bank leading to the woods where, in happier days, mother and I had walked and sung together. All I ever really had were those flowers; the annual dance of promise and disappointment of ruin. They taught me well.

Now I sit here, in my clean, clinical room, looking out upon some snowdrops, stark against the dark finality of practical hedges. Everything here is light and shade; a functional world of black and white. There are only the living and the dead; flesh and phantoms.

By next year, once the hate in my heart has seeped into the earth, the flowers will emerge, from their seeds or bulbs, and fall immediately into a brownish rot of leaves and petals. There will be nothing to see and nothing to hear. This lush world will unwork itself to a flat, sterile desert. There will be nothing but a light grey dust; the dust of countless billions of crawling, walking things; a dust lit to the brink of ignition by the savage sun of the useless day, and then frozen solid in the black cold of the senseless night. All will be gone, nothing will come again.

MIZPAH

The Lord watch between me and thee,
when we are absent one from another.
Genesis 31:49

He'd never really liked Staithes when he was a child, it seemed so boring. It was always billed as a holiday, staying at his grandmother's—his parents crammed in the tiny second bedroom and him on the sofa. He'd have preferred to have remained back in Manchester for the week, with his friends, rather than Staithes. Once he'd exhausted the pebble-throwing, the rock-pooling and the walks there were just days, frequently rainy, of jigsaw puzzles and fantasy gamebooks—and his grandmother's tales of 'better times' and complaining about all the foreigners. The odd day they had in Whitby, or even better in the amusement arcades at Scarborough, were beacons of joy in an otherwise miserable week. When he got back to school he'd hear about the kids that had gone to France, or Spain, or down to London to do sight-seeing. What did he have to write about in his holiday essay—Staithes, and grandmother. He'd get teased about it, 'Was a proper holiday too *Pricey* for poor Paddy?' the kids would jeer. It hurt him both in the truth of his family's poverty, but also mocked his name—Patrick Price. His friends knew he hated the name Paddy, as did his enemies. Now, forty years later, he could laugh about it—*Paddy Price*; it sounded like a dodgy betting shop.

When his mother had died and left him the house he was certain he'd sell it. A couple of trips back changed his mind. It coincided with his move to freelance web-design, and it proved to be the perfect place to get a break from city life and focus on projects in peace. Perhaps he was getting old, he thought. He'd never found the 'right girl' and never had any children. His time was his own and most of that was spent working. So 'Lyn Cottage' became his 'working retreat' (he was always careful not to call it a holiday home) for the time being.

One pastime he did allow himself, and one begun when he had holidayed in Staithes, was collecting postcards. When he was young he'd collect anything, from the more modern saucy seaside card to picture cards from everywhere he visited. As he grew older, and as his collection became more refined, and by the necessity of space had to become sparser, he'd begun to specialise in portraits and signed celebrity cards, especially of the silent film era. A couple of months previously, at a car boot sale, he'd acquired a number of these in a suitcase, along with quite a lot of more general interest. There was, he'd already noticed, a few from Staithes, Whitby and Scarborough. He'd brought the case with him for his stay throughout most of May. He could sort them over the coming weeks and see what was worth keeping—you never knew when you'd strike on a gem. American collectors were willing to pay high prices for them, especially older cards, and now it was easy to sell to anyone, anywhere, online. He had, of course, built his own website for exactly that purpose and it made a profitable second income.

He'd trundled his cases down the steep slope of Bank Bottom and got himself settled in. He passed by the strange shop a few doors up that was shut—again. It was an odd place. It was called The Emporium and seemed to sell all manner of things. Old toys, sun-bleached even behind yellow sun filters, sat alongside hair rollers and cotton buds, windscreen wipers were propped against a peeling poster of Marilyn Monroe pinned to the wall with increasingly sized lock knives. It had always had an eclectic display, even when he came as a child, but he had never once seen the place open. On the last few visits it had really started to bug him and he'd frequently peer into the window to try and see if there was anything going on in the space beyond. There never was.

He was working on a website for a games company and needed to complete a first version by mid-June. He was enjoying it. The company specialised in wooden board games and wanted to have animated versions of the games being played by figures made out of sticks. The animation was costing a fortune and they wanted it to be delivered in a very slick fashion. Trying to get the right kind of platform, and the right aesthetic, was proving tricky. Patrick had planned out the month and was confident he'd get it finished. After a few days he was getting frustrated though, there were compatibility problems between the formats of the video materials that were becoming insurmountable. He decided to take the weekend off; go down to Whitby for a night out for a change and then have a decent Sunday lunch. It was very enjoyable but the looming thought of starting work again on the website the following day was bothering him. On the Sunday evening he opened a bottle of red wine and decided to have a look through the postcards in the suitcase to take his mind off it.

He fished out the local cards he was keen to sort and flicked through them on the sofa. The pile grew of common cards—tatty and generally worthless. There were many scenes of the steep High Street and Bank Bottom and more of the view out to sea with The Cod and Lobster pub in the foreground. They were nearly all tourist cards, sent to relatives across the country; likewise the ones of Whitby and Scarborough. There were a few older ones that might have some value—there was a nice postcard packet, in an original envelope, of the churches in Staithes entitled 'The Five Virtues'. These were in very good condition and he guessed they were from the 1930s; maybe fifteen to twenty pounds—the whole suitcase-full had cost thirty. Then a card caught his attention. It read 'Mizpah' in ornate script, beneath which were two shaking hands within a purple heart; from the two sides of the heart sprouted flowers in delicate pinks and blues. Below that again was a picture of a woman, maybe in her early twenties, in a bonnet, and below that was a short poem,

> *Go thou thy way and I go mine;*
> *Apart, yet ever near;*
> *Only a veil hangs thin between*
> *The pathways where we are;*
> *And "God keep watch 'tween thee and me,"*
> *This is my prayer;*
> *He looks thy way, he looketh mine,*
> *And keeps us near.*

On the back it read,

> *19th February 1917*
> *Dearest Patrick,*
> *I know this is hard to read, when so much separates us. Just to let you know that I love you, however incredible that might seem. I would say that I would wait for you but you will soon know how impossible that is . . . Just as impossible as it is for you to wait for me. I will keep true to you though—I will keep true!*
> > *Goodbye my sweet!*
> > *Florence*

He read the lines again, half taking it to be addressed to him. It was odd to read his name on something a hundred years old, with the thought that it belonged to another person. The right hand side of the postcard was blank. It had never been sent. He knew there were many cards like this sent in the War but couldn't recall what '*Mizpah*' meant. It would have been more valuable if it were addressed to a specific 'Patrick'; a 'Patrick' who had been posted to a battle front—even more valuable if he had been killed heroically. The whole game was about provenance—and to get that you needed more to go on than this card offered; a surname for a start. This one might fetch ten or fifteen pounds. The only connection he could see to Staithes was the picture of the woman on the front; the famous Staithes bonnet, beyond that he'd probably never know the mysterious 'Florence'.

Something about the word, *Mizpah*, seemed familiar though —beyond his familiarity with the war cards. He was sure he'd seen it somewhere in the village, but couldn't think where. The more he looked at the woman's face on the card the more he thought that she seemed familiar too. She had kind eyes, but tinged with a sadness; unsurprising really, life had been hard here for many years—fishing hardly brought a community great wealth, but it did bring great, and frequent, tragedy. Perhaps she had lost her love to the sea—it was just as likely as the War.

He looked up 'Mizpah' on the internet and found dozens of cards, many fetching good prices, and pieces of jewellery. It seemed it had been a Victorian fad—so many things were— especially for the jewellery. It had a biblical source, as a place in Israel where Jacob and Laban had raised stones as a symbol of their bond with each other. The Victorians had sentimentalised it, of course, and then it had a revival during the Great War, especially for lovers, but also for family members. He'd have to look into it further in the morning. He wasn't sure he'd want to sell it; it was very attractive, and poignant. Florence was attractive too, in a rugged sort of way. He looked up at the clock—it was one in the morning. He'd been staring at the card for over an hour.

That night he dreamt of Florence. He was following her up to Penny Nab, above the village—no, he was chasing her; she was running, glancing back at him every now and again. It was definitely her face—that sad beauty. It wasn't a nightmare, as such. It hovered in that unnerving dream-place where there is an ill-defined sense of dread; the mood is of foreboding, as tangible as stormy air on a hot summer day. Nothing terrible happened —indeed nothing much happened at all, beyond the pursuit— but he felt it might at any moment. Consequently, upon waking, he felt lethargic, his sleep clearly having been poor and fitful. A walk out on the sea front would clear his head, as would a good breakfast down at The Cod and Lobster.

'Lyn Cottage' was the last on the left at the bottom of the High Street as it turned to the seafront. In the summer he could see all the tourists struggling up and down the steep hill, peering in the giftshops and even in the front rooms of the cottages— they seemed to view them as exhibitions in some large living museum created solely for their entertainment. He preferred to come off season when it wasn't so crowded—perhaps, in the high season, he should rent it out as a holiday cottage. He headed up to the bakers and the newsagent, past the permanently closed 'Emporium', as he mused on the pros and cons of renting out the cottage. He picked up a paper and a packet of morning rolls for his lunch. At the till in the newsagent—cluttered with lottery scratchcard units, tubs of out-of-date sweets, plastic charity boxes and other junk—he spotted a small booklet on the history of Staithes. He had quite a few of these, collected over the years as various enthusiasts had self-published the fruits of their obsessions. This looked to be a new one though. What struck him was the image on the front—the same woman in the bonnet from his postcard; she was standing on some steps, outside a small cottage with neatly ordered window boxes and tubs, with her arms crossed, in a defiant pose.

'Hey there, Patrick, you off with the fairies?' It was Rod, the owner of the newsagent—head of the local choir, chess club champion four years in a row and all-round community stalwart.

'Sorry, Rod,' he said. 'Yes, I was rather elsewhere. How much is this one, it is new isn't it?'

'Yes, it is,' Rod said, leaning forward and whispering. 'It's a tenner—very overpriced, if you ask me. It's by that chap who bought The Cobles up on Cowbar Bank a couple of years ago—Bill Jennings. I don't think it's nearly as good as Brian Verrill's one, but that's old now. Bill reckons he's uncovered lots of new stuff, but I couldn't see it myself.'

'I think I'll take one anyway,' Patrick said. 'As you know I like the old postcards and there might be some in there I haven't seen before.'

Picking up the thin paperback book he noticed a nameplate on the cottage behind the now familiar woman—*Mizpah*.

A few moments later Rod jolted him from another daze, 'You can go now, I've got your money.'

Patrick laughed obligingly but felt unnerved by the sudden rush of connections and coincidences. He headed off for some breakfast, keen to flick through the book in search of some more information on 'Florence'.

He sat at his usual table, looking out across the sheltered bay by New Landing. Further out to sea it was rough and storms had been forecast for that afternoon. He saw dots of bright tourist jackets up on the nabs; he hoped they'd heeded the warnings. A steaming plate of kippers arrived, enough to feed four, and a big pot of tea. He flicked through the book looking for any further images that would give him a clue to the mysterious woman that had now become a fixation in just a few hours.

There, towards the end, was a chapter on the local fisher-women. In amongst the many portraits of stern, suspicious faces all sporting the ubiquitous bonnet, and the scenes of them carrying heavy skeels upon their heads up steep cobbled streets, there were a number of brighter pictures in Sunday dresses; with children, with laughter. Then, there she was again—the image from the cover. The caption read, 'Florence Cole, outside her cottage, *Mizpah*, about 1920. Florence was a well-known local who never married but serviced the boats until her retirement in the late 1950s. From then on she was famous for sitting on the steps of her cottage selling "Cracklin' Toffee" to the tourists and locals alike. She is credited with erecting the stone pillars at Penny Nab, in memory of her betrothed who was killed in the Great War.'

Out in the bay Patrick spotted a coble with a man standing in it, struggling with three lines of tangled rope. It was Tommy McTeir, an eccentric Scotsman who had moved down to Staithes in his teens from Aberdeen. His coble was always immaculate, painted in bright reds and blues. He'd never noticed before though—or more accurately had never had cause to note—the name of the boat, but it struck him now: *Mizpah*.

Patrick ran out and called over, 'Tommy, Tommy, how are you today? Looks to be a storm later . . .'

'Aye, ye can really feel it out there,' he said, tugging on a length of blue rope. 'It's gonna be a bad un. I'm finished the day noo.'

'I hadn't seen the name of your boat until now, *Mizpah*; can I ask you what it means?' Patrick shouted. The boat was drifting further from the jetty.

Tommy teetered as the boat rocked from side to side with his exertions. 'Oh, aye,' he said. 'I named her after yon cottage up to Lining Garth. I was just taken with the name—sounds a bit odd, maybe, but it means to keep you safe when you're apart from each other. I named her that so the good Lord would keep her from being nicked in the night, ken?' He laughed.

He was always going on about things being stolen from him. Patrick couldn't remember a single crime in Staithes, so why he should be so concerned with that was beyond him.

'What year did you move here, Tommy?' he yelled.

'Wait there,' he replied. 'I'll pull her in a bit. I can't hear a word.' The old fisherman dragged the boat in on its line and moored up. He bounced onto the jetty like a man in his twenties.

'What's that you say, Pat?' Tommy said, wiping his hands on his jumper.

Patrick hated *Pat* too. 'I was just wondering when you came to Staithes?'

'Oh, it was 1959, day after my fourteenth birthday,' he said. 'My ma was awfa sad to come but pa was sure we'd have a better life doon here. I dinna ken if he was right or no—but here I am still, all these years on.'

'Yes, not doing too bad, are you Tommy,' he said, edging round to his real question. 'So, do you remember a woman in the village, a woman who sold toffee . . . her name was Florence Cole.'

'God, do I remember Flo . . .' he beamed. 'Oh, aye, and I've never tasted toffee that good since she died. God, old Flo, what brings you to her?'

'Oh, nothing really,' he said. 'I've just been reading about her and thought you might remember her, that's all.'

'Aye, I sure do,' he nodded. 'And that'll be why you asked about the boat too—'cause it were her hoose it were named after.'

'Yes,' Patrick nodded, watching the moored cobles bob in the tide. 'Where is the house?'

'Like I said, up Church Street, last one against Lining Garth,' Tommy said. 'Now I'm awa for a tea, you like a cup?'

'No, no, you're alright, Tommy, thanks,' he said. 'I've got breakfast waiting for me in the pub.'

Tommy shrugged and trudged off to his home on the other side of the bridge.

Patrick turned to go back and finish his breakfast. Behind the pub a figure vanished from view; a woman in a thick shawl, with a bright blue skirt, puffed out with heavy layers of red petticoats, gathered in tiers through the skirt. On her head was a grubby bonnet. In the moment he had to take in her antiquated dress she had gone. He ran around the pub to find her. There was nobody, just a large blue recycling bin.

Back in the pub his breakfast had been cleared away. He wasn't that hungry anyway. They offered to make him more once they'd realised their mistake. A glass of orange juice would be fine.

He sat there again for a good while, as the clouds gathered outside. He stared at the picture of Florence on the front of the book and was overcome by a sense of yearning for her that was so irrational but so overwhelming that it worried him. The dress—although pictured here in black and white—was exactly the same kind as he had seen a couple of minutes before on the figure behind the pub. He gazed into the eyes of a woman long dead. It was as though he knew her—as though he had always known her.

෪

For the next two weeks he thought of little else but Florence Cole. He tried to do some research into her but found little more than reference to her famous toffee. A couple of guide-books mentioned the stones up at the nab. He'd seen them before but hadn't thought much of them. They stood about six feet tall, either side of one of the pathways up to the top. Towards the end of each day he would catch sight of the woman in the blue and red skirts, with the bonnet. She would stand further up the High Street and just stare at Lyn Cottage. He watched her through the net curtains. She did not approach. She just watched for about half an hour and then headed off up Church Street. Nobody greeted her and she did not seem to acknowledge anybody either. A couple of times he went out to confront her, but by the time he'd opened the door she was gone. He hadn't seen anyone in the village wear the bonnet in years, other than on the pageant day in August. Whenever he tried to work all he felt was a spooky sense of presence. He ended up checking the window more than working on the website.

He resolved to pack his things up the following morning and head back to Manchester. This Florence Cole nonsense had become an unhealthy distraction and whoever this was that was watching him each day was surely trying to wind him up.

He slept well that night; his resolve to go home clearly bringing him back to reality. He popped up to the newsagent to get some snacks and a drink for the journey, and to say goodbye to Rod. On the way back he noticed that the window display in The Emporium had changed. The pack of windscreen wipers had been replaced by a mannequin head with a classic Staithes bonnet on it. It made him think of Florence—surely it was no coincidence; the woman that was watching him must be connected to the shop somehow. He peered in at the window again, trying to adjust his eyes to look through the grubby yellow sun film and the gaudy junk on display to the shop beyond. A dim light came from somewhere out the back, probably from a skylight. Why was it never open—who could afford to keep a shop running that never had the opportunity to sell anything? His nose pressed against the dirty window pane and he heard a voice beside him.

It was on old lady. She looked up at him and asked, 'Are you okay, dear?'

'Oh, I'm fine,' he said, feeling somewhat ridiculous. 'I was just curious why this shop never seems to be open.'

'It's been like that for years,' she said. 'David Farley owns it. He's been taken full sick now though—just last week. He only opened it occasionally even when he was well. But now they say it's the cancer and that he won't be coming home. It'll be sad to lose another shop, even one you couldn't rely on too much.'

Out of the corner of his eye he saw a flash of blue and red. He turned and saw her at the bottom of the High Street, right by his house. She was only fifty yards away. He could probably catch her. He ran—without a word of goodbye to the old lady—as fast as he was able down the steep slope.

She was away as soon as he had started, moving at such a speed—her sturdy black boots, though they looked uncomfortable, certainly could go. They must have hob nails in them because they made such a racket on the cobbles as she gathered her skirts in her hands and virtually sprinted through the warren of streets; it was the clatter of them that helped him keep track of where she'd gone. She took a turn into Barris Square and then slipped round the back of a couple of cottages; he heard her going up the steps to Gun Gutter and then through The White Horse's garden and onto Church Street. As he turned onto that road, out of breath, he saw her striding up the steep bank towards Penny Nab. He didn't fancy clambering up there right now but he had to find out who she was, and this was the closest he'd got to her. She kept looking back at him, but he thought it unlikely he'd catch her unless she started to tire. She had what looked to be an old tin tucked under her arm. He did not gain on her at all, but he was not lagging behind either. She seemed to have slackened the pace a little. She still kept turning occasionally and then stopped suddenly, near to the stone pillars. She sat down and placed the tin on her lap.

In a couple of minutes he was near her, panting and choking. She was identical to the pictures of Florence—almost as though they could be twins. She must be related, he thought. She did not seem to have even broken a sweat and looked up at him, smiling. He was desperate to speak but couldn't until he had his breath back.

'Goodness me, you aren't very fit are you?' she said. 'I'd expected someone with a bit of puff in them.' She took the lid off the tin and unwrapped a thick sandwich from some brown paper. He could smell the fish.

He sat down. The view was wonderful, with the houses sprawling down the steep banks, almost as though they were tumbling into the sea. He hadn't been up here in years. Despite the warmth of the sun the wind coming off the sea was cold. He was still huffing and puffing and the gusts took what little breath he had away. She was right; he was unfit. 'Why have you been watching my house? And I assume it was also you who followed me to the pub a while ago too?'

'I just had to check it was you?' she said. 'Do you want half of my sandwich? It might do you some good by the look of it.'

'No thank you,' he said. 'I don't really think that talk of sandwiches is quite appropriate after you've been stalking me.'

'You're not a deer,' she said, bluntly.

'I feel a bit like one,' he said. 'What is it you want?'

'What do we both want?' she said taking a large bite of her sandwich.

'You must be related to Florence Cole,' he said, 'the lady that built those stone pillars in memory of her fiancé. Now what is it that you want from me?'

'What do you mean?' she said. 'Those stones are *ours*. I had them built.'

She took another bite of her sandwich. He could hear her chewing, even above the wind.

He wasn't sure what to say, so kept silent.

'Yes, it took them five days to put them up,' she said, taking the lid off the tin again and taking out an apple. 'Good of them to do it for me really. I hadn't got much money to pay them for it. I got them a few drinks in when I had some spare, but beyond that, they did it out of compassion. Especially good of them, given that they all thought I was a looney—knowing full well I didn't have a beau in the war. Mrs Galen probably had a word with them.'

She was so casual—as though they'd known each other years.

'Who's Mrs Galen?' he asked, quietly—best to entertain her for a while, until he could get to the bottom of what was going on.

'Oh, she's our local cunning-woman,' she said, crunching into the apple and speaking whilst chomping it. 'She's how . . . I found you. Or, should I say . . . how *she* . . . found you were looking for *me*. I've never really liked apples, don't know why I keep on trying.' She hurled the apple down the nab, it came to rest on a grassy ledge and was immediately set upon by five greedy gulls.

'Right, so you used a witch to track down someone from the future?' he said, sarcastically.

'Yes,' she said. 'But she's not really a witch. She'd be very offended if you called her a witch, really she would. She's just someone who remembers old ways things worked; knowledge about people and places and ways in-between. I'm guessing you don't believe me anyway. I wouldn't if I were you. But seeing as I've been through them doors a few times now and seen what I have here—I believe it full well.'

He didn't believe her, but at the moment he had no other explanation for the recent peculiar events. He'd hear her out. She said nothing more.

'Only a veil hangs thin between the pathways where we are, Patrick,' she said, eventually—a touch exasperated. 'I think you know—or will come to know—that I speak the truth . . . time *is* a thin veil . . . *you* felt the pull to *me* . . . you felt that *through* time. I felt it to *you*. And here I am.'

He stared out at the sea—the same sea for thousands of years; the same in its difference.

'So, if such a thing is true—and I'm not saying for one minute it is!' he said. 'What happens now? You're Florence Cole, a woman from 1917, who has travelled to the future to find a man she has never met . . . Aren't there rules about this sort of thing—I've seen it on the films . . . won't you *corrupt the stream of time*, or something? You might take knowledge back that will *destroy the world*!' His melodramatic mockery did not raise any response. 'But seriously, who are you? And why do you keep following me around.'

'I *am* Florence, but I prefer Flo, it was only really my da' what called me Florence,' she said. 'And you're right, Mrs Galen warned me not to talk to anyone; not to read any newspapers; not to try to find out about anything at all about history after my time. I was just to see you . . . briefly . . . and then go back. That is what I will do. It's almost time to go. Seems funny now, after all what I've been through to get here, that we'll be parting so soon.'

'You must explain yourself properly . . .' he began, indignantly.

'Now, Patrick, you be quiet now. You can get to thinking later,' she said. He was quiet. She stood and brushed herself down and then came and stood by him. 'Now how about a goodbye kiss, my dear?'

He was astonished but struggled to his feet. She helped him up and then embraced him tightly. He did not know what to do. She smelt of fish and sweat, with a sweet perfume in the background—was it rose? She was warm—she was real. She reached up and grasped his neck, pulling him to her. It was a strong kiss.

'Remember, my sweet,' she said. '*I will stay true!*' She walked off down the nab, turned into Church Street, and was gone. He just stood there and watched her leave.

He felt weak. The gulls whirled above him, looking for more food. One perched on top of the nearest stone pillar. He wandered over. It flew off, soaring down to the harbour. The pillar was constructed of wide, flat stones laid on top of each other, and secured with a thin layer of cement between each. It had crumbled in many places and the pillar furthest from him looked quite weak about half way down. At each of their bases there was a plaque, half-obscured by soil and grass. He knelt down at the first one and cleared it away. It read,

Florence Cole
13th May 1897 – 23rd October 1967
Go thou thy way and I go mine;
Apart, yet ever near;

The date of her death had been added in a different font and still had a brassy patina to it that the other script had lost. He felt elated, terrified, confused and angry all at once. There was no strength left in him. He crawled on his hands and knees over to the other pillar, where he cleaned the other plaque,

Patrick Price
. . .
He looks thy way, he looketh mine,
And keeps us near.

His mind reeled with astonishment. His heart sank in despair.
Three cobles were heading back in to the village; another storm was brewing. They bobbed along, as thousands like them had before, over the centuries—back to the safety of dry land.

WE DON'T WANT FOR COMPANY

Welcome to you, friend! Yes, please do, please do, sit yourself down here, the fire is only just taking. This is a dark night and that is for certain. You are lucky to have made it this far without accident. You have timed it well. I have wood aplenty and a little rabbit if you'd care to.

ॐ

Oh, I see. I have always found rabbit to be almost a fruit of the earth. I have never really thought too much about meat. Everything is surely the harvest of the world. But if you have brought some of your own food then you enjoy it. It is all of the same substance in the end. We have fire and conversation and that provides wonderful complement to the glory of these stars and the hard truth of this chill wind, and the dark shadow of the hill. Let us wait for the promise of the morning.

ॐ

Ah, you have come to see the chalk figure have you—many do, many do. I seldom see them now though—the tourists. I prefer the nights myself. Or rather, I have *become accustomed to* the *gifts of the night* to be more precise—the quiet, the depths of contemplation, the revelations of a certain kind of solitude. And, I have my promises to keep and my responsibilities to the coming day to attend to. There are those of us who attend to our obligations, rather than the frivolities of leisure . . .

℘

Oh, no, I didn't mean that at all. Do stay.

Don't you find that in the night you are never really alone anyway—if you look beyond the simple aspects of it? While it appears, to the surface observer, that the dark seems to envelop one and make one feel alone it is actually the opposite that holds true. At the edges of the fire there are always shapes, gatherings of things that edge around in the gloom—works of the imagination perhaps, or hints of past events, coming to our consciousness in ways unfathomable.

I doubt you'd be able to find adequate ground to pitch a tent now anyway, I'm afraid. There's a fairly sharp incline off to the South there, which you'd need to steer clear of, and heading uphill much further it gets very steep and rocky. You were lucky to have made it up the old track from the West given how little it is used these days. I hope you didn't have too much trouble there. It wends and winds so much because it comes through the old barrows. They must remain undisturbed. Even the dead of long ago deserve their rest, wouldn't you agree?

As I said, you're welcome to share the fire, there's fuel enough until the first light and the majesty of the dawn.

℘

No, not at all. I answer what is asked of me. I have nothing to hide. I've been around these parts all of my life really. I used to work the land more. I used to dwell with others more but now I like my own space, and these old-fashioned places; they seem more homely for one such as myself.

72

I must prepare this rabbit now, if you don't mind. It needs cooking soon, and my belly is aching for some simple fare.

ဆ

You have never seen a rabbit prepared? Well, it is one of the simplest things to do, but one must be attentive to a few basic points. I prefer to leave the head on until I prepare and joint the meat. Others say that removing the head and full bleeding will give more tender meat, but I prefer the richness of the flavour and am happy to have a tougher flesh. The first incisions must be made in the back, to avoid puncturing the organs, then you can fold the skin back easily and the whole pelt can be removed in one go. With a skilled twist of the neck one should not even need to use the knife to remove the head.

After skinning and removing the head you must be careful with the evisceration. The colon and bladder, once burst, will ruin the meat entirely and must be handled carefully—discard them quickly. This is why I prefer to prepare the animal here by the fireside. Although the heart, liver, kidney and lungs make for fine eating I always cast the lot upon the fire, with the skin and the head. It is my little offering to the skies—that their smoke might fuse with the rain and fall again to the ground to bring forth more creatures to turn the great wheel of existence.

Then . . . four . . . swift . . . stokes . . . and you have removed the fore and hind legs and have the torso remaining whole. All can be popped straight into the pot, with herbs and a few vegetables, and the fire will take care of the rest.

You look pale, my friend, are you alright?

ဆ

Oh! That is a terrible bite. Yes, these flies can be a curse, especially on these autumn evenings. I have never been bitten

73

but have seen many who have. I know of leaves, you see, that, once rubbed all over, will keep them from the skin.

ℰℭ

Yes, they are a very particular kind of river fly, found only round these parts; they seem drawn to the hills in the evening and stay active throughout the night, perhaps more so even than in the day.

That will come up well and bring much pain. It will seem to be more of a blister for a day or two. It will subside though, once you've returned home. Some folk round here take it for a sign that you are not welcome in a place, and that there is witchcraft afoot. But it is a kind of witchcraft that can heal up such things—so what does that say of silly gossip, eh?

ℰℭ

No, how can one be lonely in a place such as this—a place that echoes with the memories of a thousand dead souls all crying out to have their pasts recalled; all clamouring for the light of day again; to be reborn, whether it be through the composting of the ground, or the ebb and flow of tide on shore, all things are reformed and reshaped into everything else, each blade of grass was once the bone and blood of living beasts that grazed upon it in another incarnation. No, my friend, we don't want for company—none of us do. You must listen for the voices that are always speaking about you, and watch for them that comes to visit, even when you cannot see them.

Wouldn't you say that something of what I speak is in that hillside figure you've come to see? What might he be saying to them what comes to look upon him?

ℰℭ

No, I do not care what your books say. The figure is not that old at all. What it speaks of—what it shows us—is ancient indeed, though. The men that carved it, that brought it back to our minds when we had all but forgotten it, were working with the old lore. They hoped they might recall something from the darkest places of our minds and make us see again, and listen again, to those things that compel us to join together; to seek shelter from the night; to sow seed; to celebrate the harvest; to revel in the sun . . . to enjoy the precious fruits of the world.

℘

That is most kind of you. I shall have a handful if you have them to spare.

℘

Ah, such ripe and beautiful fruits. Don't you feel they are the very quintessence of Autumn—dark, juicy, rich and so complex; a sharp tang of the violence of the summer heat followed by those hidden flavours of earth and thorny hedgerow. The blackberry unfolds the flavours of the damp darkness that heaps itself upon us all eventually.

But these really don't belong to you, do they? You picked them on that path that leads up by the old chimney stack. Did you see it?

℘

Yes, indeed, it is charred. I'm surprised you noticed it to be honest, with all the brambles and bracken that have grown around it after all these years. Few come up here now, and of those few that do even fewer come by that almost forgotten path.

No, that is not entirely true, it is not so much *forgotten* as *remembered*. But what *is* remembered, by *most*, has become a silly thing of rumour and tall-tales, fireside stuff for the children really—not like a campfire tale at all; a tale where you can feel the darkness of the night about you, rather than see it through the comfort of your window panes. Wouldn't you agree; do you like a little campfire story?

ဢ

Well, why not tell it to me?

ဢ

Ah, yes, I heard it before, many, *many* times, in different forms, from different mouths. But I can tell you that those men you speak of where not like other men. They were my brothers. They were my kin.

ဢ

No, no, of course, it was many years ago now—but what are centuries, my friend, in this endless circle of life. Kin can be more than just blood you know. There is kinship of the mind, and of the soul. They were men who knew the ways of the earth and all of its abundance. They knew what plants could cure and what could harm; what might open the eyes to other places just on the edges of our own, and what might shut those eyes forever.

And what of it that they did not drink with the slobs that surrounded them and found their fellows to be nothing but fools and scoundrels? They chose a life of the true wilds and worked in isolation to restore the old laws to this impoverished land— and their thanks for their sacrifices? Hah! Unmarked graves at the crossroads; the subject of petty superstitions and wilful misrepresentation by the barking congregations of a new God they could never even comprehend. But still the heavens moved about those treacherous villagers, the day dawned on their deeds and they felt ashamed. They shunned the path you came here on, filled with guilt and the terrors of false tales told beside their Grandmother's fireside. They let it go wild and return to the land and they closed their eyes to reality, and to their true ancestors.

But, I grow angry. I apologise.

I yearn for a world of tolerance and understanding, not one of venom and revenge.

I will take a drink of a little herbal remedy to ease my spirits, would you care for some?

℘

That is entirely your choice my friend. I find it strange now that people do not chose to enjoy the nectar of the land and prefer water from plastic bottles and cans. A few sprigs of this, and leaves of that, mixed with the fresh water of the hillside spring will revitalise many an ailing body. Yes, all about us is a rich garden of medicine. These plants are a gift of the heavens. Without the rising sun and its benevolent light there would be nothing on this wretched earth but a frozen wasteland. And that is why we must ensure that the dawn will always rise.

Have you ever been gripped by the fear that the dawn would never come? I mean a *real*, unshakeable *terror*, that you would never see the light again—that the future of the world would be unending darkness of a kind that this moonless night would make seem as though it were the brightest summer day. Imagine if the world stopped turning. Imagine the freezing cold. Imagine

77

the perpetual night. Imagine the mad packs of humanity turning upon each other like feral creatures, in fear and hunger, as every crop failed, as the animals died about them and the flies and insects, viruses and bacteria, seized hold of the planet. In that eternal, black night man would descend to the depths and chaos would return.

So there are those of us tasked with the sacrifice of keeping watch upon the night and ensuring that its tyranny will end. There are others whose sacrifices are that much more straightforward. They are the blessed.

You would have done well to have drunk a draught of this, my friend. It soothes all pain and would have made the next part of our tale that much the easier for you. Well, now we've had our fill perhaps we should begin that new story, it won't be long in the telling. It won't be *long* in the telling, *at all*; they never are. An event is only ever the prelude to the real, eternal performance of history. It is in the *retelling* that all stories properly begin to live.

OPHELIA

I have seen great castles rise and fall. I have seen dragons breathe fire and giants tumble from clouds in the sky. I have seen frogs turn into princes, and princes turn into frogs. I have seen a dwarf spin gold. I have seen geese lay golden eggs. I have been witness to the greatest battles ever fought; Agincourt, Hastings and Gettysburg. I have dined with maharajas, princesses, dukes and emperors. I have dug for buried treasures across all of the seven seas. I have ridden elephants with Hannibal. I was at the court of Queen Victoria. I sailed with Magellan into history. I have climbed Everest and swum the wreck of the Titanic.

We had such times! And there were the parties, of course, the endless parties, day after day. I was clothed in rich gowns; blues, crimsons and rich creams—you dressed and undressed me a dozen times in an afternoon. We would dance and talk until your eyes fell heavy and you would have to sleep; weariness, our perpetual nemesis! I watched you as you slept—always watched you, guarded you.

How can we have known such joy; watching birds from the window, walking the gardens in spring and gathering kindling in the winter. Everything was dusted with magic and the simplest of tasks became infused with heroism and the mythic power of a fairy-tale—we transported the dull world into mystery. Nowhere was hidden from us, all of history our playground— we travelled its wonders together. What you did not know you invented. Anything that can be thought I have enacted—all with you, my beloved; all with you, my loving mistress. Our days were not metered by the pendulum of the grandfather clock and its ominous hourly lament; our time was a gust of summer wind, the opening of flowers in the morning sun, the flick of a cat's tail, dew on spiders' webs, rime on a shadowed sundial, the gradual slowing of a spinning top; our time was crayon and chalk, not pen and ink—it was erased and reformed a thousand times within an instant and an afternoon might last three months, or be gone in a blink of tearful eyes.

It was the day that you found me that you gave me my name. Your father thought it odd and tried to dissuade you. We knew it was right—we knew I was destined for greatness. I knew you had chosen well and that we would live out our days together in sunshine and bliss. I did not know that after sunshine comes the dark. I did not know that after bliss comes woe.

As the years massed you grew tall and strange, and with the years came responsibilities. Rather than our joyful hours and days there were the tutors, with their bags of books, their maps, equations, languages, etiquette and the teachings of dust. You exchanged our world for a new one—one where the demands of order hold sway; you watched the clock, you were diligent, obedient and polite. The savage passions subsided as you entered the grim hallways of reality. I had waited for you patiently. I hoped that one day you might hold me as you had before, and try again to return to our domain of dream and fantasy.

ᏸ

One day, in the depths of a sweltering summer, two of your friends arrived. They carried with them their beloveds—a monkey and a bear. We all took tea, as we had in the old days— we were happy and you all laughed. Your gangly arms knocked dainty cups and saucers aside carelessly. You were becoming accustomed to new limbs and the three of you tucked your long legs awkwardly, and uncomfortably, beneath your thighs. There was something amiss though—something in the way you played was forced, your smiles were tinged with sadness; rather than the enthusiasm of creation there was a formulaic adherence to structure. You deemed, at some point, that the tea was over and we were hoisted into the air by your spidery fingers and we all raced out into the scorching afternoon.

We sped through the fields and soared up the hills—all our old places were revisited as your laughter was absorbed by the heavy, hot air. Frequently you all sank down in exhausted chuckling heaps. We were thrown about in flowers; we danced through tall grasses and clambered upon the boughs of great trees, whose frames had known the scramble of your feet from their tiniest cautious step to their current confident clamber. We leapt from the branches and lay in the shade—in the distance, thunder.

Once your energy had returned you skipped, hand in hand, through the woods towards the old bridge. The trees were jittery with rooks, cawing and squawking, screeching their cackling warnings to each other, or out into the mad air. Bright green leaves fluttered down around us, dislodged by the frenzied passions of the birds. Was it this storm they feared, or something more menacing? Did they sense—in your gait, or your forced joy—that something more serious; something weightless, yet terrible, was approaching?

At the bridge the three of you placed us in a heap by some nettles and sat on the wall, watching the waters below. Desperate clouds of mosquitoes swarmed about you, mad with heat and hunger. Your bony arms waved about like sticks in a storm, but still you all giggled and squealed, the children hiding somewhere deep inside your new skins. You all ran to the other side of the bridge. An argument began. You were angry. You folded your arms in that petulant way I remembered so well. Inside me I yearned for those days again—your scuffed knees, grass stains, tantrums and the elation of snow. You lost the argument—or you relented, having learnt the necessity of negotiation. The three of you returned—you stern and regretful, the others with malicious grins.

You took us to the stony wall and perched us there in a row, looking down at the river. The thunder rolled closer and closer—the air was fresher, rain was coming. You seized me and clutched me to you in a desperate embrace. What was happening? One of your tears landed on my hard, cold cheek. I could not cry, I could not blink; but what passed for a heart within me was breaking. I did not know why. Your friends laughed and jeered. Shaking, you placed me back on the wall.

The air was a great breath, held for an hour. The sky groaned its displeasure and a flicker of bright light surged through the dark clouds above. The rain disgorged itself upon us all. The three of you howled like witches and with a shove we were launched into emptiness.

Our stuffed arms waved their helplessness. Our useless legs flailed in the rain. Our fixed stares looked on as the scene tumbled between the river, the banks, the sky, the bridge and your three faces, looking down with torturers' glee, at our lifeless forms.

Splash! We were in—we were under. We bobbed and rocked on the surface, rolled and swirled in the eddies, surging now with the violent storm waters. You all waved and screamed. This was our savage goodbye was it? This was all of our past rolled into a great sacrifice. New worlds lay ahead of you and we were no longer a part of them. It was time to move on. We did move on, racing faster than you had anticipated. You sprinted to catch up with us.

I watched as you ran along the bank. You squealed and laughed and jumped and danced. You shouted my name, over and over and over; urging me on; further on through the tumult. I would sink, sodden and heavy, into the green murk of the river, and then, a moment later, I would be thrust up again into the light and you would cheer again. The others would pass me and you cried out in disappointment. Your friends were running with you; they too cheered us on. Their beloveds were beside me one moment and gone the next. We tumbled through the increasing currents, collided with the muddy banks; our limbs would catch a while in tree roots but then we would be taken again, back to the watery maelstrom. All was grey sky, rain and muck; leaves plucked from their branches by the sudden winds vied with us in the race downstream; twigs, like little toy boats, floundered and were pulled below.

And then we were at the weir. You all cried out. You had forgotten the weir. Down and down we crashed, against the stones and the white foam, and then under the water, carried deep into the still, wide pond beyond and we were lost. From amongst the murk and filth our eternally open eyes peered out to catch one last sighting of you, but there was only the grime and green gloom. No doubt you cried that night, and many more besides. Perhaps you dragged your father and mother down here to look for me; probing the reeds with long sticks. They never found me. Perhaps you wandered the banks for months, hoping to catch a glimpse of my soggy frame. You never found me. I lay there as the seasons came and went—as the years came and went.

§

I am just a little thing; a thing made of cloth and thread. My once beautiful porcelain face and hands are crusted with filth but yet my eyes still see; out into eternity. I see again all of our joyful hours—the colourful toys, the dolls in their house, the teddies at tea, the train on its track. That playroom comes to me as a vision of heaven. How did I fall from grace? What sin lay so dormant in me that I did not know it? Is this judgement?

PETALS AND VIOLINS

But my sight is not like your sight. I see all things at once and the future erupts as easily as any other time. I see you, in years to come, standing on the same bridge where we were last together. It is night, bright with a great silver moon. You cry and cry. You cry so much it seems the river might burst its banks with the torrent of your tears. Perhaps your lover has jilted you; perhaps your beloved father has died in the wars—these things I cannot see. As the time passes you calm and gaze into the water—the beckoning water. You resolve to cast your body into the river, and with it your miseries. You drop like a flailing animal into the flow—and in that instant do you regret your decision? I cannot know this either. Only facts are given to me— the facts of a vision. You follow the same journey I took, sinking and surging, smashing and struggling. Your body, unlike mine, is made of flesh; you bruise and break, thrashing and screaming against the flow. The roots cut and scratch, a hundred lacerations etch a record of your last moments; your fingers claw at the muddy banks; your nails break against the stones. The current is too strong for you though and your ragged body is dragged back under. Your mouth fills with silt and decaying leaves, the water surging into you, filling your nose, ears, eyes and lungs.

At the weir your bones are broken against the steps. You would feel the pain if your flesh were not as cold as ice. Once the white havoc of the course subsides you drift out into still water. You float there, the last sparks of life fading into the chill of the water. You bob into the reeds and we meet again, my great love, my mistress. The last astonished flicker of your eyes sees the rotten tatters I now wear; you recognise my porcelain face, caked with mud. My glassy stare will last millennia—in sad exhaustion, yours closes for the last time.

DOREEN

'The soul is a terrible reality. It can be bought, and sold,
and bartered away. It can be poisoned, or made perfect.'
                    Oscar Wilde, *The Picture of Dorian Gray*

Doreen was watching Steve eating his bacon sandwich. The red sauce was running into his two-day old stubble, as was a slimy trail of yellowy, melting margarine that looked like milky pus. He gave a little snort and choked.

'God, took a bit of a big bit there,' he said, wiping his greasy face with the back of his hand. 'Good bacon though.'

He continued his munching. Doreen sipped her tea and poked at her poached egg on toast with her fork.

'I love coming here on Sunday mornings,' Steve said, taking big gulps from his mug of steaming coffee. 'Feels like a proper treat, wouldn't you say, love?'

Doreen stared out of the window of the café at the launderette over the road, watching Mrs Chatterjee lugging two vast blue Ikea bags of clothes home. She wasn't any taller than five foot but she seemed to have mastered the painful art of balancing the weight of a bag on each hip and sort of waddling along with them, like a pregnant duck.

'Don't you reckon, love, a *proper treat*?' he repeated.

'What . . . *a proper treat* . . . *what's* a proper treat?' she said, half listening.

'*This* . . . *this* is a proper treat,' Steve said, pointing at the remains of the sandwich with his greasy fingers. 'I love a Sunday morning nosh-up.'

'Yes . . .' Doreen replied glumly. 'Do you think we could do something else one weekend? It's just got a bit boring, going down to The Bluebell and watching you play darts until chucking out time, and then down here the following morning. Maybe we could go up to Hunstanton one weekend, or Skegness, maybe Scarborough—we haven't been there in ages now have we.'

'Oh, it'd just piss with rain, it usually does.' Steve said, taking another gulp of coffee with that long slurp that had so irritated her for years. 'Anyway, what's wrong with The Bluebell, you have a good time with Karen and the girls, don't you? You don't go short on drinks neither, I see you alright.'

'I know, love,' she sighed. 'I'm not complaining about that, you buy me lots of stuff. But I've got my own money anyway; you don't need to buy me drinks.'

'My wife and daughters aren't going to buy their own drinks while I'm around, that's for sure,' he said.

She knew it wasn't worth pursuing, Saturdays belonged to The Bluebell, and that was that.

'So how was that then?' a loud voice called from over at the till, it was Shirley, the café owner.

'Oh, it was a beut', Shirl, an absolute beut',' Steve shouted. 'In fact, I think I'll have another. Dor, you want anything else at all?'

'No, ta,' she said.

She resumed her watch over the launderette, it was getting busier and she could see a number of her friends huddled outside having a cigarette.

'I think I'll just pop over and have a fag with the girls a moment, love,' she said.

'You do that, Dor, and say hi from me,' Steve said.

Doreen lit a cigarette on her way over and they all called their hellos as she joined the group. Most of them had been in the pub only the night before but there was a real gossip going on.

'Oh, have you heard, Dor?' said Kate Wright, her neighbour. 'Steph's back from Spain, you know.'

'Yeah, she got back last night,' agreed Sue Carter, who ran the hairdressers. 'Terry died a few months back and she's sold up everything and come home. She's staying with Mark and Angie, 'til she can find her own place.'

'Don't blame her,' said Jasmine Walker, from the flats. 'I wouldn't want to stay out there without my hubby. Then again I'd have stayed pretty much anywhere with Terry Stephens—as long as the place had a bed.'

They all laughed.

'You dirty bitch, Jas,' Kate said playfully. 'Mind you, with Terry, I wouldn't have been bothered whether there was a bed or not.'

They all laughed again.

Doreen was stunned. Stephanie was her oldest, and greatest, friend, when they were children. Her mother had died when she was ten and Doreen's mum was always cooking dinners for Steph as her father frequently worked lates and hadn't coped well with the bereavement. Steph often stayed over; they had been more like sisters. They had fallen out over Steve, who Steph accused Doreen of having 'stolen from her' more than twenty years ago. It hadn't happened like that—not as far as Doreen was concerned; although she'd always had her eye on Steve, and was terribly jealous when Steph had started seeing him. It was a couple of years after a massive row over it that Steph had married Terry and moved to Spain, as he'd set up a construction company over there and was building flats for ex-pats. The last she'd heard was that they were pretty well off. Why would she want to come back to Leicester, Doreen thought, if she's got the money to move wherever she wants?

'What d'you reckon, Dor, Terry Stephens . . .' Kate said, prodding Doreen's arm with her green e-cigarette. '*To bed, or not to bed*, that is the question . . .'

'What?' Doreen hadn't really been listening. 'Where did you say she was staying?'

'At Mark and Angie's, you deaf bugger,' Kate said. 'You two probably best have a go at patching things up now, if she's sticking around.'

'Yes, I guess so,' Doreen said thoughtfully. 'I never did anything wrong though. She was the one that never answered my calls, if you remember.'

'I know, love, I know,' Sue said. They all looked at each other awkwardly.

'Anyway, I'd best get back to Steve now,' Doreen said. 'I'll catch up with you all later.'

A chorus of cheery goodbyes followed her as large drops of rain began to fall, driving the group back into the launderette.

Back in the café Doreen rushed over to the table just as Shirley was bringing Steve his second bacon butty over.

'Have you heard, Doreen . . . ?' Shirley started.

'Yes, I blooming well have. Have you heard, Steve?' Doreen said.

'Heard what?' Steve said, shaking the last of the red sauce out of the bottle onto his bacon. 'Have you got anymore red, Shirl, love?'

'I know,' Shirley said. 'Who'd have thought she'd come back here after all these years. I'd have stayed out there in the sun if it were me, what with all of Terry's money—it's like winning the bloody lottery. I'd set up me own restaurant, I would. I wouldn't be coming back to this bleeding place, that's for sure. You finished with that egg on toast, Dor, you've barely touched it?'

'Yeah, I know, I'm amazed,' Doreen said, passing her plate to Shirley. 'I've finished, Shirl, thanks. I just wasn't very hungry. Do you really think she'll stay?'

'I don't know, Dor, I really don't know,' Shirley said. 'I guess it depends on why she's come back in the first place.'

'Can someone tell me what the bloody hell is going on?' Steve said. 'And can I also have some more red sauce before this bacon's stone cold?'

'I'll let Dor tell you all about it, Steve, but *Steph's* come back home, *Steph Stephens*,' Shirley said, passing him another bottle of red sauce from the next table.

℘

Doreen filled him in on the little she knew on the way back home. He didn't seem too surprised, or even particularly interested, but Doreen had a feeling that he already knew about it somehow. She'd work on him over the coming days to find out if that was true, she thought. Entering their front room they found their daughter, Anna, and her two boys, Jayden and Joshua. The kids were playing with Doreen's knitting bag and had taken a number of balls of wool out and were in the process of tangling them all up together.

'Oh, Anna, what have I said before about watching what they're doing with my wool,' Doreen said, gathering up the cloth bag and trying to prise the strands from the boys' tight grips.

'Oh, mum, they're only messing about,' Anna said, casually. 'You've got to let them play.'

'Well, buy them some toys to play with,' Doreen said. 'Besides the needles in my bag could be pretty dangerous for them; you need to watch them every moment at this age, Anna, honestly you do!'

89

'Lovely to see you, dear,' said Steve, suspiciously. 'But we normally only get a visit from you these days when you need these monkeys looking after.'

Anna looked guilty, 'Ow, dad, that's a mean thing to say, I'm always round here.'

'I know,' he laughed. 'And we're *always* looking after them.'

'A little correction there—*I'm* always looking after them,' Doreen said, unravelling Jayden's feet from a chaos of wool.

'It's just that Dave has got a last minute gig on in Melton tomorrow,' Anna said, busily texting away on her phone. 'And I really want to go and see him playing.'

'What, a gig on a Monday, must be a pretty crap venue!' Steve said, turning on the telly. 'And anyway he's just a kid, you need to grow up, love and look for a proper man, with a decent job, like your sister's got.'

'Whatever, dad, you don't know anything about him,' she cut back. 'He's training to be a plumber, but he won't need that anyway, because I reckon they'll make it big. So, mum, what do you say, just for this one night, I promise; *please!*'

Doreen sighed. Joshua had climbed onto her back and was bashing her head with some pattern sheets for a cardigan.

'Yes, ok then, but you're really going to have to start cutting back on your socialising you know,' Doreen said.

'Thanks so much, mum,' Anna said. 'Oh, yeah, I saw Kelly earlier and she said that some old mate of yours, Steph *Somebody*, is back in town and staying with her mum and dad for a bit.'

'Yes, I know, love, Stephanie *Stephens*,' Doreen said, sadly. 'We were best mates years ago.'

The doorbell rang. Doreen looked urgently at Steve. He was engrossed in a programme.

'Steve,' Doreen implored.

'What . . .' Steve muttered.

The doorbell rang again.

DOREEN

'Are you gonna get the door, mum?' Anna said, looking up from her phone.

'Steve, it's *her*,' Doreen said, some awful fear beginning to grip her.

'Who?' Steve said.

'Oh, for *fuck's* sake, Steve, who do you *think*—Steph!' Doreen said. 'I just know it's her. Get the door will you, for once. I'm just going to brush my hair quickly.'

Doreen extracted herself from the crawling clutches of the boys and raced through to the kitchen with her handbag where she quickly did her hair and put on some more make-up in her compact mirror. Her hands were shaking and she kept slipping with the lipstick.

'Doreen, love,' Steve's voice called through. 'You were right, it is Steph. She's just popped by to see us.'

In burst Stephanie Stephens in a cloud of perfume, shedding a kind of sunny brightness with her colourful clothes and loud joviality.

'Oh, my darling Doreen, it's been so long,' Stephanie said, running over to her and hugging her tightly. She was darkly tanned and Doreen could almost smell the sun upon her. 'Let me look at you, my Dor, let me look at you. Don't you look a picture, love! Doesn't she look a picture, Steve—You lucky bugger you!'

Steph was gripping Doreen's shoulders tightly, staring at her intently. Her green eyes were like pale, shallow Mediterranean waters, her golden hair shimmered like shards of late summer sunlight through olive groves, her soft brown skin was healthy and glowing. She looked as though she had walked off a film set.

'Hello Steph, I'm so sorry to hear about Terry,' Doreen stuttered, tucking a strand of dark hair behind her ear self-consciously. It felt greasy. She felt dirty. She felt old.

'Oh, yes, poor, *poor* Terry,' Steph said, an air of performance about her. 'It has been a *dark* time, Dor, a dark and difficult time indeed. But I'll get through it. I'll get through it with the help of my *lovely old* friends.'

Doreen was just staring at her. She looked no different really. There were no wrinkles to speak of. Didn't they say that the sun dried your skin out, Doreen thought. There was no grey streaking in her hair—she must dye it, she must! Her skin looked firm, no sagging jowls, no double chin. She was as thin as when she was a teenager.

'You alright, Dor?' Steve said from the kitchen doorway. 'Maybe Steph would like a tea or something? I could do with one myself too. Anna, you want a tea, love?'

'Yeah, cheers,' came the slightly distracted reply.

'I'll leave you girls to catch up then,' Steve said, sloping off.

Doreen turned the kettle on automatically and started getting the mugs out. There was a silence. Steph paced about the kitchen on the size of heels most people had left behind in their twenties.

'You've got the place looking lovely here, Dor,' Steph said peering into cupboards and looking about the small kitchen diner. 'I love the tiling and this wood effect floor is great.'

'Glad you like it,' Doreen said, still a little suspicious. 'We bought it off the council just before mum died and done it up as and when we could.'

'It's nice to have a place of your own, isn't it,' Steph said, looking at a photo of Anna her sister, Jodie, and brother, Andy. 'Lovely to finally see the kids too. I heard a bit about them through Terry's folks.'

The kettle boiled. Doreen felt she had to say something.

'I can't just pick up like this, Steph,' Doreen said, almost on the verge of tears. 'It's like there's a massive elephant in the room. The things we said to each other all those years ago. How can you just waltz back in and act like nothing's happened?'

'Oh, Dor, my little cupcake,' Steph said. 'Don't you worry about all that nonsense. Those waters are all long gone under

92

the bridge now. Let's just make the next few years happy ones and try and get back to where we were. I'm not one to bear grudges, not at all. I just want to be back in my own country with some familiar faces around me. What's wrong with that?'

Doreen nodded and poured the tea.

As the afternoon passed by Doreen relaxed more. They laughed again together. Anna seemed to get on wonderfully with Steph, and she also had a way with the grandchildren. They agreed to meet up again on the Wednesday and go for lunch together. Steph left just as it was getting to teatime and Doreen had quite forgotten about a meal. She said she'd just get some ham salad together. Anna and Steve grumbled a bit.

'If that's all you've got, mum,' Anna said.

'Yes, it is love,' Doreen snapped. 'You could, of course, go back to your house and get your own supper if you'd like to.'

There was a silence, interrupted by the boys crying.

'Might have a beer with it, if you can find one for me in the fridge, love. Mind, Steph's looking pretty good for her age ain't she, Dor,' Steve said.

'Get your own bleeding beer, you've got legs haven't you! You'd look bloody good too if you hadn't had three kids and weren't constantly looking after two grandchildren whose mother is too busy having a good time to do it—oh, and doing a cleaning job at the school in between all that shit!' Doreen snapped, and stormed through to the kitchen from where she yelled through to the front room. 'Yeah, and I bet she wasn't making loads of food for greedy gannets that never clean up after themselves neither!'

Steve and Anna looked at each other and raised their eyebrows in playful conspiracy.

ℰ

The next few weeks saw a flourishing of Doreen's social life as Steph got settled back into life on the estate. They were always out and about, Steph with a glass of Prosecco almost permanently in hand and Doreen drinking the kind of quantity of Bacardi and cokes that she had never even managed in her late teens when she was still going clubbing. Steph was incredibly generous and Doreen felt guilty about the constant lunches, nights out and fancy frocks she bought her—from little boutique shops that Doreen had never even dreamt of entering. Doreen also accompanied Steph on her hunt for a nice house, near the estate (but not in it), and eventually they found the right place; a new build, four-bedroomed detached, with a bathroom that seemed as big as the whole upper floor of Doreen's little house.

They were as good friends now as if the terrible dispute all those years ago had never happened, but something still worked away at Doreen inside, some kind of envy that occasionally gnawed at her and dug itself deep into her mind. It could have all been so different, *their lives*; Doreen could have married Terry just as easily as Steve. She knew he'd had a thing for her in the last year of school but she'd dismissed him because he was a bit fat; Steve was fit, and was saving up for his own car. And now look at them both; Steph awash with money, and as gorgeous as she ever was—Doreen still struggling with her few hours of cleaning and trying to make ends meet, her looks long faded and every day another ache or pain emerging. She tried to put such negativity from her mind and focus on Steph's generosity, but it kept returning—the wretched jealousy—and with each return it became darker and more resentful.

As the months went on Doreen really began to struggle to keep up with the pace of the endless drinking and partying. Every weekend was like being on a hen do and any day she wasn't working Steph whisked her about the city shopping and socialising. It was those long walks about the city centre that really showed how unfit she was. She quickly got out of breath

94

and soon her legs and hips ached, even when she got up in the morning. Every afternoon she seemed to need a little nap to be able to get through to the evening, if she missed it she would be in bed by eight o'clock.

Finally Steve confronted her and suggested she ease up a bit as she really wasn't looking herself. She agreed and started to cut out the drinking while she was out with Steph, and limited meeting up with her to just once a week, usually at the weekends.

After a further few months things weren't any better. She went to see the doctor who ran tests, all of which came back negative. Further investigations were called for, at the hospital. Steph was very supportive and drove her back and forth for various scans and appointments with consultants. Cancer was ruled out, as was heart disease. The aches, and trouble walking seemed to suggest arthritis, but X-rays could find nothing. Other more obscure diseases were monitored for their symptoms and then rejected. By then Doreen was walking with two sticks and had trouble even getting up the stairs at home. Steph would often come round to help clean the house or cook a meal and Doreen really wondered what on earth she would have done without her.

Finally the doctors concluded that it must be psychosomatic and recommended a psychiatrist. The morning after that diagnosis Doreen looked into the bathroom mirror as though it might magically reveal whatever aberration of mind was affecting her body. It did not. It showed a woman in her early forties who looked as though she should be on the verge of retirement; her hair was grey and hung in long greasy strands beside her wrinkled and blotchy face, her eyes were pale and haloed by dark red and blue circles, the skin on her neck hung in loose folds and her lips seemed to have withered to two faded lines lightly scratched onto the surface of her drooping mouth.

She brushed her teeth—even they ached—and went downstairs to start her miserable day.

As she went into the front room she caught sight of her wedding picture and burst into tears. What a lovely young thing she had been. Ok, not a patch on the delights of Steph, but she'd still been a looker. How different she was now—just twenty-five years, how could it be. She thought of all the stars on telly, with their money and their entourage of helpers, stylists and make-up artists; what a big, bad lie it all was. A sham world where most people ground themselves into the dirt while everyone else larked about to their heart's content—people like Steph; people just like *fucking* Steph!

Doreen burst into tears again. Not only had her looks faded rapidly, so had her character. She used to pride herself in her generous spirit, her ability to forgive—to love. Now she was a bitter ruin encased in the shell of a little old woman. The tears flowed on.

Then a text came in from Steph, 'Meet up tomorrow at that new wine bar in The Walk for lunch? My treat. Can't pick u up, sos, am going away for a while on little hols and will leave for the train straight from there. How about 1 pm? xxx.'

Doreen was tired, and knew she would be tomorrow too, but she'd best see Steph off before her break, at least she'd have a rest for a bit while she was away.

∞

Steve was back from work a bit late that lunchtime and it wasn't until one o'clock that they left the house. Doreen was there by half-past though and had texted on the way to let Steph know she'd be late. She struggled along the pedestrianised area of the road on her sticks and found the wine bar—it had been a small cinema when she was a kid. There was a large trolley case on wheels by Steph's side and the small corner table was filled with dainty sandwiches, fluffy cakes and the ubiquitous bottle of Prosecco in an ice-bucket.

'Lovely spread there, Steph. So are you off somewhere nice then?' Doreen puffed, easing herself into the chair. 'God, I don't know about forty-three, I feel more like ninety-three these days.'

'Oh, my dearest Doreen,' Stephanie said, sipping at her glass of bubbly. 'One of the saddest things I ever heard was from Terry's mum, before she had to go into the home. She said that the worst thing about being old wasn't *being old*, but that she had stayed *young*. You're not really even managing that are you, love? You're still young, *relatively*, and yet you're already old. Look at the way you tottered in here as though you were eighty-five. You want to take a look at yourself in the mirror, if you can bear it. I don't know how Steve can stand it—you're a fucking mess, Dor, totally fucked.'

Doreen stared at her in disbelief; at that pristine face—her plump, bright pink lips, her sparkling, terrible eyes, fierce with false pity and delighting in vicious triumph. A tear fell on Doreen's cheek and she wiped it away with a sniff.

'What . . . what do you mean, Steph,' she whimpered.

'You know, darling Dor,' Stephanie said with a sneer. 'I'm so grateful for what your mum did for me all those years ago. She did me a proper service. You did me a *disservice*. I never forget a slight. Not that I ended up too bad, after all. Terry was just as much of a slob as your Steve is—all men are—but at least he made a fortune; plenty enough to allow me to spend my time doing whatever I liked. I didn't spend my life in the local bars drinking lager and eating shitty fish and chips, acting as though the place were little old England with a bit of sun. No, I looked into lots of different things about the culture out there. I found out some things, some *other* things. And I found ways in which my greatest wish could come true.

'I don't want to crumple up like you, Doreen, like some rotten grape in the hot sun. I want to go on forever—who wouldn't!—and all I need is to find someone like you, every now and again, someone whose jealously is such that it can sustain me a while longer. Every glance you throw at me that questions and envies, every thought that wishes you could look like me, sends a little strength my way and diminishes you a little more. But we're nearly at the end now, my little cupcake. I wish I could say you look a picture—like I always did when we were kids—but you don't. In fact you look fucking awful, Dor, an embarrassment. I won't be taking you down the doctor's anymore; what's the point, there's nothing they can do for you now, there's nothing anyone can do for you. Thanks for your envy though, it's helped me get my zing back. These few months have been like a lovely little holiday, and now I've got that mojo back I'm going on a little cruise for a few months. You won't be here when I get back, *I think you already know that don't you.* So I guess this is, "goodbye".'

Doreen sat there, slumped back in her chair, tears quietly dripping down her face.

'Are you mad, Steph?' Doreen whispered. 'How can you say these things, you must be quite mad . . . mad . . .'

'Oh, I'm as mad as a bag of cats now, Dor,' Steph said, grinning. 'It isn't easy coping with this strangeness, with this *power*, I can tell you. Anyway, that's enough chit chat, we've wasted enough of each other's time, not that there's much of that left for you now.'

Steph got up and pulled the handle out of her case with a determined click. Her face, although beautiful—more beautiful now than ever before—was so filled with malice and hatred Doreen felt that she might melt before its ferocity.

'I never knew you loathed me that much, Stephanie,' Doreen sobbed.

'Goodbye, Doreen,' Steph spat. 'I'll let you pick up the bill for this one seeing as you've been sponging off me all these months.'

DOREEN

She left and Doreen watched her saunter down the street as though she were on some Parisian boulevard, heads turning to follow her as she passed them by, on into her own lonely, cruel future.

Doreen didn't really know what was real now. Certainly the waiter presenting her with the bill was real enough. She scraped together enough from her purse to pay for it. The walk to the taxi rank, though short, was also painfully real.

The following few days were like a terrible hallucination. Doreen could barely get out of bed and she kept drifting off to sleep and waking with a cry, Steph's green eyes haunting her nightmares. Steve and the kids really rallied around her for once—she knew things must be serious. She couldn't tell them what Steph had said—they'd think her insane. She didn't want to go to hospital, despite the doctor's recommendation. She finally, inexplicably, drifted away from the world a week after her last meeting with Steph.

On a small balcony of a river boat near Lübeck Stephanie Stephens gazed up into the sunset to see Venus appear. She ran her soft hands through her bright, blonde hair and took another sip of Champagne; she smiled her perfect, poisonous smile, before heading in to her cabin to get dressed for dinner, at the Captain's table.

Conflagration
Immoral Vignettes

Dramatis Personae

Angel – August Strindberg
An aigrette of iridescent flames – Maurice Maeterlinck
Priest – Antonin Artaud
A long shadow cast against the cyclorama – Edward Gordon Craig
An infernal propeller – Filippo Marinetti
Language professor – Samuel Beckett
Violent shout (from the wings) – Alfred Jarry
Red flowers – Jean Genet
Macbeth or *Clytemnestra* – Tristan Tzara
Man bearing a placard with a Chinese symbol – Bertolt Brecht
Trumpet player – Václav Havel
Hanged Man – Stanisław Witkiewicz
Pierrot and *Juggler* – Vsevolod Meyerhold
English schoolgirl – Eugene Ionesco
Charon – Tadeusz Kantor

CONFLAGRATION: IMMORAL VIGNETTES

This is not a manifesto; it is a dance of desire.

You know the old days are over; the playing with costumes and the giggling with make-up; the green room banter and the old rivalries; the useless mantelpiece acting and the puffing on chalk cigarettes.

The wonderful baritones have degenerated into wheezes and groans; even the audiences are aged and their eyes no longer distinguish the players—all has homogenised into a colourful blur; widow Twankey has fused with the castle door frame and the props are dust in your hands.

The old days are over, burn your photo-albums!
The playbills have been whitewashed and their ridiculous names are now just a smutty rumour.

PETALS AND VIOLINS

20th April 1889
Braunau am Inn

Amidst the screams and the blood there is a desperate creature, beckoning for sustenance. Swaddled in a blanket his face is framed—a portrait. His mouth is the pit; his tongue, a flame.

CONFLAGRATION: IMMORAL VIGNETTES

15th March 1895
Rue de Clichy, Paris

You are an Old Man. I am a Young Man, though a stranger to you.

We crouch in the garden of a modest home. There are willows that billow their long tendrils about us, shielding us from the family that are gathered around the fireplace within. We see them. They cannot see us. We are in darkness. They are brightly lit.

They are a father, a mother, two daughters and a young boy. The father, as is a father's way, sits beside the chimney corner. He does nothing, his hands in his lap. Similarly the mother, seated at a table, gazes blankly into the nothingness of the windows (but still she does not see us). The girls, dressed in white, are at their embroidery. The child is sleeping, his head against his mother's arm. All is tranquil, tinged with the sadness of fate. They wait for someone, but not for us.

We cannot hear them. We merely watch. We debate how best we are to proceed. How to approach them with the terrible news; news that will shatter their lovely home, news so frightful that their little home might crumble with the telling of it.

It is only a short while since we found her in the river but already we do not agree on the details. How could we even begin to tell them if we cannot agree on the details? You say her arms were clasped before her; I say they floated by her side. I was there first but you can claim seniority and, knowing them, must be the one to speak to them first.

During our discussions the girls look to each other, rise, and come to the central window. They gaze out into the relentless emptiness.

'She was as beautiful as they are,' you say, in a hushed tone.

Still they do not see us.

The family all turn to look at the sleeping boy.

I say that it is strange they do not know we see them. You say that all of us are being watched. That is true. We turn to look behind us and hear murmurs in the darkness. Eyes are everywhere.

A girl appears from the blackness—a newly made identity. You know her. You call her Mary. You are kin.

She tells us that many of the village are coming. They are bringing the bier to the house; her hair made pretty with marguerites as there was nothing more majestic to be found.

The three of us are filled with dread. It would have been better to have told them already but we lack the courage. The others must know all this as we watch. The others must know all this as we talk.

The silent scene plays out in the flickering firelight.

The father stands and opens the front door. The entire house shakes, as though he were a circus strongman about to pull the whole structure asunder. Beyond him there is a painted backdrop—a fountain in moonlight, a lawn, a starry, starry night. Nothing moves upon it. It is false.

Suddenly all about us swarm people—the villagers we have been expecting, and as they see the family leave the house through that door, obediently following the father, they flow, like a flood, towards the front of the house. Maybe they will tell them and we have been relieved of our responsibility.

As all falls silent we look to each other and approach the lit window.

You say, 'Look, the child; he still sleeps.'

I nod to you and behind us a great yellow curtain falls.

CONFLAGRATION: IMMORAL VIGNETTES

We collapse out of ourselves and leave the scene. Somewhere in the distance we hear a roar—of applause, or perhaps a distant collapse of masonry, or the sea has surged inland and a new deluge has begun.

In our dressing room we look into the decaying, cheap mirrors and begin our transformations.

My task is relatively brief and soon I am in a battered leather armchair reading old news from the morning's papers. You begin the tedious process of removing make-up; the nose, the beard, the chin, the thick eyebrows, the dark lines of age, and finally the wig that makes you sweat and itch. You unfurl your hair and you are, once again, the young woman I married last spring. We chat and laugh as you prepare yourself for our return home to a late supper. You pinch out the candle and we leave the dressing room hand-in-hand. We will return tomorrow and light it again. Tomorrow we will do the same thing, all over again, until there are no more tomorrows.

PETALS AND VIOLINS

10th December 1896
Théâtre de L'Oeuvre, Paris

He stood there before the full house; friends, foes, and critics (the latter falling into neither of the first two categories being altogether more loving and more hateful than either of them). He had bothered to put on some new clothes, for once, and looked quite the twit. With his grotesque chiffon scarf and his face made up like a Geisha he proceeded to lecture his audience on what was to come.

As he droned on with his monotone description the audience's eyes fell upon the crude set before them; a gigantic bed with enormous bed pan was painted on a flat to the right of the stage. From the foot of the bed there grew a great tree in full green leaf, but heavy with snow. To the left, another flat depicted a row of palm trees, around which coiled great brown and yellow snakes, from the middle of the flat there was constructed a gibbet, from which hung a skeleton. Against the back wall was painted a rolling, idyllic landscape of fields rich with crops, leading off to calm seas in the far distance. Before this stood a large flat with a grand fireplace and an oversized clock and candelabrum on the mantelpiece. Painted flames roared from crudely drawn logs that seemed to have faces scribbled upon them, but it was difficult to discern these clearly in the gloom from the footlights, only half of which were lit.

The instructions had finally come to an end and as he folded his papers and tucked them into his pocket he turned to the set.

'And now, without further ado, I give you Père Ubu,' he said, scuttling off into the wings.

CONFLAGRATION: IMMORAL VIGNETTES

A man burst through the centre of the fireplace, which opened on a spring. He wore a great strap-on belly and had a huge conical bald head on top of which teetered a bowler hat. He had a large mask with a pendulous nose—like an elephant's trunk, or a great tumorous cock. He strode to the front of the stage with a large bottle of green liquor swinging from his belt.

'Merdre,' Père Ubu yelled at everyone.

That set the fuckers off!

Mon. Duclois hit Mme. Lefebvre squarely on the chin just because she was smiling across at Mon. Fouquier, a couple of rows behind. Mon. Fouquier in turn had been smashed over the head with a bottle by Mon. Mercier (who had never forgiven him for that article he wrote about him years before in *L'Echo*). Near the orchestra pit a large fight had broken out between two factions, one in support of the production, the other opposed. They were battling over a certain Mon. Sauvageau who seemed to belong to neither group—being deaf he had not heard the outrageous first line and was now bewildered by why he had become the object of a tug of war. He was also more bewildered by the general goings on as he had thought he was coming to a production of *Cymbeline* but had arrived at the wrong theatre entirely. Each side had an arm and the poor man was on the verge of being torn apart. Mon. Bauer (an idiot!) had brought his attractive, young and intensely religious new wife with him to see the performance and was now so terrified that she might divorce him he had covered her in a coat and was dragging her through the mêlée whilst trying desperately to make sure she neither saw, nor heard another word of the production or the pandemonium that raged about them. Reaching the end of his row he was almost within sight of the doors when he was brought down by Mme. Hébert, whose coat it was he had taken. She was having none of it, that coat was a gift from her late husband (another idiot!). With a stout kick to the knackers

Mon. Bauer was on the floor and the coat retrieved from the head of his poor wife who had been struggling to breathe.

After about ten minutes the fighting was over. Those too badly injured to remain, or those too appalled to stay, had left. The show went on, as they so inevitably do.

'*Merrrrr-drrrrre!*' Père Ubu screamed.

The whole thing kicked off again, with dwindling enthusiasm this time, and for a shorter period.

Once the second round had subsided the dissenters relaxed into wolf-whistling and booing as the play charged through its obscenities.

Ubu became king and rounded on his noblemen—over forty of them—that had been laboriously crafted over weeks from wicker and wire (flesh and blood being far too pricey!), each in a pompous military costume (it had still almost bankrupted the production). Cardboard cavalrymen were led on by teams of stage hands and everything ended up being cast into the audience as each scene raced by amid the swearing and shouting of the childish mother and father Ubu.

At the end of the show there was a ripple of applause followed by a renewed round of combat. Many seemed to have changed sides—some converted to the savagery of the play, others now shocked by it. As the din abated he took his opportunity to survey the carnage and peered out from the wings.

The whole place was a litter of wooden nobles, trombones and violins, cardboard horses and broken chairs. Amidst all of the wreckage one could occasionally make out an arm or leg here or there, fighting or tickling, or clawing for some safety, or simply waving ridiculously. It was an orgy of limbs, wood, instruments and cardboard. *It would be interesting to see the progeny of such couplings*, he thought.

The battle gathered momentum again and he beat a brave retreat.

CONFLAGRATION: IMMORAL VIGNETTES

He sat and drank absinthe with the stage manager until the morning came. Their cheeks flushed so red they thought they might ignite.

PETALS AND VIOLINS

3rd October, 1905
The Theatre Studio, Povarskaya ulitsa, Moscow

It is now the dress rehearsal. All of reality is in turmoil. The workers are about to riot. Strikes are imminent. The whole world is driving for the abyss in a carriage garlanded with rotting white roses. But here in the studio all is calm because it has purpose. Everything here is meaningful while all about meaning is lost in the fatal rush of existence and the feeding and fucking and shitting. Everything here is constructed and managed, mastered and crafted. Beyond the door is chaos, where one might just as easily slip on a banana skin and break one's neck, or swallow a fish bone during a simple supper and choke to death.

He nods at the beauty of his vision. He smiles at the perfect forms of his actors; the low light; the portentous choral framing of postures and words; gestures overpower all of language—a pointed finger more significant than pages of poetry.

He had to have his chorus of souls. They must bring forth the songs that would enthral and wound. There would be no false words though, heightened by the polarities of emotion. There would be the stark control of feeling, so that the violent shudder of deep tragedy can be understood through the body; the trembling, almost imperceptible body that would release the true music of the play.

Let the old ways of working die, he thought. *It is time for new patterns and systems!* There can be no more ridiculous synchronicity of words and actions; the two must move to their own rhythms and when these work against each other new significations emerge.

CONFLAGRATION: IMMORAL VIGNETTES

The three maids enter, moving as one. They speak as one, but each is living their role rather than allowing it to live through them.

'No, no, no!' he cries. 'Why can you not relinquish your *desire* for these characters? They are nothing! They *mean* nothing! They are only the *symbol* of the Queen. They are the conduits of the tragedy of this little prince about to be destroyed. If you insist on maintaining this charade of realism I will . . . I *will* . . .'

He stormed off and headed for the workshop. He thought an hour or two elsewhere might calm him, and give these actors time to reflect on the new opportunity that was being offered them—a break with the tawdry emptiness of Naturalism; a flourishing again of true performance, at the threshold of truth!

'What have you done?' he yelled, as he saw the designers working on some of the flats and screens. 'Why have you added these crude details to these panels?'

He pointed at a door knocker that had been painted onto a brown screen and a small block of castle brickwork that had been added to a grey panel that was meant to be flown in place beside three others.

'These are not *things*, they are the *implication* of things,' he said, his face flushing red with rage. 'They do not *clarify*, they offer the chance to contribute to the awe of the events that are unfolding.'

'Oh, right you are then, sir,' one of them said. 'We'll paint 'em back again.'

Outside, in the streets made of hard cobbles, barricades were being erected and bonfires began to burn.

PETALS AND VIOLINS

11th March 1907
A boarding house, Florence

He has his head in his hands. His pen sits idle beside the stack of pages.

'Why, why, oh *why* must it be so!' he laments, the clock progressing as it always does through sadness or joy.

He pauses long enough to consume a glass of wine. He resumes his stricken position.

'But how can it have come to this?' he sobs.

His upset was not of the usual order; an ailment, a bereavement, financial calamity or public humiliation. It was having witnessed, earlier that terrible morning, a children's puppet booth at the corner of the marketplace where he saw a crowd of eager faces alight with joy, their little hands clasped in occasional, awkward applause and voices raised in gleeful, anarchic abandon. This eternal picture of childish delight had filled him with the deepest dread.

It was not a terror of the fleeting, carefree pleasures of childhood or the horror of mortality, but rather the diminished role of the jiggling puppet that so troubled him.

'Oh, how terrible that the perfect form of *you*, once venerated in the shrines and temples, has been so reduced to this crude thing—this *puppet*!' he bemoans.

Another draught of wine restores to his tortured mind the memory of a thousand actors and actresses, smiling and strutting across the stages of a thousand theatres of Europe. Anger overcomes him and he springs up from his seat with the vigour of vengeance.

'Arise and triumph, great emissary of death!' he booms, the floorboards and the rafters quivering. 'Come with your battalions of wooden warriors, faces fixed for ever into ferocious snarls of war! Come and overthrow this vulgar thing called LIFE with the beauty and form of ART! Arise, great über-marionette and lay waste the cities and avenge your forgotten Gods!'

There is a loud knocking at the door.

'Are you alright in there, sir?' a concerned voice calls out.

'Oh, yes. Yes,' he says, composing himself. 'Do come in. Do come in. I was just carried away with the passion of my writing.'

A short, plump woman enters—his landlady. She looks nosily around the room before nodding to him, 'Is there anything I can get for you, Mr Great Director, your highness, your mightiness, *sire*, while I'm here?'

'Oh, that's very good of you, Signora Geppetto,' he says. 'Another jug of wine would be most welcome—most welcome indeed!'

She shuffles off to fetch the wine.

'Yes, *arise*, perfect über-marionette, and reclaim what was rightfully yours,' he whispers to himself, picking up his pen and beginning to write.

Out in the courtyard, beneath his window, there is a log store. Within it is a neat stack of kindling. It had heard the call to arms. Little twigs, shards, splinters and curls of wood shavings begin to twitch with life. All through the night they gather together into a crude shape—a form almost human and strangely other. As the dawn breaks, and he slumbers at his desk, this newly born *thing* totters to its 'feet'.

At that moment Signora Geppetto arrives and with a small hatchet and shovel collects what she needs to get the fires lit for that morning throughout her boarding house—the guests must be comfortable, after all.

Within minutes the embryonic wooden existence—a new form of an old god—is sooty residue on a chimney wall. The ink is dry now on another essay.

CONFLAGRATION: IMMORAL VIGNETTES

17th April 1907
Somewhere in Blasieholmen, Stockholm

All through the vision he had seen miraculous images and witnessed many things. He had seen a God made flesh. She came to earth to redeem mankind. He had seen many wondrous characters and heard many things he did not understand. There was, as there always is, unrequited love. There was a man with a green fishing net. There was everything.

Against a screen of dancing light he had seen castles rise and fall. He had seen the stars of heavens and the billowing clouds of a tormented sky. He had seen gigantic flowers bloom and trees bring forth leaf in seconds. All was colour and noise, song and celebration, but behind it all a great sadness moved through everything—pity for the sad and wretched human! Compassion for the low and weak!

Now he watched the final moments of the world. A great swell of organ music. A burning fortress collapses into a wall of faces; questioning, grieving, despairing, laughing, screaming. They disintegrate into the petals of a great chrysanthemum that withers into blackness.

He has decided. He will conjure such miracles. His pen will be the origin of mystery and through such ritual as this he will generate such flames as will make dreams live again.

PETALS AND VIOLINS

1st November 1907
The Grand Chasublerie, 7 Rue Cassette, Paris

They were gathered around his bed, some kneeling, some leaning, some sitting upon his writing desk. They looked like figures in 'The Anatomy Lesson'.

They asked him if there was anything he needed.

'A toothpick—what else could one require at a moment such as this!' he replied, closing his eyes—all the sound and fury gone from his voice.

A toothpick!—they laughed so long they thought their bellies would burst.

And with that his brief candle flickered its last and went out.

CONFLAGRATION: IMMORAL VIGNETTES

12th January 1910
The Streets of Trieste

The performance was over.

He led his followers on for their meal.

The performance was never over!

The Caffè Milano wished they'd never agreed to the banquet now.

He announced each course with a sounding of a gong and a loud shout.

'And now for *The Coffee*, you bitter bastards!'

'And now for *The Sweet Ices of Remembrance*.'

'And now for *The Marmalade of Bygone Glories*.'

'And now for *Roast Mama and Professor's Liver* (lightly sautéed).'

'And now for *The Salad of Archaeology*.'

'And now for *A Goulash of the Past with exploding peas, smothered in Historical Sauce*.'

'And now for *The Dead-Sea Fish*.'

'And now for *The Congealed Blood Soup*.'

'And now for *The Annihilation Entrée*.'

'And now for *The Vinegared Vermouth*.'

With that it was over, the bill flung in the faces of the waiters and they moved on to taunt the soldiers at the Caffè Eden. After their fists and faces had had a good workout it was on, and on, and on, each establishment greeting them with nervous laughter until they had drunk their fill and rolled on to the next one.

On and on they went, on and on—you'd think their guts and livers would burst. Even the police had to watch helplessly as the growing throng became more like a great slick of oil that oozed

117

across the city, bringing with them new ideas and new ways to play at being serious.

They carried on long into the night, many other revellers joining the rabble as they woke the locals with their chants of 'Long live the Futurists! Long live Futurism!'

At the back of the line a young man, for a joke, yelled, 'Long live the Passéists! Let yesterday rule over the disappointment of today!'

They all laughed as they set light to his trousers and watched him run for the safety of the river, where he bobbed away to the sea like yesterday's newspaper. They found him weeks later in the marina in Ravenna, his dead mouth home to a form of seaweed never previously known to marine biology.

CONFLAGRATION: IMMORAL VIGNETTES

14th November 1912
Northern Cemetery, *Solna*

In the middle of a crisp winter's night an invisible hand etches upon his gravestone:

O Crux

Ave   Spes

Unica

In a far corner of the cemetery three witches were stirring a cauldron. They were somewhat lacking in their usual ingredients; fillets of fenny snakes, eyes of newts, toes of frogs, bat's wool, tongues of dogs, adders' forks, blind-worms' stings, lizards' legs, owlets' wings. They had also forgotten to bring the bags of rarer components; scales of dragon, wolfs' teeth, hemlock root, livers of blaspheming Jews, gall of goat and slips of yew. And it had become nearly impossible to find any Turk's noses or Tartars' lips these days, as everybody knows. Instead they had to make do with the whisperings of Christ and Buddha, some sprigs of Cabbalism and a shard of an unknown rune. They added a drop of Swedenborg, lashings of Nietzsche and a grating of Schopenhauer and finished it with a jus of the tears of neglected children and the shadows of ex-wives and allowed it all to simmer.

They stoked the flames of the fire with bones from the charnel house. By dawn there was nothing remaining in the cauldron but vapours of bitterness and dregs of sorrow. They tipped them on his grave and went back to their work in the factory.

CONFLAGRATION: IMMORAL VIGNETTES

5th January 1912
MAT, Moscow

He is a thousand miles away from where it is happening. *Hamlet*, again. *Hamlet*, as never before. *Hamlet*, as never will be again.

It is late afternoon in London. Over *there* they will be taking their seats ready for it to begin. There will be much anticipation and terror in the dressing rooms. They will be unsure whether the new forms will be accepted, whether the *very idea* will even be tolerated.

He can see, in his mind, those first moments . . .

Gertrude and Claudius sat upon huge thrones, almost floating in the middle of the stage; Ophelia in green, flecked with white sequins that flicker like stars in the yellow lights. Hamlet sleeps and behind him the dream of power dreams itself in a swath of golden cloth. Bodies emerge like spring flowers from the folds to attend their lords, their masters. Attendance is everything. To be present. To be on hand. The dream still dreams and everything folds in upon itself in preparation for a hard winter.

There is the drama—enough drama for a lifetime. Armies enter—armies leave.

His thoughts drift, as the show too must drift away from him—its reality unshackling itself from his authority.

He thinks instead of the simplicity of a tall stairway, and the sketches he had made years before—sketches that pared the drama down to its very core.

The stairs can be lit in ways that move the shadows about and bring us to a participation in time, nothing more than that—time.

At the beginning three children play upon the lower steps, what they do is of little importance—they play.

Then the scene moves to a row of children dancing along at the top of the stairs, moving from left to right, or right to left—it makes little difference. Down below, on the lowest step, there is a ripple of light, so as to suggest water. It flows in the same direction as the children dance.

Then to adult figures—a man in darkness at the bottom of the stairs. He moves aimlessly, as though lost. A woman, in a white robe, descends the stairway slowly to him. All about them is the eerie eternal aspect of death, but they are quivering with the vibrancy of life.

Finally, where the children had played at the beginning, there sits a figure, head sunk upon his chest. All is in darkness, save for a lit archway at the top of the stairs. An indistinct shadow passes across this and the lights go out.

One day, he thinks, everything will be the passage of light upon a staircase.

Meanwhile, back in Moscow, they are taking up the bodies. In London they are lighting the lamps.

CONFLAGRATION: IMMORAL VIGNETTES

5th April 1914
Sprovieri Gallery, Rome

They had decorated it themselves. He had overseen the work. They were very proud of themselves. They hung up their overalls and washed out the paint pots and when they were ready they surveyed their masterpiece.

The backdrop was a hastily-splashed piece that evoked the mood of a Neapolitan carnival festival and all around the walls hung pictures that were nothing but the force of speed and the energy of vehicles, the surging of movement and the violence of colour. They depicted only the passion of their own inception. Red lanterns gave the place a dingy, brothel light.

The performers donned their bright costumes and tousled their hair into bizarre shapes using egg white and spittle. They made their faces up into grotesque clownish masks and even before the audience had arrived had begun marching around with their cacophonous blather and ludicrous songs. They were joined by a troupe of performing dwarves, as the onlookers began to gather, each handing over their two lire with suspicion.

The dwarves played on tuneless homemade instruments and pinched the bottoms of the crowd as they traipsed around and around until there was hardly an eardrum left that could stand the din.

They were accompanied by a master pianist, who played on a broken piano they had found outside a music shop the previous day. With a grand fanfare of paper trumpets all fell silent.

He stood up, the only one in a black suit and bow tie, and shouted, 'Now it is time for *the poetry*—pray silence for genius! This is called *Oombala Foroomcaka*.'

A loud, wolfish howl came from the back of the gallery.

'Lolooloolooolooo / Oomba oomba, ickackooo / Fckack Kckaf fckaf / It was a sombre moment.'

Half the audience barked like dogs and the other half applauded politely, flicking their delicate hands back and forth like butterflies wings—producing just as much silence.

They flung confetti at him and as it fluttered through the warm air each piece transformed into rotten fruit and gravel, bunches of flowers and empty wine bottles, bicycle wheels and mummified cats. He ran through the barrage of objects behind the curtain at the side of the gallery and found himself transported to the wings of a conventional theatre. He saw the stage manager slumped in his corner reading a newspaper. Its pages were blank.

All around him there were flames, leaping into the rigging and licking, like chorus girls' keen tongues, around the flats propped against the wall.

'What's wrong with you man?' he screamed. 'Get out, the place is alight. Get everyone out . . .'

'Yes,' the stage manager said, reaching for a thick crusty beetroot sandwich wrapped in greaseproof paper. 'It's been on fire for years, you're the first one that's noticed. I'd get out there, if I were you, they love you. You'll be quite the new thing, I'm sure of it.'

And so he returned to the stage, bemused.

It was a grand auditorium, so vast he could not see the gallery. An eager mob awaited him. They had heard rumour of his appearance through the ghostly whisperings of history. As the tomatoes hit his face, and the eggs slid down his lapels, he saw all the angry, laughing, leering, crying faces melting in a mass of red, orange and yellow flames. The future was upon him.

CONFLAGRATION: IMMORAL VIGNETTES

22nd September 1914
Zakopane

He opened the door to find a boy, maybe a young teenager. He has been sent with a message.

He listened to the boy.

'They found Miss Janczewska at the foot of the cliff this morning. She had shot herself. She shot herself in the head—with a gun!

'They told me to tell you that she had placed flowers beside herself. She had prepared well for it.

'They told me to tell you this. I am sorry. I am so sorry. Do you have a message I should give to them?'

He stood there a moment, thinking of her blood against the rocks, the flowers withering in the cold night air—the endless night hours that must have gone on forever. The night. The night.

'Eros and Thanatos,' he said.

'Is that what I should tell them, sir?' the boy enquired.

He shut the door and slid down behind it, tears trickling down his face.

In the kitchen a sausage he had been cooking for breakfast began to burn.

PETALS AND VIOLINS

17th February 1915
A dreaming mind, Milan

He smiles, his mouth covered in drool, pinkish from the red wine. He giggles. It is a silly dream—perfect!

ℰ

The curtain rises on a man. He is a plump operatic type, used to a grand performance. He reads his script from a napkin stained with vomit.

He describes the scene, pointing to an empty stage. It is, apparently, a road at night. As such roads often are it is deserted. It is—as deserted places at night often are—cold.

He looks at the empty stage and turns to his audience who, because they are a dreamer's audience, are multitudinous. They applaud appreciatively.

You have imagined it well, the man declares. *You see it now, the dark road—the emptiness. You feel the cold don't you*, he says. *You feel the chill of a wintery night.*

Another ripple of applause.

He waits a minute, standing with his stinking napkin by his side, as though awaiting the entrance of nobility.

From his jacket pocket he takes a revolver. From his other pocket he takes a clean handkerchief and polishes the gun. He replaces the handkerchief and takes up his napkin again to read. He points the gun to the ceiling and fires.

The curtain falls and after the applause and the polite exit to the foyer and the waiting carriages only the smell of the brief

126

detonation remains. It is almost undetectable, but stains everything for eternity.

စာ

He begins to choke on his own joke and turns over in bed. A loud fart erupts from his fat arse.

PETALS AND VIOLINS

23rd May 1921
The Schoolhouse, Wielopole

He sits at his school bench nursing his sore hands from the whack of the cane. He copies out lines from a history book where all is borders, and dates, and names, and births, and marriages, and deaths, and war, and famine. There is no laughter here, only the ticking of a great clock that is wound with ceremonious performance every Monday morning.

He looks up at the old man who reads at the front of the room. He is very old—at least forty years old, maybe more. His fat face looks like a red balloon that has been stretched to bursting point.

He wants to go and play in the cemetery with the people who live underground. If only this wretched old man was gone he could enact his dreams.

Then, puff, in a cloud of smoke the old man was gone and he skipped joyfully out of the room and into the brighter than bright sunshine to enjoy the rest of his day.

CONFLAGRATION: IMMORAL VIGNETTES

10th June 1921
Galerie Montaigne, Paris

The greatest three act hoax of the century, he read in the programme for the entertainment he has been invited to. *This should be interesting*, he thought.

He didn't find it so though.

To keep himself occupied while the nonsense plodded on he drew a large cock and balls on the back of the programme, turning the pubic hair into a tropical jungle through which large crab-lice with monkey faces swung in the trees, grabbing at breast-shaped coconuts. He named it, 'The Copulation of Goats on the Shores of Antiquity', for no other reason than that the thought of goats copulating amused him. He had completed it just as the performance was over and the baffled spectators were ambling out. He signed his name to his little sketch and jumped up, applauding vigorously.

'Bravo! Bravo! A work of mind-altering genius!' he cried, and marched out with his programme under his arm.

Later, back at home, he used the rolled up programme to light a small fire in his sitting room and made thick slices of toast that he spread liberally with dripping. He enjoyed these with a jar of pickles whilst reading Aeschylus.

PETALS AND VIOLINS

26th November 1921
Kantstraße, Berlin

In that rotting black jacket, its fur lining sticky with every fluid imaginable, he trudged his stink through the rainy streets—at least it washed the piss from the gutters. The Theater des Westens imposed its pomp on his crusted eyes, the street echoing with the screeching of fat opera voices that grated his ears and scrambled his brain.

How much he hated. How much he loathed. How much he needed a beer and the warm stink of genitals.

He slipped around the side of the building and down into the basement of the theatre where a little hell burnt beneath the grand works above. The cabaret had better live up to its name 'The Wild Stage', he thought. He was not disappointed.

As he took a table near the door—to benefit a little from the breeze that wafted through the thick curtains with the arrival of each new patron—he had a large beer plonked before him by a plump little waitress who waited for payment before flicking an ashtray across the table just in time to catch the taper of ash from his cigar.

The beer was foul but the entertainment was promising.

An elderly man came tottering onto the low stage and with a flourish of animation, as though he had been wound up by some invisible props' mistress, he excitedly proclaimed the arrival of one, 'Magnesia, the tattooed lady', at which point a podgy man appeared in a flamboyant drag costume, edging his way on stage through the blue drape that hung raggedly behind the older man. The elderly compère shuffled off, bowing profusely as 'Magnesia' made grotesque curtseys to him—made all the more awkward by the huge papier-mâché bodysuit that served to emphasise 'her' femininity, in the form of two gargantuan breasts that wobbled about beneath a purple negligee that concealed nothing. All across this fake body there were scrawled various slogans that he could not read from his far table.

This looks interesting, he thought, clearing his drink and calling for another.

'Well, *hello* ladies,' Magnesia squealed in a nasal voice.

'Hello *MAGneSIA*,' the place roared, sounding like a disturbingly drunken and orgiastic class of children responding to their teacher with a sing-song refrain.

'And hello there, *boys*,' Magnesia said with exaggerated coyness.

'Hello, *MAGneSIA*,' the place roared again, with much banging of tables and whistling.

'She' pointed to her left breast and sang, 'I've come to tell you about the mark, which was a funny little currency, it flew so high, and grew so big, that none could keep it down.' And as she sang her left tit gradually inflated with each line until, with the words 'it was so loved by all who got it, that they couldn't do without more of it,' the thing burst, showering the first few rows with cognac that had partly filled the thing.

'Oh, no, my bubble's burst,' Magnesia cackled. 'Fetch me another will you Herr Shäfer . . .'

On hobbled the old man and helped her shove another breast under the suit.

It went on like this for some time, as different 'tattoos' were highlighted to assist in the mockery of one, and then another, politician or public figure.

After a while the crowd were growing restless and began to call out and sing over Magnesia's act. She judged them well, and took some on, but knew when it was time to bow out, so with a little parting ditty about the ritual circumcision of General Ludendorff, she was gone.

He ordered another drink, and finally yesterday's hangover had begun to abate.

Herr Shäfer had shuffled back on and then sprung into life to bring in the next act; a stout woman, accompanied by a street organist belting out moritaten at the top of her voice, so loud in fact that he was sure the opera above would be entirely drowned out. As the verses flew by and the crowd's imaginations dripped with blood and savagery he was moved to order some brandy—a bottle—and set to it with enthusiastic abandon as the twangling whine of the organ stirred his soul with violence.

The next performer bounced onto the stage—a strange clown, with blank white face and shocking wig of bright red hair. His expression was flat and dead as he began to recite lines from Wedekind—*Spring Awakening*, *The Dance of Death* and *Franziska*.

He sat enthralled. Wedekind was a genius, and this recitation, with the ridiculous contrasting buffoonery was perfect. As he allowed the last few lines to soak into him, with the harsh alcohol, he thought he might take a gamble before the old man was up announcing another turn.

What the hell, either I chance my luck or remain a useless spectator, he thought He got to his feet and began his 'Ballad of the Dead Soldier'.

At first there were heckles and a few bottles flung his way, but once he'd lured them with his story of the heroic corpse dug up to fight again, and sent off in a cloud of incense by the priest to mask the stench, they'd come round to him and even joined in on some of the last choruses of ludicrous oom-pah-pahing, that he played for all it was worth.

By the end they were calling for more, so he gave them a dose of 'Apfelböck, Lily of the Field', about the boy who killed his parents for no reason at all. They loved it—*who can resist such sweet sentimentality.*

Before he could begin another little song a woman caught him by the shoulder and pressed him firmly down into his seat.

'Now, what a lovely voice you have my darling boy,' she whispered to him, her hair tickling his cheek, the smell of cheap perfume and cheaper wine swimming around her. 'There is a touch of the demonic about you and I'd love to hear more of those dangerous melodies. But this is my place and you'd better play by the rules for a while, before we set you loose on them. Come to an audition at my apartment tomorrow, and I'll see if we have time to fit you in to our schedule.'

And she was gone. He held a printed card with her name and address. Either it was the brandy, or the fumes of her perfume, but his throat was burning, as were his loins.

PETALS AND VIOLINS

6th July 1923
Théâtre Michel, Paris

Barely five minutes into the performance Nose, Ear, Eyebrow, Neck, Eye and Mouth are attacked by a man who leaps up on the stage shouting, 'Frauds! Ignorant swine! Swindlers!' This is soon followed by others who begin setting about the audience surrounding them. Another man is standing on his seat yelling, 'Down with Dada! Long live Surrealism!' He gets a jab in the guts from one of the lamps that the stage manager is now using to clear a path through the brawling mob.

Nose has fallen off the stage and lies in a heap of broken wooden chairs. His cardboard costume is in bits about him and he appears like a newly hatched chick from within. His fists flail around attempting to strike anyone nearby. He attempts to drag himself up by the torn curtain but succeeds only in bringing a rigging bar crashing down upon the stage, narrowly missing poor Neck who, straightjacketed in rolls of packaging, is being spun around and around by five men with a long rope.

Ear, Eyebrow, and Mouth are huddled in the wings in tears. Eye has vanished entirely.

The hubbub continues, everyone merrily thrashing each other. Soon nobody knew whose side anyone was on, if there had been clear sides in the first place.

He sat watching the whole thing, unsurprised. As the police burst through backstage and began to beat all of the combatants he popped his last grape into his mouth and stood up to leave.

'What is that smell?' he said to one of the ushers who stood there passively watching the fight. 'It's like burnt hair'.

'Yes, it is curious isn't it,' the usher replied. 'It is either the smouldering beginnings of love or the ashen embers of hate—it does not matter which really, they both smell the same.'

He nodded his agreement and left to enjoy a carafe of red wine and *Le Figaro*, for although he could not read he did enjoy the cartoons.

PETALS AND VIOLINS

A day that never was, 1926
Théâtre Alfred Jarry, Paris or Hell

He is where it should have happened, if it had happened. He sits where others would have sat, had they been there to sit. He sees the stage hand mopping the boards, readying the empty space for the next performance; for the building and playing, the furnishing and frolicking.

He imagines him to be a young lover, the broom his beloved. They declare their love for each other and that the world is beautiful. They repeat their love. They repeat the beauty of the world. It is intense. It is as ridiculous as reality.

Then a great gust of wind blasts the stage. The storm arrives and blows them apart. The stars are exploding in the canvas heavens, great columns are falling in upon them, pillars and statues crash to the stage, a temple is in ruins, and with it comes a shower of limbs; of hands and feet, torsos and scorpions, frogs and beetles, until slowly, slowly, everything calms and he can see the wires and the pulleys; the mechanisms are laid bare and it is all make-believe again.

Characters churn in his mind—ludicrous jokes of existence; a knight in full armour struggles into the scene, his labours false as his breastplate is paper, his chainmail knitted. Alongside him comes a wheedling wet-nurse, her tits as vast as camel humps. A priest blathers about the confessions cried into volcanoes. Night descends and hair bursts into flame. A gigantic hand is flown in to grasp at a strutting strumpet, she bites it and a great jet of blood showers the stage.

Everyone dies at the sign of the cross.

They rise again and dance the dance that the dead do the best—the copulation waltz. Vaginas burst amidst a spattering of spiders and crabs.

The lights burn as bright as the sun, for a moment.

It was a good show. Some will complain there was no interval, but you can't have everything.

The working lights go out and he is in darkness.

A gentle, flickering yellow glow comes from the wings. The stage hand emerges with a small lantern—how quaint—its stubby candle's weak flame shimmering slowly against the decaying mirrors of the shuttered lantern.

It is as though he has fallen back thirty years, to before he was born, to a time before trenches and tanks, gas and mud, and the chaos of his mind.

'Will you be much longer now, sir?' the stage hand says. 'I'd like to be gone soon.'

'No, I shan't be long,' he says, gathering his coat and bag. 'We'll all be gone, sooner or later.'

PETALS AND VIOLINS

9th December 1926
The Meyerhold Theatre, Moscow

He is in the auditorium, amongst the crowd. From the moment the curtain went up there has been a mixed reaction. This is what he wanted. Half of them are delighted and awed by it. The others find it crazed and abstract. This is no longer some provincial comedy but a sculpture being formed before their eyes. What is needed is a real government inspector to come and set things right.

But they will have a while to wait for that. In the meantime there will be experiments again, there will be play with form and expression.

And now to the final scene.

This will really start the fireworks, he thought.

It is The Dumb Scene.

After the moment of revelation all of the actors are to stand in complete silence, unmoving, unblinking, until the very last moment that the audience can endure and then—curtain!

But he has done it differently, very differently indeed. There is a curtain before the final scene. There is much shuffling about and muttering. Some begin to gather their belongings with frustrated expressions on their faces, thinking it is over.

Then, the curtain rises again, slowly.

Before them they see double, questioning their eyes. Each character is reproduced in perfect stillness—in eternal stasis—in the form of a mannequin. They stand in tableau in poses of shock and surprise and could stand there until the theatre crumbled into rubble, and they along with it. Beside each of them is their actor, peering at themselves in this frozen pose.

138

CONFLAGRATION: IMMORAL VIGNETTES

They contemplate the image of themselves as another and one can only wonder at what goes through each of their minds as their own face peers on into forever.

They all stand there, each beside their own effigy, and as they wait the delicate tremors of the human body begin to overtake them so that the mannequins seem strangely ghosted by a quivering echo of themselves. The whole scene begins to ripple with a pulse of life, either fading or emerging.

The audience rub their eyes and sneer. It is too much; the silence that is not silence and the stillness that is not stillness. Instead everything becomes more apparent; the fat man in the third row is choking down a cough; a lady in the gallery has ornate pearl earrings that seem to jangle as loudly as a dinner service being dropped in a stuffy restaurant; every movement in the auditorium is now under the scrutiny of the gaze of hundreds of eyes, and every breath is being monitored by hundreds of ears, tuned like wirelesses to the slightest of murmurs.

A century or two later and the curtain goes down. In tomorrow morning's papers the firestorm will begin.

PETALS AND VIOLINS

30th September 1935
Malet Place, London

He had heard Jung's lecture and, whilst most of it had been of little interest—it was something to pass the early afternoon—something had struck him, a comment that he knew would haunt him forever.

The girl had *never fully been born.*

What on earth did it mean?

The girl had dreamt of mythology before she had died. This had foretold her death, apparently.

He looked about at the tall buildings surrounding him as he headed for Hyde Park . . . *not fully born.* Everything took on a sense of a façade; the iron railings edging the stone steps that led up to fine front doors might all be made of papier-mâché for all he knew and unless you tested each one for its truth it might just be a stage prop in an elaborate play.

It was a common enough feeling of estrangement, he told himself. At times the world feels oddly beside itself, especially when one encounters something that makes a deep incision into one's psyche.

Never fully born. But lingering *where?*, and what *part* of a being might not be *fully born* . . .

There had been mention in the lecture of the characters of a play, or novel, or poem—that they might have a life of their own; that they bring themselves into existence through the author's unconscious mind. What is revealed is the psychology of the author, through the manipulation of these characters.

'Pfft!' he exclaimed, causing an old lady walking in the other direction to look up at him in astonishment.

CONFLAGRATION: IMMORAL VIGNETTES

What complete piffle, he thought.

It was a wonderful, bright day and as he quickened his pace, eager to get to the park and clear his mind—a walk he had taken these last three weeks while formulating his novel—he removed his coat and slung it casually across his shoulder, looking every bit the dashing young literary type.

Not fully born. Halfway between full existence and none.

He felt his walk was under the watch of those about him. He suddenly felt awkwardly tall and thin. He hung his head down, as though attempting to vanish into himself. He had not felt so disturbingly self-aware in years. He spun around suddenly, his mind crying out—*who? Who is watching me? What can you want from me, whoever you are?*

There was nobody there, and everyone. That is to say that there were people, as ever, but they were going about their business, clearly unaware of him, until now. A few passers-by gave him a stern look, similar to the old lady minutes before, but nothing more serious than the kind of frustrated pedestrian commonplace in cities across the world; people whose busy movements from A to B, or Z to Y, are interrupted by one who goes against the flow.

He collected himself for a minute or two and hurried on, thinking only of the park, and the greenness, and the fresh air.

After a carefree hour of aimless wandering there he headed on to Kensington Gardens, where he had spent the latter part of recent afternoons watching groups of kite flyers. They took their play very seriously indeed and he thought how much they were like clumsy overgrown children . . . *never fully born* . . .

He tried again to shake the idea from himself as he watched the dishevelled old men assembling their kites, untying knots and teasing out ribbons and stretching the coloured cloth over frames until it was taut and firm. He watched as the first gusts of the late afternoon breeze arrived and carried the colourful things into the sky. He watched as the last moments of a late summer decayed into autumn. He wanted then to either live forever in that bright and beautiful September as a carefree kite or die where he stood.

He watched, *never fully watching though* . . . maybe watching himself more.

In the distance, above the treeline of the park, a curl of black smoke rose from a dirty chimney somewhere around Victoria Road. It coiled about in the gathering wind and formed, for a moment, what he thought was the face of a little girl, before disintegrating into the ruins of his imagination.

CONFLAGRATION: IMMORAL VIGNETTES

18th September 1939
A lonely place, Jeziory

They jump down from the wagon. It clatters into the distance; into the mud and destruction. She nods to the driver with gratitude. He manages a pathetic wave, his arms barely able to lift themselves from the side of his body. He carries the pack as though he were about to collapse beneath the weight of it. He wheezes and groans with every step as they set off into the wood.

After an hour he says, 'This is fine. This is far enough.' They are in a little grove. They sit beneath an oak, as though somehow symbols might save them.

He takes a variety of pill bottles from his pack. He opens a dark brown bottle, Ephedrine, and begins to take the pills, one by one, each with a pause—a thought—a swallow—a pause—a thought—a swallow.

'What are you taking those for?' she asks, to confirm, perhaps, that this is really about to begin.

'This will make the blood flow quicker,' he said—a pause—a thought—a swallow. 'It will drain fast and sure.'

He counts out eighteen Luminal tablets and two Cybalgine and grinds them to a powder with a stick in a battered metal mug. He adds water and they dissolve. They share the mug, as lovers do.

Each says, almost whispering, 'Good-bye.'

He begins to slit his wrist with a razor. The blood does not flow. It is the cold. It is the terror.

He takes the razor to his leg. The blood does not flow. It is the terror. It is the cold.

Her head nods. She is drowsy.

'No! No, please, do not sleep,' he says. 'You cannot leave me alone!'

For a while there is only the silence, the darkness, the cold and the terror.

'When you are asleep I shall slit my throat,' he announces, sure of his plan. 'There is a vein that, once severed, will do the necessary. It will not be a long cut. It will not look too terrible.'

She cannot fend off the sleep any longer and crumples onto the damp ground.

The night moves on and she does not see him. None but the oak tree sees him in that blackness. It sheds acorns upon him as he passes; final meagre gifts of the world.

In the morning, damp with dew, she wakes, vomiting.

He has folded his coat beneath her head to make a pillow.

He lies beside her, eyes and mouth open, staring up into the trees. He looks relieved, almost smiling.

She begins to yell—incomprehensible things of love and sorrow. She drags dirt together to try to bury him, but her hands cannot break the ground enough for anything more than a thin layer of soil. She scrapes it off desperately and instead washes his face with water from the mug and lays ferns upon him.

She sits helplessly beside him. The quick and the dead.

Away to the East the sky glows red; not with the dawn, but with the flames of towns and cities—the bombing has begun.

CONFLAGRATION: IMMORAL VIGNETTES

2nd February 1940
The Cellars of The Military Collegium
of the Supreme Court
of the Soviet Union, Moscow

They came for him in the night, or in the day—in this lightless, airless place there was neither, so it made no difference. There were three of them, young men in ill-fitting green uniforms. His feet and legs were so ruined by the torture he could not stand. Two of them dragged him along, like a sack of coal, as the other strode along gloomy corridors and staircases—down, down and down into the damp cellars of the building that reeked of death and boot polish.

He was thrown before a metal door as keys were jangled and bolts were unbolted.

They dragged him into the tiny room, bereft of furniture. Its floor was freshly mopped and the low lamplight glistened across it like a glimmer of dying stars.

He could barely breathe with the pain.

'Give me a smoke,' one said to another.

He heard the spark of the match and the long exhalation of pleasure.

'You always have good cigarettes,' the one said to the other. 'I wonder if you have been seeing someone you shouldn't have.'

The three of them laughed. He began to fall asleep.

A kick woke him.

'So, how many do we have today?' the other one asked his fellows.

'Oh, not many today, maybe thirty,' the smoker said, checking his revolver. Click, clack, clunk. 'We should be done by lunch. I have to meet with Irma this afternoon anyway, so it will be good to get away early. Get him up and let's get on with it.'

They lifted him to his knees. His head sank to his chest.

'I wish you wouldn't beat them so bad as this,' the one with the gun said. 'If you get slightly the wrong angle it makes such a fucking mess.'

'Just because you're such a piss poor shot, don't blame me,' the other chuckled.

He looked down at himself. Beneath the rags his skin was a thin, translucent costume that fell awkwardly about his bones. It was yellow and purple, blue and black; blood adorned the garment and stale sweat held mud and dust to it like a crust.

He knelt on the cobbles like a beast at the sacrificial altar, or an initiate to a long forgotten but pointlessly enacted ceremony. There was only the final act left now; after all the acting and playing at life, only the *final, inevitable* act.

He pissed himself and laughed.

'Oh, God!' spat the one with the cigarette. 'We have to clean this place up don't you know—selfish cunt!'

The final scene was an explosion of senses. He heard the crack of the shot. He tasted the blood as it boiled in the back of his throat. He smelt the burning powder. He felt the bullet as it sped through his brain. All the lights went out forever.

CONFLAGRATION: IMMORAL VIGNETTES

12th October 1943
A deserted farmhouse, Roussillon d'Apt

He had agreed to take the message out to the waiting contact. It was a simple enough errand, and one that contributed a little to the efforts of the Resistance.

He was to make his way south about two kilometres and to take a dirt road to the east for about a further kilometre. There he would see, by a small wood, an old farmhouse, with a barn, the roof of the latter having caved in.

He was to knock three times (he objected to the ridiculousness of this, but was overruled). The man who answered it would ask him a question, 'Was it you who came before?', to which he was to answer, 'No, sir, perhaps it was my brother.' The man would reply, 'But I'm sure it was you. Are you sure you have not seen me before?' to which he would reply, 'No, sir, I have not seen you before, I am a stranger to these parts and as you are the new tenant here I bring you some news.'

If this dialogue was conducted correctly then he was to deliver the man the message, 'He will not come today—perhaps tomorrow.'

That was all. There was no expected response he should bring back and he should return immediately upon delivery of the message.

That evening he set off, as instructed. Unfortunately the moon was almost full and it made it difficult to conceal himself. Wherever possible he stuck to the deep ditches and hedgerows. He passed a couple of patrols, but they were more intent on getting back into the village to enjoy a break.

The farmhouse was as described and there was no other building in sight, so he was sure he had the right place. Rows of withered vines climbed up a hillside beyond the buildings and perhaps the tall, ruined barn might have once produced a good yield of wine. But now all was strife and its previous occupants were probably lying dead in some unmarked grave.

He approached the farmhouse through an orchard that had also fallen into neglect. Although now bare of leaves at least there was some cover from the twisted branches.

At the door he paused a moment and chuckled—*knock three times*—how silly!

He knocked three times.

Instantly the door was opened by a man who might have been Charlie Chaplin himself—bowler hat, threadbare suit and little moustache. He must have been in his late fifties, perhaps early sixties. He looked over his visitor with a bored glance and seemed to be chewing on something.

'Was it you who came before?' 'Chaplin' said, flatly.

'No, sir, perhaps it was my brother,' he replied.

'But I'm sure it was you. Are you sure you have not seen me before?' he said, mechanistically.

'No, sir, I have not seen you before, I am a stranger to these parts and as you are the new tenant here I bring you some news,' he said, completing the required words.

'Good,' said 'Chaplin'. 'What's the message?'

'He will not come today. Perhaps tomorrow,' he said.

'That's all?' 'Chaplin' said. He seemed suddenly quite desperate. 'Is there nothing else?'

'No, I'm afraid not,' he said, now concerned that he might have forgotten something. '*He will not come today. Perhaps tomorrow.* That was all they said, I'm certain of it.'

There was a long pause. The man stared at him. He looked down at his shoes to avoid the gaze.

'Tell them . . . tell them . . .' 'Chaplin' murmured, tears forming in his eyes. 'Tell them that you saw me here. Tell them that you gave me the message and that I will wait. Tell them that . . . that you *definitely* saw me . . . be *sure* to tell them *that*.'

'I will,' he said, turning to go.

'You will remember . . .' 'Chaplin' said, taking his arm. 'You will remember to tell them, won't you? You will remember . . . you will remember *me*?'

'I will,' he repeated.

'Chaplin' nodded, tears now sliding down his grubby cheeks, and closed the door.

The air was still. The sky was cloudless. The moon still shone brightly. The whole place looked like a ghost of a world that had existed a thousand years before.

He made his way quietly back to the road through the untended orchard. The layer of autumn leaves beneath his worn-out boots looked like ashes in the moonlight.

PETALS AND VIOLINS

22nd June 1944
Ul. Grabowskiego, Cracow

YOU
CANNOT
ENTER
THE
THEATRE
WITH
IMPUNITY

This was written on the door of the flat to which the audience had been invited. He was sitting inside with the others, huddled at the edge of their crude set. Across the road the Schutzdienst Polizei outpost was alight with schnapps and cruelty. It was the very same outpost from which they had stolen the loudspeaker that peered down from the corner of the dingy room.

As the guests took their rickety wooden seats the performance began as Odysseus returned through the front door in a muddy uniform with a battered helmet—back from Stalingrad.

Phemius was a crude mannequin, swathed in military tatters. The song from his wooden lips masked by orders boomed from the loudspeaker.

But the characters were outshone by the power of the objects that littered the space; a rotten board from an outside toilet; a length of rusted riverboat cable; a pile of dusty sacks discovered in the attic that were offered to the audience to ease the discomfort of their chairs; a huge wheel from a rural wagon was propped uselessly in the corner and on the other side of the room a cannon—made of rolled cardboard and propped on trestles.

How little is real.

As it unfolds people barely breathe and they leave as soon as it is over, waiting a few minutes before each of them exit the building so as not to arouse suspicion.

Odysseus returned that day and with him the stench of the crematorium.

PETALS AND VIOLINS

This is not a manifesto; it is a hymn to eternity.

Pray to the clowns and the troubadours.
Worship in the stalls of the music halls and venerate the Punch
and Judy booths.
Let the puppets man the barricades; they are immortal, no bullet
can harm them.

Every harsh word screamed at the dancing bear is met with only
a blank stare.
In the heart of the inferno the girls still spring lithely upon the
trapeze.
The true theatre of ages is as ancient as a glacier and will freeze
any heart as it adores the marvellous.

CONFLAGRATION: IMMORAL VIGNETTES

Before 1947
Anywhere

With a simple dress he becomes she. She has invited two friends to join her. They shave together for their stubble grows swifter than . . . than . . . *how do they say it* . . . swifter than . . . swifter than . . . yes, swifter than the weeds on a rich man's grave.

They are all beautiful now. They were beautiful before.

Madame is a tyrant. Claire and Solange are her servants. They all have their roles to play. Their words are poems; their movements, dance.

Claire says devil, nobility, tatters, gown, scrape, precious, exile, love, veils, humbleness, gladioli, glory, blissful, legacy, respect, mistress, dreaming, boxwood, image, lovelier, salvation, burden, imagination, game, impudence, dominate, expression, pretty, strolled, gesture, kindness, virgin, voyage, ceremony, stifling, halo, pink, menagerie, flustered, vengeance, peacock, deed, sullen, crown, flabby, poisoner, scrub, clothespins, ghost, and tears.

Solange says ivory, orchestra, silk, perfume, stockings, powder, furs, rebellion, wrath, sacrifice, dazzling, radiant, destiny, grandiloquence, flowers, defile, delicate, mingling, garret, butler, balcony, velvet, noble, jewels, chandelier, holy, anteroom, slaves, conquerors, loathe, carnation, God, joy, lover, petals, worm, dove, waltzing, kindness, delirious, foetuses, grotesque, bosom, mourning, darling, abbesses, sweet, diamonds, and grace.

Neither comprehends. It is their catechism to questions never asked of them.

Madame is not the tyrant *she* might have been. He simply enjoys the feel of tight knickers rubbing on his cock. *She* appears briefly and flits about like a clumsy tart.

Claire and Solange drink their *final* tea, their fresh stubble scratching on the fine china teacups. They are dead now. What a beautiful final pact—what sadness, what strangeness, there is in death; little playtime death.

They stand and remove their dresses, shake hands and smile. They use wet cloths to drag the sticky make-up from their lips and eyes. They do not talk. This is part of the ritual. Be patient, they are almost done.

They will play at being themselves again soon. The costumes will be brought out from the cupboard and Claire and Solange will live again until the agony of servitude drags them to oblivion. Madame will be as cruel as *she* can muster. They will all be servile to other ways of being.

Their lives are no more unreal than our own (turn your face again to the mirror and admire that fetching profile). As any of these supposedly reluctant actors might say, *who knows what dramas are unfolding behind the door of any home, in any town, at any time*, all as though written by another, for their amusement, or the amusement of others, or *other* others lounging in fiery pits or radiant heavens.

They flick the switch as they leave. The lights fuse and the ancient wiring in the wall begins to smoulder. As they drink weak lager in a nearby bar the fire brigade is called.

CONFLAGRATION: IMMORAL VIGNETTES

28th November 1947
A white room, Paris

He is with friends but he does not like this cell he has found himself in. He does not like the black wires trailing about the scuffed white floor. He does not like the black microphones and their stands that seem to perch like herons above the instruments, seeking to catch each stray morsel of their sound. This should have been an impromptu event, its very existence to become a rumour that would fuel arguments for decades. There should have been no record of it. It should have been offered to the silence of the mountains and have its words cast into the wilderness of forest winds. Instead it is saved for the dull catalogue of the avant-garde and passed around the mouths of the chattering artists as though it were a fine wine. It should be spat upon the pavements with force enough to make them splinter. It should be screamed from rooftops in unknown languages. Instead a grinning man with headphones on, his dirty black beard littered with the remnants of a hasty lunch, raises his thumbs behind a glass wall—the performance must begin.

Kettledrums and gongs, and a xylophone, accompany the friends as they screech and cackle their way through words that are carved from rock and turn to dust and dreams on their tongues. Their throats ache with the utterance of noises that have not been heard upon the earth since the times of dinosaurs and angels. Everything is as dark as tar and as bright as heaven. The tumble of cries begins the work of killing the sun and sundering the cross, all the horse bones rise up again as sunflowers and the drum beats as fast as a virgin's thrusting pelvis. Everything is iron, arseholes, earth, fire, blood and meat.

From this infernal invocation springs a rat, and God, and armies, and an invisible world of endless, pointless consciousness that laughs and laughs at its own voice that sounds so much like a squeaky toy mouse being savaged by Cerberus.

They are searching for a thousand other shrieking forms of life; through hunger and desire, the revolting unfolding of the inner places of the body. They juggle pain and milk the intoxicating gases of putrefaction. They are cruel animals that throb with diseased bites of ideology, their skin heavy with proliferating microbial existence that jitters its erotic dance into their voices and through the brains of a billion hallucinatory animalcules. They wear their own organs like jewellery and burst them like balloons.

'Great,' the bearded guy says, popping his head round from behind a copy of *Paris Tabou* and dragging his muddy feet off of the mixing desk. 'That's in the bag.'

He looks up from his drum and feels the flames in his heart flare into ice.

CONFLAGRATION: IMMORAL VIGNETTES

2nd February 1948
Throughout the empty air, Paris

There was nothing but the everyday sounds; the animals, the machines, the people. There was no crackle of radio waves setting fire to heaven. They had not yet done with the judgement of God.

PETALS AND VIOLINS

23rd July 1948
A study, *Paris*

The package had arrived for him that morning from Assimil. He waited until after his lunch to unwrap it and begin. Inside the package there was a large further package of records, twenty in total. Unfortunately two of them had shattered in transit, despite the thick brown paper around each one. More unfortunately these were the first two recordings of the English language course he had ordered. He would have to begin on a more advanced stage. At least he knew a little English, hopefully it would not set him back too much. The rest were intact, if a little scratched. There were also five thick workbooks and a set of instructions on thin yellow paper, and a typed receipt for his order and payment.

He set up his desk with the gramophone, the first workbook and a notepad and pencil. He made a pot of coffee and opened a fresh packet of cigarettes and began to play the first recording on the third record.

There are seven days in a week, a slow, deep voice boomed out, with precise received pronunciation.

'There are sivin days in a weeek,' he repeated.

The days of the week are Monday, Tuesday, Wednesday, Thursday, Friday, Saturday and Sunday.

'The days of the weeek are Maunday, Toosday, Weynedesday, Thursday, Freday, Sayturday and . . . ,' he repeated, running out of time to complete the sequence before the next one began.

He reset the needle of the record.

. . . Thursday, Friday, Saturday and Sunday.
Thursday, Freday, Sayturday and Sunday,' he repeated.

On a Monday morning a man, Mr Smith, goes to work.
'On a Maunday morning a man, Mr Smeth, goes to work,' he repeated.

Mr Smith works very hard for the Post Office . . . click . . . Post Office . . . click . . . Post Office . . . click . . . Post Office . . . click . . .
He lifted the needle a moment.
'Mr Smeth works very hard for the Post Offace,' he repeated.

Mr Smith is married to Mrs Smith.
'Mr Smeth is married to Meesess Smeth,' he repeated.

Mr Smith is Mrs Smith's husband.
'Mr Smeth is Meesess Smeth's hoosbund,' he repeated.

Mrs Smith is Mr Smith's wife.
'Meses Smeth is Mr Smith's wyfe,' he repeated.

Mrs Smith looks after their three children, Timothy, Matthew and Mary.
'Meses Smith looks after their three children, Teemothee, Matt-hew and Mary,' he repeated.

Mr and Mrs Smith have two sons and a daughter.
'Mr and Meses Smith have two sons and a dogter,' he repeated.

Mr Smith enjoys reading the newspaper in the morning and the evening.

'Mr Smith enjoys reading the noospaper in the moorning and the eeeveneeng,' he repeated.

Mrs Smith enjoys making the family dinner after she has been to the greengrocer and the butcher.

'Meses Smith enjoys making the family deenner after she has been to the greengrocer and the boocheer,' he repeated.

Mr Smith enjoys his pipe after the children have been put to bed by Mrs Smith.

'Mr Smith enjoys his pipe after the cheeldren have been put to bed by Meses Smith,' he repeated.

In the city of London there is a river called the Thames.

'In the seetee of London there is a river called the Taames,' he repeated.

In the suburbs of the city there live many people.

His repetition was interrupted by the clock in the apartment below, which seemed to operate on an entirely different system of chimes to those relevant to the time of day. One, two, three, four, five, six, seven, eight . . . When he was sure it was over he played the track again.

. . . of London there is a River called the Thames. In the suburbs of the city there live many people.

'In the supurps of the sete there live many people,' he repeated.

People who live in the city travel to work on the train.

'People who live in the sete travel to work on the traayne,' he repeated.

The houses in the suburbs are spacious with large gardens.
'The howssess in the supurbs are spay-shush with laarge gaardens,' he repeated.

Mr and Mrs Smith live in the suburbs and they have three bedrooms in their house.
'Mr and Meses Smith live in the supurbs and they have three bedrooms in their howsse,' he repeated.

Mr and Mrs Smith have a kitchen, a sitting room, a dining room, and a bathroom.
'Mr and Meses Smith have a kitcheyn, a sitting room, a dining room, and a barthrooom,' he repeated.

Mr Smith smokes his pipe, and reads his newspaper in the sitting room.
'Mr Smith smowkes his pipe, and reads his newwspaper in the sitting room,' he repeated.

Mrs Smith makes the family dinner in the kitchen.
'Meses Smith makes the family dinner in the kitchen,' he repeated.

He stopped the record and stood up. He stretched his arms and yawned widely. He went to the mantelpiece and looked into the mirror.

'I am Mr Smith, from London,' he said. 'I have a wife, Meses Smith, and three children, Timothy, Mary, and . . . and . . . er . . . Martin. I work very hard all day at the Post Offace and I like to have a roasted beef dinner, wearing my English sleepers, every eeveening.'

He went back to the desk and rummaged a moment in the top drawer. He found his old pipe that he had not smoked in years. He returned to the mirror.

'I am pleesed to meet with you, Mr Smith,' he said to his reflection. 'I too am Mr Smith. I live next door to you but I do not like roasted beef.'

What a ridiculous little sketch he had enacted, he thought.

He looked at the gathering baldness on his head. His face was pale; he had been indoors too long—a clown's face, before the joyous application of the reds and blues of garish joy. A tear trickled down his white cheek.

He heard the wail of sirens from a fire engine in the street. In the apartment below the loud clock struck seventeen. He burst into a fit of uncontrollable laughter—thoroughly un-English laughter.

CONFLAGRATION: IMMORAL VIGNETTES

15th August 1956
Theater am Schiffbauerdamm, East Berlin

He is not really there. He is more a lens that drifts through the world, haunting old places, watching, and weighing, the work of the world.

He is watching old friends as they sit in a dimly lit room and read, half-heartedly, from books. They are trying to stick to the task at hand but it is not in them anymore. They want to cry. They want to wail and beat their fists upon their chests, but instead they must stand beside themselves and be critical, be perceptive—it is what he would have wanted. It is what he wants. There should be no tears. He is just a fact of history now and it is their task to locate him thus; to make of him a character for others to reflect upon and to draw their own conclusions. Who knows what he might have become? Who cares? All that matters now is history, refracted into today, and analysed.

They get back to their work, after a long silence. They are showing what it is to be The Philosopher, The Dramaturg, The Actor and The Actress. They are not these things, although all of them have been, at some point or other. They are showing to each other the difference between being something and showing something. They are weighing up the importance of the theatre and its usefulness to life. They are beginning to agree with The Philosopher and thinking that their work must be about how best to imitate and demonstrate to enable a critical viewpoint from their audience.

Their audience are outside in the broken streets, struggling with their wages in shops that have nothing. Their audience are waiting for their words to become bread and fishes to fill the bellies of their children. Their audience lusts for big red American cars and houses with hallways bigger than their own cramped apartments. Their audience aches for the frivolity of ice cream and the dreamland of movies rather than the dirt of newspapers and the thumbscrews of Stasi-men. Their audience dreams of the tenderness of death rather than the uncertainty of life.

They close their books and they are no longer showing themselves as The Philosopher, The Dramaturg, The Actor and The Actress. As themselves, not quite themselves, they discuss Shakespeare and Naturalism, history and the Nazis. They talk about the usefulness of theatre and the importance of life.

He is proud. They are testing their art. They are feeling how solid it is. They do not admire trumpets, they work with the solidity of metal. Their voices are guns and their bodies are tanks. Their work is a war without blood; their battlefield is the mind of every citizen that will witness them in action.

Each of them takes from their tatty clothes a thick cigar and lights it, puffing columns of blueish smoke into the cold room, almost indistinguishable from their breath. He rises through it and is gone into the still air, rank with the fumes of practical vehicles.

CONFLAGRATION: IMMORAL VIGNETTES

29th-53rd Enuj, 1960
On Charles Bridge, Prague

He makes his way into the old town through the gradual heat of the morning. By the time it is unbearable he will be inside a dark studio, or in a workshop tacking canvas to large frames, or dismantling a lantern. He will not know his task until he arrives there and the jobs are allotted for the day. He likes to arrive early so that he can have some time alone, in the spaces, before others arrive. Empty theatre buildings are a joy to him—resonant with the past and yet aching to explode into the future; spaces of pure presence that reform themselves infinitely.

Halfway across the bridge he bumps into a stocky man in a thick coat (quite inappropriate for the weather).

'Sorry,' he says and makes to go on his way.

'Oh, don't be sorry,' the man says, with a rural accent, maybe Hana—it sounds false, put on. 'You're just the man I was looking for.'

'Really, why?' he said.

'I have a letter for you, from your employers,' he says, taking from his pocket a folded piece of paper.

It is without an envelope and he is immediately suspicious.

It is with regret that we have had to close the theatre for refurbishments. These were essential works that could no longer be postponed. We received final confirmation of the funding for these late yesterday and have been forced to close the theatre without delay. We hope that these renovations will not take long and we look forward to working with you again in the near future. Do not fear though, your wages will be paid to you in a timely fashion during these works. All we ask is that you meet each morning at the time and place that you received this communication to await further instructions.

He nodded at the man.

'You understand?' the man said.

'Oh, yes, I understand fully,' he replied.

The man nodded back at him and waited a moment before turning to leave.

'I'll see you in the morning,' the man said as he marched away.

He stood a moment gazing into the languid warm shallows of the Vistula, then re-read the letter.

What a load of nonsense, the theatre was only refurbished two years ago, he thought, and continued his walk to work.

He arrived at Anenské and found the theatre shut. A sign hung upon the door saying, 'Closed for Refurbishment.'

He tried the door—locked. He knocked and waited. Nobody came. He put his ear to the door. No sound.

He made his way home and spent an uncomfortable day alone—due to the heat and the boredom.

The following morning he met the same man at the same place on the old bridge, at the same time. He read the same message on new paper, save for one line, scribbled out with a thick pencil.

It is with regret that we have had to close the theatre for refurbishments. These were essential works that could no longer be postponed. ~~We received final confirmation of the funding for these late yesterday and have been forced to close the theatre without delay.~~ We hope that these renovations will not take long and we look forward to working with you again in the near future. Do not fear though, your wages will be paid to you in a timely fashion during these works. All we ask is that you meet each morning at the time and place that you received this communication to await further instructions.

That day he spent in a similar fashion to the previous one, sweating and dissatisfied.

As the days went on he decided to fill the time by writing a few lines of his own; lines that soon coalesced into dialogues; dialogues into scenes; scenes into acts, acts becoming units within a number of possible plays.

Each day followed the same pattern with the man. The same letter (with its crossed out line) was received at the same time and the same place. On Fridays he received, in addition to the letter, his wages, in crumpled notes, in a roll secured with a rubber band wrapped repeatedly around the bundle.

After what seemed like months, but had in fact only been a few weeks, a morning came when the man did not arrive at his usual time. The weather had turned colder and the morning unusually dark for the time of year.

When an hour had gone by and the man still had not appeared he decided to walk on to the theatre again. Perhaps they had completed the work.

When he arrived he found a smouldering ruin, a blackened hole of rubble stood where the theatre had once. The buildings either side were unaffected, it seemed, and the people in the street went about their business as usual.

Am I the only one that sees this? he thought.

'Hello there,' that rural voice called softly behind him. 'I'm sorry I was late. So many things to attend to these days. I see you've found it then. Such a shame. But have no fear, I'm sure you'll find work soon. And anyway these sort of places are everywhere really—empty spaces.'

He nodded his agreement, quite at home in the absurdity of it all.

Yes, he thought. *There are many empty spaces all about us. It will not be long before another one is discovered and work can begin again.*

He turned around and the man had gone. It was an unusual time in an unusual place. He did not quite feel himself.

CONFLAGRATION: IMMORAL VIGNETTES

15th November 1975
Krzysztofory Gallery, Cracow

He is at the front of the schoolroom, sat on that chair, playing at being old. The roles have been reversed. But this is only a role, and not a *rôle*.

He attempts the séance—not to bring back dead spirits, but to resurrect youth in the old bones of his actors. They sit before him at the school desks, each with a dummy of their childhood self. They will search for themselves tonight—for selves that are as lost to the world as the sound of chariot wheels on Roman roads.

Has it begun yet?

How does memory begin?

Their faces are pale. Their clothes are black. They are rendered into characters. Some are tall and some short. Some are fat and some are thin. Some are men and some are women. They are barely there.

Out of their nothingness the performance explodes.

He conducts them like a mad orchestra from the asylum, the pupils: a woman with a mechanical cradle and the charwoman, an old man on the toilet and the old man with his bicycle, the somnambulist whore and the endless repeater, the beadle and the woman at the window. What a grand parade!

They sing-song, sing-song, rhyming and blowing raspberries, they show their dirty arses and pull faces, using their fingers to stretch their mouths wide. They bare their teeth like animals and then cry. They stomp around and throw their arms about for no reason. One minute they are on someone like hunting hounds and then on to the next until they have all had a piece of the misery.

It is all grammar and Cleopatra's nose. It is all legs and bums, feet and genitals—this is the map of the human. It is all King David and an ark, and Hannibal and elephants and something about the eyes of March—whoever she is! She ISN'T, she ISN'T. Then it's camels and needles and haystacks and eyes again— eyes, eyes, eyes! Then it's moons and toilets, professors and princes.

'Gott erhalte unsern Kaiser . . .'

They grind on until their joints are all rusted with arthritis, until the dawns and evenings have come and gone and all that is left is the sound of their shoes falling to dust.

Then all is silence and the shimmer of windows.

Quiet. There is nothing left to see. There is nothing but the sound of the clock. There is nothing left but the sweepings of memory and the sound of the clock. There is nothing but the fading sound of the clock and even that ticks itself to silence.

They are gone, only the desks remain. He stands and walks slowly to the dark opening. He turns a moment and looks about him. Then he is gone. He joins his fellows huddled in the darkness and waits.

What is this purgatory? There in the silence they yearn for the green places and the cool mountain air. They want to see the animals and the blue skies. They need to feel the rain on their skin and the prickle of the burning sun.

But no, all is ashen. They wait still, in the shadows.

CONFLAGRATION: IMMORAL VIGNETTES

17th July 1986
The Spanish Cemetery, Larache

He is lying in the ground, beneath a whitewashed stone. The sandy ground is littered with the butts of discarded Gitanes and the stains of dried tears. He is oriented to Mecca, for no reason. He rots.

A goat wanders between the graves, it tugs and chews at weeds and gazes out at the calm of the Atlantic.

A fat woman drapes her washing over the taller stones and stands waiting; she too is a monument.

The tableau waits for the sea to erode the low cliff away, for all of this is as eternal and as transient as the waves.

In the distance is the old prison and brothel. A breeze brings the scent of roasting meats up from the medina.

The woman's nostrils flare.

The goat sighs.

The sea is still, still.

PETALS AND VIOLINS

7th December 1990
Ul. Sienna, Cracow

Another pigeon flew down and awkwardly landed amongst the others, setting a couple to flight. Its right foot was little more than a stump and badly charred. A fleck of pinkish colouring gave his wingtips the appearance of a kindling flame in the dull light from the window.

Ah, he thought. *It is the phoenix returned. The rehearsals are over, it is time to begin the show.*

He sketched the birds with a shaky hand. His chest hurt again and he was tired.

He telephoned Wanda. She said she'd come by to check him over and take him to the hospital if necessary.

Good, he thought. *It is very reassuring to have these good friends around me at this time.*

He signed the sketch and pushed it to the side of his desk.

After a minute or so of aimlessly wandering around his apartment he lay down amidst the paraphernalia of an artist's life and slept. Outside, on the roof, a blackened chimney spewed its smoke into the freezing night air.

CONFLAGRATION: IMMORAL VIGNETTES

8th May 2010
Str. Jean Louis Calderon, Bucharest

He had gone there to see *Hamlet*. He saw a version of *Hamlet*. It was something dragged out of the past. Someone had been back to 1964 to coax a dead man to life again. On a screen the black shadows moved so as to suggest a face; the lips parted and closed and the arms made their mechanical gestures as though there really had been skin and bone beneath the tight garments. Everything suggested that this was real.

The actors, if such they were, sped about moving chairs and scenery, frames and bodies to re-enact each scene, their mouths echoing the echoes that already echoed from the loudspeakers, the cracking of electrical cables all about them, sending pulses of history to everywhere at once. We are all condemned to repeat. The seat beneath him feels warm from the person who sat there the night before—a world of warm arses, eager eyes and deaf ears.

He saw *Hamlet* and was back on the street again, as though *Hamlet* had never happened. *Did it ever happen*, he wondered, *or has it always been* Hamlet—*is everything just* Hamlet *in disguise?*

Outside the theatre there is a burnt square on the broken tarmac—a shadow of a car that had parked there once. He had not noticed it on his arrival. Perhaps, during the performance of all performances, a nuclear blast had erased everything and there were now only dark marks to outline all the things that ever were.

He must get back to his small rented apartment but does not really have the inclination, everything is paused—life becomes an interval.

The streets are mazes and he lingers in them for many hours. He hears, always behind him, the barking of angry dogs—or maybe they are the echoes of dogs from long ago. Maybe there are no dogs, and never were, only the sound of dogs.

CONFLAGRATION: IMMORAL VIGNETTES

28th June 2014
The Latin Bridge, Sarajevo

After a few failed attempts he strikes a damp match and lights a cigarette, the dead June air carrying the stench of the waters of the Miljacka into his nostrils as he fills his lungs with smoke and sewers.

A swirl of plastic bags and bottles bobs slowly downstream as though, at any moment, the flow might be reversed. Is the river playing? A milk carton jiggles about, telling some ridiculous tale to the carrier bag that lounges nonchalantly atop a thick ripple of muddy water. It seems these things are speaking to him, in the way his children make their toys come alive.

He watches until the play is over.

The rubbish is gone from sight.

I will go home, he thinks. His favourite television show will soon be on. He flicks the match into the river—it swirls a moment, pirouettes with a crisp packet, and is lost.

He leaves, murmuring a little ditty—*hey! diddley de!* He cannot recall where he heard it, or the lyrics. It is stuck there in his mind and will not go away.

PETALS AND VIOLINS

This is not a manifesto; it is a love song.

What was this terror, theatre?
It was the soul of humanity; mystery, bodies in torment and
flux.
What is this luxury, theatre?
It is a place in-between; the eruption of the crude and the
incredible.

Theatre?
Cardboard and twine; rose petals and violins.
Blood and betrayal; hope and empires.
Sun and candlelight; oil on water and the magic of sweat.

Theatre: *conflagration*—the future!

OH, PRETTY POLLY!

PUNCH. When the heart of a man is oppressed with cares,
The clouds are dispelled when a woman appears . . .

That Roseanna Robertson should have had an affair at all was shocking enough; that it should be with that poet and ne'er-do-well Simon Symington was too much. It really was just too much, *indeed*! It was the talk of Wickhampton and had no doubt already reached the ears of the gossips in Baseford and Newbly; by noon it would be on the eager, blathering lips of the social set throughout the whole of Nasleshire and would spread on from there, like a plague, to other counties. Within a month, or perhaps six, it would have reached the ears of his few friends in London. There it would die a death within a day, but Rupert Robertson was not to know that, was he, poor chap. For now, in the depths of his misery, calamities of all proportions were seething through his head, along with the image of his wife and her lover making the devil with two backs within his own marriage bed.

And to make matters worse, wasn't Symington a notorious homosexual? Hadn't he been associated with the Brockington Club and the Boothington Boys, and everyone about town knew where all that horrid debacle had ended up; not only in the law courts but finally out on Dumpington Heath in the morning mists when young Worsley's father shot dead both Brockington and Boothington, one after the other, in a duel at dawn.

Rupert Robertson was day-dreaming of Captain Worsley sending a shot through the temple of Simon Symington when he

177

arrived at the premises of Achington, Takington and Back-scratch, where he had an appointment with the clerk, Mr Stitch.

So it was, with a heart wounded with betrayal and a head buzzing with ludicrous dreams of vengeance, that he entered the accountants and was drawn back to reality by the tinkling of the tedious little bell, that seemed to sound so long, and so loud, that it had been deliberately calculated to irritate. The place smelt, as it usually did, of musty ledgers, ink and boredom. Ducking into the main office, and keeping his head beneath the low beams that had often caught him Mr Robertson began to feel the weight of his other worry—money.

Mr Stitch was in his usual position, one that he had occupied since the Fall, at a low desk near the fire. He was always an eager and over-welcoming sort and today was no different.

'Why, Mr Robertson, *sir*, how wonderful to see you on this *fine* morning,' Mr Stitch said, hurrying to shake his hand and take his hat and coat.

Rupert Robertson failed to see what was so fine about the morning. He thought it rather looked like rain. But then for Rupert Robertson even the clearest of days was almost guaranteed to become gloomier.

Fawning over him quite unnecessarily, and after proffering a tall stool opposite the desk, Mr Stitch pulled out a sheaf of papers.

On taking his seat poor Rupert managed to smack his head on one of the beams, dislodging a cloud of dust that scattered across the desk.

'Oops, mind yourself there, sir,' Mr Stitch offered, cheerily.

'So, how are things looking for me?' Rupert asked, knowing Mr Stitch to be one notorious for circuitous discussions prior to addressing the business at hand, and a fellow in need of fairly firm prompting unless their meeting were to be unduly lengthy.

But today was different.

'Well, I can't say that it looks as bright in here as it does out there, and that's for certain, sir,' Mr Stitch said, shaking his head and running his fingers down columns of figures that looked heavy in entries on the right hand side of the page and rather light on those on the left. 'Without you finding something in the region of five hundred pounds by the end of the month I'm afraid to say the cause is lost.'

He had never heard Mr Stitch be so blunt. Certainly he'd been in financial difficulties before, but never to this degree.

'And what of the sale of Mrs Robertson's land in Bullingham?' Rupert enquired.

'Well, sir. There we have encountered further difficulties,' Mr Stitch said, again shaking his head forlornly. 'On the very morning of the arrival of the signed contract they had another messenger come in minutes later withdrawing it, before anyone had chance to complete it. It seems Mr Gruff is dissatisfied with the potential flooding risks and has put in another offer.'

'Well, how much is he offering now, may I ask?' Rupert said, abruptly.

'Sadly, he can only see to paying two hundred pounds for it,' Mr Stitch replied.

'Two hundred pounds!' Rupert screeched, jumping up and banging his head again. 'But that land is worth ten times that amount, the scoundrel.'

Thus it went on, for an hour or so, as Mr Stitch elaborated the complexities, and ramifications of Rupert Robertson's financial mire.

On shutting the door the rain began to fall, to the muffled sounds of the jubilant bell behind him. The intensity of the downpour was such that great streams were running from the brim of his hat and splashing into his face as he headed home. He could already feel his undergarments were soaked. Ordinarily he would have hailed a cab, but given his predicament some frugality was required.

Besides, with any luck, the deluge would soon overwhelm the river and the whole town would be drowned in the flood. He would have thereby saved himself a few pence, hopefully mitigating any impact his prior wastefulness might have upon the record of his immortal soul.

So, desperate, angry, bewildered, and achingly alone he hoped desperately for another Flood, or at least the first trumpet of the apocalypse, to save him the bother of addressing his multiplying worries—his wife was embroiled with the town's most notorious sexual deviant and he would soon find himself in debtor's prison.

Rupert had to say that he did not think the day was fine at all, quite contrary to Mr Stitch's assertion. But, realising it would be rather unfair to subject the entire world to annihilation due to his misfortunes, he wondered if he might perform some slight upon Captain Worsley's honour and thus unburden himself of otherwise having to devise the means by which to do away with himself.

He made to cross the street at this point and finished his *fine* morning by stepping, ankle deep, into a pile of fresh horse manure.

ℰ

The evening had been tortuous, with the maid-of-all-work, Alice, barely able to stifle her giggles. Little did Alice know that should he be unable to muster some support from somewhere she would be on the streets within a month. He certainly hadn't employed her for her skills at keeping the home, and it had been the topic of constant arguments with his wife. Alice was tolerated in his household solely because she hadn't the wits to negotiate a higher wage. He thought it unlikely she would find other work, at least not in a respectable household, should such a situation befall them both.

OH, PRETTY POLLY

The night brought only further horrendous rain, drumming against the windows of the master bedroom with the urgency of insistent creditors. Roseanna had not returned home and no word had been sent of her whereabouts. No doubt she would be in some wretched garret, reading Symington's own poetry back to him, before fornicating on a sweaty, lice-infested mattress. Let her have her little dalliance, he thought. She would soon learn what it is to be the fleeting passion of a poet. If she was not cast aside within a week, she would soon be acquainted with the horrors of poverty. Let consumption take them both!

By morning Rupert had, despite his lack of sleep, resolved to make a further appeal to his uncle, Reginald, to help him. It was unlikely to be successful, as their last meeting had ended disagreeably, the result of a bond that Rupert had 'forgotten' to honour, causing substantial losses for his uncle on a shipment of sugar. Still, there were few other avenues available to him and so he took his cane, and most importantly, a sturdy umbrella, and made ready to brave the day.

An hour or so later found him at his uncle's sumptuous home, amongst the other fine residences of Cummerbund Square.

A few minutes after admittance he was assisted in his departure by the butler.

Now, to accompany the relentless rain there were angry growls of thunder and frequent flashes of lightning—still, at least these brightened the sky that seemed as dark as the inside of his hat, which lay in a puddle at his feet, having been delivered to him by the swiftest of methods by the butler, along with a parting gesture—one best left to the imagination and of a character that Rupert thought beneath one in his uncle's employ.

He began to make his way home, hoping that a bolt from the heavens might put him from his misery.

Then, as suddenly as such a strike would have been, the clouds parted, the rain stopped, and a burst of sunshine was cast upon the wet street, which shone like polished jet. And to add to the beauty of the moment a vision of wonder appeared.

Stepping into the street from the pharmacy opposite him was a woman, the like of which he had never seen. She was wearing a simple blue dress, with embroidered ruff cuffs and topped with a beautiful pink bonnet. Her eyelashes curled up like feathered fans from her great blue eyes, which caught the sun and reflected it on into the depths of Rupert Robertson's heart. She laughed too, to see the bright day that had been revealed. It was a great rolling song of joy and delight. Its melody followed the light of her eyes into him to begin its echo and start his yearning.

'*What a beauty! What a pretty creature!*' Rupert thought, his mind fashioning the words into an odd, sing-song rhyme.

Teetering behind her as she made her merry way along the street was her maid, who carried two great wicker baskets and two umbrellas under each arm. But Rupert's eyes followed only the woman in the blue dress, and his ears heard only that rapturous laughter.

He had wits enough about him to stop a passing gentleman and enquire as to the identity of this angel.

'Why, sir, that is none other than Miss Pollyanna Pickering,' the gentleman said. 'She is the darling child of Colonel Pickering. Have you not heard of the Pickerings, sir? They are the wealthiest family in the county.'

Rupert Robertson had returned to his reverie though and did not even hear the man depart with an offended 'Good-day!'

Rupert stood there muttering under his breath, as a light drizzle resumed, 'Miss Pollyanna Pickering, darling child of Colonel Pickering. *Miss* Pollyanna Pickering, indeed! *What a beauty! What a pretty creature!*'

OH, PRETTY POLLY

From that day on, for two weeks, not a day passed without him catching sight of Miss Pickering; in the park, taking coffee with friends, alighting from cabs, or hailing them. But then, not a day passed when Rupert Robertson did not wander aimlessly about the town in the hope of catching sight of her, so the coincidence is hardly remarkable.

At each of these 'chance' encounters he only glimpsed her from afar, and heard once more her wondrous laugh, which set his spirit soaring. He forgot his debts. He forgot his wife and her ugly affair. He could think only of Miss Pollyanna Pickering, and soon he was so consumed by her that he knew he must effect some means by which to be introduced.

Lieutenant Simeon Smythe was a man who knew about women. He had been a dashing young cavalryman in the Sixteenth Lancers, and had seen action in many battles, eventually sustaining a wound to his leg on the first charge Kitchener made at Paardeberg. But a slight limp, a military background, and a fine family upon which one can draw a steady income, are a boon to any young man aspiring to play the town's eligible young ladies. In company with fellow soldiers, and with Robertson himself, the limp was inconspicuous. However, around any attractive young girl, and even her mother, the leg seemed to seize, enabling the deployment of the story of the wound to great effect, and much sympathy.

What Rupert Robertson needed, he resolved, was some heroic deed to bolster his agonisingly dull history.

Smythe lodged with a Mrs Keepum, whose third husband had recently passed on—as a result of her fish soup, Smythe had quipped, saying that you had to add a little arsenic to make it taste of something. Although, joking aside, there *was* an air of the sinister about Mrs Keepum and Rupert preferred not to dine there, or even take drinks with Smythe unless it was in a nearby tavern.

It was a late November evening when finally he could meet with Smythe, and only on the promise of a hearty supper at The Toby Jug. So there they were, quaffing their ales and picking over a chicken and a hock of ham. Rupert Robertson dominated the conversation, with brief talk of Roseanna, and his financial predicament, but mostly with a lengthy description of his sightings of Pollyanna Pickering, her attire on each occasion and the enchanting nature of her laugh. Finally losing his steam, and sliding back into his ridiculous fantasies, he became despondent.

'Oh, there's none like Pollyanna Pickering,' he said, wistfully. And then, humming an old melody that he could neither recall the name of, or its original words, he began to softly sing. *'Of all the girls that are so smart, there's none like Pretty Polly. She is the darling of my heart. She is so gay and jolly.'*

'Good Lord, Robertson,' Lieutenant Smythe gasped. 'What a strange little song. You really have got it bad haven't you, my poor fellow.'

'Oh, goodness,' Rupert blushed. 'I didn't mean for you to hear that. Well, it must be said, it is *true*! I have fallen for her with all of my heart. I adore her. What more can I say? It will have to be a love that remains forever hidden unless I can find some means of gaining an introduction. If all else fails I shall worship her from afar and be content merely to glimpse her angelic form around the town, as God wills it, occasionally having chance to be near enough to her perfection to catch faint echoes of her melodic laughter.'

Lieutenant Smythe raised an eyebrow at the gushing speech but sympathised, having been besotted for many years with a young milk maid from his uncle's farm. Although the infatuation had not lasted long after he had finally enjoyed her one stormy August afternoon in a convenient haystack. So, already sensing that it might be a mistake, but compelled by sympathy for his poor, wretched friend, Smythe offered to help.

'What say I arrange for you to go along to Colonel Pickering's ball this Christmas?' he said, taking Robertson squarely by the shoulders and looking intently at him. 'But you must promise me you will, between now and then, put your mind to all efforts at resolving your financial dilemmas, and putting Roseanna as far from your mind as possible.'

'Oh, would you, Smythe—*could you?*' Rupert squealed like a schoolboy with a penny liquorice. 'I shall make preparations for a fine costume with which to impress her.'

'Did you hear what I said, Robertson?' Lieutenant Smythe sighed.

'Yes, yes, you will get me an invitation to the ball,' Rupert jabbered. 'And I shall have my chance to speak to Pollyanna, to tell her my hopes and my dreams.'

'Yes. But did you, by any small chance, hear the second part of what I said?' he asked, watching the face of Rupert Robertson light with the fever of his imagination.

'Oh, yes, certainly. I shall re-open my negotiations with Mr Gruff, concerning that plot of farmland. That will buy me some time,' Rupert said. 'That should leave me just enough for a costume and the household expenses until the New Year, by which time I will have met with Miss Pickering and our courtship will have begun. Roseanna will not pose any problem, although I do wish she'd get what she deserves. I have already received a letter from her concerning the divorce, which she wants resolved as soon as possible before she departs for Italy. Oh, Smythe, *who'd be plagued with a wife, that could set himself free . . .*' And here his mind danced again with thoughts of brutal revenge and, what he considered rightful, bloody justice.

'Well, as long as you remain calm and measured it sounds a good plan. But, could I enquire . . .' Lieutenant Smythe began.

But Rupert was already off again with dreams and fancies.

'Now do you think it would be best, for my costume, to go for something contemporary and quirky, say from a novel, or for a more historical character?' Rupert interrupted, beginning the second phase of what was, for Lieutenant Smythe, a very boring evening.

ఴ

The evening of the Pickering's ball arrived, and Rupert Robertson took a cab—he had to really, it would not do to arrive on foot. He was dressed as Pierrot. It was not a costume he had chosen, but had been the only one that his new tailor had been prepared to make for him, on credit. He was clearly a suspicious and overly materialistic man, Rupert thought. The irony of the costume had not occurred to Rupert, for this evening was to be, he believed, a glorious unification of lost souls, parted only by the vagaries of family and social circumstance. It was more likely to be the sustained elaboration of an entirely one-sided obsession.

He entered the fine mansion of the Pickering's. One day it would fall to him, he thought. It would be a burden, but it was a responsibility he would have to bear if he were to be with his Pollyanna. And that is exactly what he intended. She would feel the same.

The servant announced his name in a hushed voice, barely audible even to Rupert, who was stood only feet from him. But he was not here for social climbing. He was not here to mingle with the great and the good of their feeble little town. He was not here to play the guessing game of those who had chosen masks. He was not here to listen to music, and drink, and dance the night away. He was, most certainly, not here to celebrate Christmas. He was here for one thing only—to meet his Pollyanna.

As he descended the stairway into the great ballroom he scanned the crowd, searching for her. There were costumes from all ages, but many dwelt upon the French Revolution. There were some military men who had elected to come in their uniform instead of costume; although to Rupert their clothes seemed just as ludicrous a plumage as the other fancy dress. Lieutenant Smythe could be seen, with his usual gaggle of attendant ladies. There was a small orchestra, dressed as performing monkeys, with red tunics and fez hats. But nowhere could he see his Pollyanna.

He almost tripped over a group of young children, dressed in endearing animal costumes, who were dancing around in a ring, singing, '*Dancy baby diddy, / What shall daddy do widdy? / Sit on his lap, / Give it some pap; / Dance baby diddy.*'

It was that awful old ditty that had been ringing through his head all these weeks. It had the air of a fairground song, repetitive, insistent, and maddening. That, or a rhyme that grubby street children scream at the top of their voices as they play with their crude toys, fashioned from sticks and stones, dead cats or whatever materials may be to hand. Strange that the sons and daughters of wealthy Wickhampton folk should be singing it, at Colonel Pickering's Christmas ball.

They had planned—that is, Roseanna and him—upon having children. They had agreed upon four, and God-willing, two of each—enough to make for a lively nursery. Their offspring would not play in the grimy alleyways and dangerous streets. They would have a nanny and a tutor. They would have discipline, and set hours of study and relaxation. It would not be a hard regime, but regimented enough to give them purpose and aspiration. Pollyanna Pickering would share his beliefs, of that he was certain, and they would have six—no, *eight*!—children to show the world their love for one another.

And then she appeared—Miss Pollyanna Pickering, attired so lavishly that Marie Antoinette would have balked at the extravagance. Her wonderful locks of golden hair were braided up into cascades of ringlets around a silver filigree frame, with little nodding birds perched amongst the coiffeuse's artistry. Her gown was of a pale blue, as light and delicate as a promising spring sky, with wide panniers that billowed in great waves about her. And the lace that edged it were the delicate clouds flitting through that painterly scene. Her pointed bodice was a light yellow, with an almost invisible grey embroidery that echoed the birds in the frame of her hair. The colours reminded him of that first morning he had seen her step from the pharmacy, like a proud, exotic bird. And in doing so she had ignited within him fire enough to rise from the ashes of his misery, in the hope, one day, of soaring through the air with her, both dematerialised through the intensity of their passion.

She glided, his perfect *baroque dream*, through the magnificent ballroom.

She floated, a *glorious bird*, alighting here and there amongst the guests to curtsey and greet them.

Interminably slowly, but as though drawn, she made her ethereal way towards him. As she came closer he heard her beautiful laugh, those notes of supreme joy that had held him captivated for these long weeks.

'Oh, how is it possible that perfection could be further perfected? *What a beauty! What a pretty creature!*' Rupert thought, the infernal, unknown melody jingling through the back of his mind.

And soon, very soon, he would hear her charming voice. A few more pleasantries with the other guests and she would be with him. He saw their faces around hers, some masked, others thickly daubed with make-up. They looked as one to him though, as useless as peg dolls, gruesome nothings that merely squandered the time that could be taken up by his first meeting with his exquisite queen.

'*There's dead folk here, all stiff and dolly,*' that tedious music rang in his head as he mouthed the words. '*I'll dance and sing like anything, with music for my pretty Polly.*'

The orchestra began a waltz.

Miss Pollyanna Pickering finally arrived, a *graceful swan*.

'Why, Mr Robertson,' she curtseyed, her thin lips sneering. 'What a pleasure to have you at our little gathering. It is strange though not to see your wife here with you, or has she been detained by the delights of the muses and the hidden charms of Apollo?'

Rupert Robertson heard not a word of what she said though. His mind, so disassembled by the madness of these weeks of fantasy and desperation, permitted only a seraphic choir to play to his ears, further confirming the heavenly being that his crazed eyes had fashioned.

'Might I have this dance with you, my lady,' he burbled. '*I can dance and sing like anything, with music for my pretty Poll!*'

He did not comprehend the shock upon her face and heard, instead of her indignant reply, the poetry of a psalm, set to the music of the cosmos. His enfeebled mind could discern only assent to the dance, and he frantically grabbed Miss Pickering for the embrace he so richly deserved after these weeks of ignominy and anticipation.

He twirled her into the waltzing crowd and laughed, crying out to the tune that played through his brain like a broken mechanical organ, '*At long last, I'll dance and sing like anything, with music for my darling Polly. All night, I'll dance and sing like anything, with music for my only Polly. Oh, look you fools, I'll dance and sing like anything, with music for my pretty Polly.*'

They danced and danced. He danced and danced her.

The music had stopped but the insane jig in Rupert Robertson's mind was still in full flow.

And he continued to dance and dance her, and chant and chant his demented song.

PETALS AND VIOLINS

The peg dolls stood about the ballroom, their blank faces as dead as everything else in the world. There they were, in the centre of the room—the new Mr and Mrs Robertson—their predestined union finally confirmed.

Pollyanna Pickering's breathless body was slumped in his arms. As Rupert rocked her back and forth a thin line of red liquid trailed from her still lips. He did not hear the shouts of outrage from the men, the agonised screams of the women, nor did he hear the steely swish of Colonel Pickering's sabre being unsheathed, or the great bellow of his martial voice as it broke from the might of his moustache.

No, in his last moments, Rupert Robertson focused only on the gentle kiss he bestowed upon his sleeping beloved as he whispered into her sweet mouth, '*I love you so, I love you so, I will never leave you; no, no, no!*'

THE ROCKING HORSE

It would have been possible to have stayed in York, given that I mostly worked from home, but we decided the move to Wales would be good for the children, so they could experience a more rural way of life. My job was chasing grant money and I was often referred to as a 'bid-fixer'. I knew the right jargon to get funding and that was what mattered most nowadays. That I could combine those skills with my previous work in earth science, at a place as prestigious as the IBERS research centre at Aberystwyth, was something of a dream come true. We found a beautiful house in a small village, Clarach, north of Aberystwyth. It was a half mile walk down to a pebbly beach, just beside a picturesque church and small hump-back bridge, the kind of location you see in those period dramas. Leaving city life behind was not a struggle, for either us or the children. Marion, my wife, illustrated children's books, and she was delighted to be somewhere more peaceful.

After we had moved I was full of enthusiasm. I thought I might even learn Welsh. Something in the language fascinated me and on the page it looked like a secret code—a childish reaction to a rich and complex history but sometimes the frivolous leads us to more meaningful discoveries. Marion was less keen. She said it would take us years to get the hang of it, and even then we'd have only the most basic grasp of it, and from what she understood the locals would just get frustrated with your faltering attempts and switch straight into English. Such pessimism was confirmed, or certainly deepened, one evening when we had Ann and Derek over for some drinks; they lived in the small cottage opposite us and had once owned the house we now had, before they had downsized a few years previously. To start my 'course' I'd purchased a set of CDs and a book, *Welsh in Six Weeks*, and had left it out on a bookshelf. Ann spotted it and laughed.

'Oh, God, Mike, you're not going to learn Welsh are you?' she scoffed. 'Do you know what, Derek has lived here for over fifty years; he moved to Bow Street when he was three, didn't you, Derek . . .' Derek sipped his wine and smiled. '. . . and do you know what they call him . . . *The Englishman*. He speaks fluent Welsh and still he's *The Englishman*. No, love, if I were you I wouldn't bother wasting my time.'

'Well, it was also for the kids,' I countered. 'They'll learn it at school, and their friends will all be speaking it. I'm hoping that we'll be here a good few years and I thought it'd be good to . . .'

'Oh, don't even try to fit in,' she interrupted. 'There's really no point. You'll always be an outsider. Even the kids . . . *especially the kids* . . . they're ten and five aren't they?'

'Nine and four,' Marion said, I could hear the frost in her voice.

'Yeah, that's what I mean,' Ann said, oblivious to the mood of the room. 'If Derek can't get any further with them in fifty years, and he started when he was three, then you've got no hope starting now. Best get used to being newcomers.'

Quiet descended. Derek smiled his ineffectual smile and just sipped his wine; he was used to it. I could almost hear Marion's fury pounding through her though. I found Ann irritating, but she was jovial enough and we had so few acquaintances, even after six months, that it seemed best just to put up with her casual racism and occasional rants.

Derek started to talk about work. For once I was grateful. I kept one ear open for anything that might kick off between Ann and Marion. One more glass of wine and Marion would go for her. Thankfully Ann started on another subject and the tension dissipated. They started chatting about furnishings and decorating and got up to walk about the lounge a bit. They seemed to spend a lot of time over by the window. I thought they were probably hatching a plot to convince me to go for some expensive curtains. Derek warbled on about cell wall degrading enzymes and I allowed my mind to drift. I was thinking back to our time in York, just after Eva was born. We'd had a party there for friends and family. Eva cried the whole time. She was only just six months old. Our house was overflowing with people. We'd had caterers in and they'd put on a marvellous spread. We'd build up a good network of friends here too, given time.

'Don't you think, Mike, that the use of ryegrass in the first place was a mistake?' Derek asked.

I stuttered a bit, coming back to my senses. I hadn't been listening to a word he'd said.

'Well, Derek,' I said. 'That's a good point you make, but . . . well . . .'

I was saved by Ann and Marion.

'Ann has had a lovely idea, Mike,' Marion said, seemingly happy again. 'Haven't you, Ann?'

'Yes, I think it will look lovely in here,' Ann said. 'You've got all this gorgeous wood on the walls and it will be such a treat for the kids. It's very reasonably priced too. I think you should snap it up, before someone else does.'

'Snap what up?' I said, suspicious that I was being set up for further unnecessary expenditure.

'A rocking horse!' Marion said, triumphantly.

'Yes,' Ann said, grinning. 'I saw this gorgeous one down in town at that house clearance place. Andy just wants rid of it. It's all handmade and he's giving it away at five hundred quid. I hear that Marion has always wanted a rocking horse for the children and it really would look gorgeous here in the bay window, wouldn't it Mike? You go and have a look at it tomorrow; you'll fall in love with it.'

Marion had indeed been on about a rocking horse for years. Thankfully the place in York just wasn't big enough so I didn't have to discuss it that much whenever she spotted one and started cooing over it. But here we had plenty of space—if not in the window it could go in the playroom, or even Eva's bedroom, which was vast. I'd have to think carefully about how best to play it. I'd always found them rather sinister things and the creaking noise they made really put my teeth on edge.

'Well, that's still rather a lot of money,' I said.

'Not for a full-sized one that's handmade,' Marion said. 'Some of them cost over two grand. You never know, we might make something on it when the kids are older and we sell it on. Would anyone like more wine?'

She turned on her heel with a cheeky smile. She knew full well that she had planted the idea of making money on it and that I would be unlikely to resist that. To be fair to her, if it proved to be the real deal, she was probably right.

I managed to fend Marion off each time she mentioned going to look at the rocking horse though. I really wasn't sure that five hundred pounds, even if it was a bargain, was a sensible investment. But over the next couple of months I kept finding myself thinking about it. The summer holidays arrived and, knowing that I had a big bid I was working on Marion offered to take the kids to her mother in Lincoln for a week. It was a great idea—I'd have some peace and quiet and they could go to some of the East coast beaches for a change.

ॐ

With Marion and the kids gone I thought it would be the perfect time to go and see the rocking horse for myself; to be able to make a decision on it without the hindrance of nagging and emotional blackmail.

I'd been in the shop a few times, poking about for furniture to fill up the huge rooms of our virtually empty house, but most of it was just modern junk that falls apart as soon as you touch it. As soon as I walked in I saw it. It was just behind the door as you walked in, jammed between a grubby grey sofa and a folding dining room table that had four chairs stacked on top of it. A head popped around from a low counter further into the shop. It was a guy in his late forties or early fifties with a neatly trimmed beard and a bald head.

'Oh, hello there,' he called out, in an overly familiar way. 'How's it going?'

'Er, okay . . . thanks . . .' I said. 'I just thought I'd have a browse . . .'

'You go ahead,' he said, ducking back behind his counter. 'Just shout me if you spot anything you want to haggle on.'

I didn't go any further in; I was only interested in the one thing. I had been fairly certain I would not like it at all and would have to prepare a list of reasons why we couldn't have it to ward off Marion. But looking at it now it struck me as rather beautiful; it was larger than I expected, its head reaching to my chest, and quite wide, Carl would struggle to get up on it without assistance. The wood had been built up in layers and then planed and shaped and this gave it a striped effect that ran the length of its body, with flowing contours of darker grains that had then been further emphasised by coats of light stain. Every detail had been attended to, not just in the physique of the animal—its muscular legs giving it a power I had never expected—but also in the tack and accompanying paraphernalia. The saddle was soft red leather, tacked down with brass studs. The bridle and reins were black and the buckles were bright gold, as were the stirrups. It looked as though it had hardly been used; that certainly wouldn't be the case for long if we got it, Eva and

Carl would soon have it covered in scratches and dirt. Its eyes were painted and they were the only element that I found disconcerting. They were very lifelike and something about them was familiar; a curious shiver of déjà-vu came over me but I could not fathom its origin—this horse was so unlike any of the others that we had looked at, and I had not had one of my own as a child, nor had any of the children I played with, as far as I could recall. I stroked its mane. The coarse hair felt odd beside the smoothly varnished body. The horse sat upon a large frame that had also been worked to a fine finish, with large metal clips that allowed it to move freely. I pushed it. It clunked back and forth a couple of times and then came to a stop. It was that noise that I really didn't like—it sounded so like the rhythm of a horse's canter, but there was also a resonance in its repetition, like the monotonous pendulum of a gargantuan clock. Despite being a little unnerved by it I still found it striking, and knew that Marion would adore it. I was not sure about the children. Eva was getting to the kind of age where she might find it wonderful for an afternoon and then never ride it again; Carl would love it, no doubt, but soon the lure of the computer would make such a quaint plaything redundant. It was more for us, I thought—a beautiful, nostalgic object.

'How much for the rocking horse?' I called out.

The man poked his head round again and looked at me curiously. He didn't say anything.

I pointed to it and called again, assuming he hadn't heard me, 'The rocking horse; I can't see a price ticket on it. How much is it?'

He walked over to me slowly, with a very puzzled expression. He stood there looking at it for a moment and then asked, 'You're interested in the rocking horse?'

I felt awkward; either he was being deliberately obstructive in an effort to push me for more money than I knew it was going for, or he was a little crazy.

'Yes, *the rocking horse*,' I said, with an emphasis that leaned more towards sarcasm, 'it is for sale isn't it. How much is it?'

'Yes . . . yes . . . it is,' he stuttered. 'But . . . I don't know . . .'

'Look it's a very nice piece and I can offer you a fair price,' I said, trying to force him out of his odd daze.

'Well, I had said five hundred . . .' he said slowly.

'Will you take four-fifty?' I said, keen to just get it concluded. 'I can give you a deposit of a hundred now and then the balance on delivery. I assume you deliver.'

He stared at me in amazement. Perhaps he was unused to such a swift negotiation.

'If you're sure you want it . . .' he mumbled.

'Yes, of course I'm sure,' I said, handing him a card with my address and phone number on. 'Now I'd like to have it by the end of the week, if possible; my wife and children are away at my mother-in-law's and I want it to be a surprise when they get back.'

He looked at the card and then looked back at me. Again, he didn't speak but just looked perplexed.

'You can deliver, can't you?' I said exasperatedly.

'Er . . . yes . . . we deliver . . . usually on Friday's,' he said, again looking so confused that I wondered if he might be ill.

'Are you ok?' I said, taking the hundred pounds from my wallet and offering it to him. 'I think four-fifty is a fair offer, it'll free up some room for you in here.'

'Yes . . . I'm fine,' he said, taking the money hesitantly. 'If you're *absolutely sure* you want it.'

I decided not to react any further. 'I look forward to seeing you on Friday then, I'm Mike, by the way,' I offered my hand.

He shook it, rather limply for someone of his size. 'Er . . . *right* . . . yeah, *Mike*,' he said. 'I'm Andy.'

I left the shop quickly and headed off. About halfway down the road I realised I hadn't got a receipt for the deposit. I really couldn't bear the thought of going back for one and just decided to leave it. It was a fairly small community and if he diddled me then word would get round. I had to trust that he would deliver it.

Back at the house I looked at the empty space in the bay window. Yes, it would look quite stunning there and be a wonderful surprise for Marion when she came back. I spent the next few days working on the bid for an EU grant and needed to prepare too for a trip the following week to the South of France for a conference on soil erosion. The evenings were spent with ready meals and DVD boxsets. It was very quiet without Marion and the kids but it was also quite enjoyable having some time to myself for a change.

The only problem with working from home is that you can go a bit stir crazy and by the Friday I was walking up the walls. I wasn't sure what time Andy would be delivering the rocking horse but it wouldn't be too early, I hoped. I decided to have a walk down on the beach, to get some fresh air and clear my head a little for another go at number-crunching and converting the proposed project into funding-attractive gibberish.

I walked for a good hour along the pebbled beach, right to the end where, with just a little more beach one would be able to walk all the way round to Aberystwyth. There was a large caravan park and small complex with a café, amusement arcade and gift shops that catered for the tourists. I stopped off for some toast and a coffee. Just as I was finishing Ann appeared in loud yellow shorts and a t-shirt that read, 'I'm wiv stupid' and an arrow pointing sideways. She really was a peculiar character. She sat down at the table with me looking quite sad.

'Are you okay, Ann?' I asked.

'Yes, *I'm* fine, I was just dropping some of my fresh scones in here and spotted you,' she said. 'How are *you*, more to the point? I'd seen your car go out of the drive a couple of times but I didn't want to trouble you, you know. How are you getting on? You can always pop over to us for a meal if you don't fancy cooking.'

It was an odd comment really. 'I'm sure I can manage, thanks Ann,' I said. 'I'm a big boy now and there's always the trusty microwave.'

'Yes, *I know*, I don't mean to pry,' she said, somewhat gravely. 'But do let us know if you need anything.'

I thanked her and said I had to get back for a delivery. By the time I was heading up the drive it had clouded over and a light rain had started. There was a van outside the house—it was Andy. He was banging on the front door and there was a younger man with him who was peering in the lounge window. It was only just gone nine in the morning.

'Hello, you're a bit earlier than I expected,' I called out.

'Oh, hi there,' Andy called out. 'We decided to do this as the first call of the day.'

'Hello there,' I said to his colleague. 'I'm Mike.'

The guy looked surprised and turned to Andy who gave him a little nod.

'I'm Ioan . . . Andy's son . . .' he said.

'Right then, I'll show you where I'd like it,' I said, unlocking the front door.

'I'm sure we can guess,' Ioan said.

I turned to see Andy give him a shove in the back. 'What do you mean, you can guess?' I asked.

'Well, er . . . it's just that . . .' Ioan stuttered.

'Most people put them in a playroom, or kid's bedroom,' Andy interrupted. 'Don't they Ioan?'

'Yeah, that's right,' Ioan said. 'So is it going up the stairs then?'

'No, it isn't,' I said, leading them through to the lounge. 'It's going just there.'

'Righto! Let's get it in then, dad,' Ioan said heading back out in a hurry.

I watched them from the window and saw that they were having an argument as they lowered the tailgate of the van. I couldn't make out what was being said but it seemed quite heated. They were speaking in Welsh and despite the fractiousness it still had that poetic lyricism. I resolved to have another go at learning it, despite Ann and Marion's cynicism. The rocking horse was covered in a grey blanket and even with the strength of each of them it was a struggle getting it into the house. After much grunting and swearing they placed it in the window and took off the blanket. It looked magnificent.

'It's a lovely piece of craftsmanship, even if the kids aren't fussed I know my wife will fall in love with it,' I said. There was no response. 'Well, I'd best settle up with you hadn't I?'

I went through to the kitchen to fetch an envelope with the balance I owed him in cash. I heard that they'd resumed their argument, but they stopped as soon as I came back.

'There you go, Andy, three-fifty.' I handed him the envelope.

'Cheers,' Andy said. 'But three hundred is plenty.' He opened the envelope and gave me back fifty pounds.

'Right then,' I said. 'Well it's a double pleasure doing business with you.'

'Yeah, that's right, a *double* pleasure,' Ioan said, then turned to his father and spoke quickly in Welsh. 'Mae wedi colli'r plot, dad, gadewch i ni fynd . . .'

Andy gave him an angry look and headed straight out to the van.

Once they'd gone I made myself a coffee and settled down in the lounge to watch the news, before starting on the funding bid again. I kept glancing over at the horse, admiring it—a part of me even thought of having a quick ride on it, but then thought better of it; I'd likely break it. I then noticed something protruding from the belly. I hoped it wasn't damaged—I hadn't been able to see underneath it in the shop for all of the furniture it was jammed between. I knelt down and found a small cork bung. I took it out and there seemed to be some kind of cavity inside. I went and fetched a small torch but it was so awkward to see inside, even if I lay on my back beneath the horse. The torch showed that there was something inside, it looked like rolled up pieces of paper. I tried a variety of things to get them out; kitchen scissors, a screwdriver, a ruler, but nothing worked. Then I remembered that Marion had a set of tweezers in her bedside drawer. They worked perfectly. I soon wished that they hadn't.

There were two sheets of thick cream-coloured A4 paper, the kind that Marion used to do her initial illustration sketches. Each was written in the lovely calligraphy she used for important things, and in the same dark purple ink. The first one read, 'Eva Sarah Wallis, Born 13th June 2007, 6.07 am, York, 6 lb 7 oz'. Taped to the bottom of the page was a small envelope. I opened it and found a lock of hair. I glanced quickly at the other sheet—Carl's birth details and another envelope. This was bizarre; my hands were shaking. I didn't know what to think. I quickly tried to rationalise it. Marion must have already been to Andy's shop and agreed to purchase it, and prepared a surprise for me with these lovely keepsakes inside. That's what his son meant by a 'double pleasure' was it—to take the money from both of us! I was fuming.

I looked up the number for the shop online, thankfully it gave Andy's name on a very basic website and a mobile number for him. I rang it immediately.

'Hello, Andy's House Clearance,' he answered, a rumble of traffic noise in the background.

'Look here, it's Mike, the guy who just bought the rocking horse off you,' I said, trying my best to contain my rage.

'Oh, hi, Mike,' he said. 'Is everything ok there?'

'No, it's not, if I'm honest,' I said. 'I think you know what's going on. I have found some personal effects relating to my children in a cavity inside the horse. Clearly my wife has been negotiating with you on this already and I think you need to come clean with me right now what is going on . . .'

It was clear that I was on speakerphone because his son then started speaking in Welsh. Another brief argument between them and then Andy was back on in English. 'Look, Mike, I know things have been hard for you recently. I don't want to cause you any more bother. I just don't want to get involved. I checked with you whether you really wanted the horse back, or not. You sold it to us a month ago. You said you wanted it back—we brought it back! If it's about the money I don't understand why you didn't just say you'd changed your mind, rather than offering to buy it. I'll drop the extra hundred we made on it into you next week. I don't know what else to say. I feel for you but it's really none of our business.'

'What do you mean, *I* sold it to *you*—*you* sold it to *me*!' I shouted.

'Ok, that's enough . . .' he said, angrily. The line went dead.

I rang back a couple of times but he didn't answer. I'd go in to the shop first thing in the morning and confront him. In the meantime I'd give Marion a call and find out what had been going on.

I called her but all I got was a recorded message saying I'd dialled an unrecognised number. I double checked her number, it was correct. I tried again from the home line—the same message.

I thought I'd try her mother; hopefully they weren't all out for the day. At least that rang out properly and she answered.

'Hi, Eleanor, it's just Mike,' I said. 'I wondered if Marion was there. I keep calling her mobile and there must be some problem because there's no dial tone. Can I just have a quick word with her?'

There was silence.

'Eleanor . . . Eleanor . . . are you there?' I said.

'Yes . . . yes, I'm here,' she said quietly. 'Are you alright, Mike? Are you at home? Is someone with you?'

'Yes, of course I'm at home, just needed to ask Marion something before she comes back on Sunday,' I said. 'What do you mean, *is someone with me*? I'm not having an affair you know . . .' I laughed. There was another silence. 'I think there's a problem with the line, Eleanor, I'll call you back.'

'No, the line is fine,' she said, her voice breaking a little. She began to cry. 'What do you mean, Mike? What do you mean?'

'Are you ok, Eleanor, I just called to speak to Marion . . .' I said, confused.

'I know how you feel,' she sobbed. 'I can't cope with it either. You know though . . . you *know* what happened . . . you *do* remember . . . Mike?'

'I don't *know* what *you're* talking about, Eleanor,' I said. '*Know* what?'

Another long silence followed. 'Mike, I think you need to call someone for some help. I tell you what, why don't you come over to Lincoln for a while and I can see what can be arranged here.'

'I think I must have entered some bizarre parallel universe . . .' I said, flippantly.

'They're dead, Mike,' Eleanor said sternly. 'You know that. Marion and the children died two months ago in an accident in the centre of town. A bus mounted the pavement and they died. Now, you have to get a grip on things . . .'

I dropped the phone on the sofa. I could hear Eleanor's voice calling my name. I looked out from the lounge and across the hall at the dining room door. It was shut. We normally left all of the doors open as they tended to get very musty if shut up for even a short time. I couldn't remember when I had last gone in there. I felt nauseous, as though I teetered on some huge precipice. I opened the dining room door; my stomach heaving as I began to recall what had happened.

PETALS AND VIOLINS

On the dining table there were two large bouquets of flowers in tall vases. One had been lilies, the other an arrangement of white and purple hyacinths. They were rotten now, most of their petals withered and browning, many fallen onto the table cloth. On the mantelpiece, and on every available surface around the room, there were cards—so many cards. I picked one up that was near me; there was a silver cross on the front with an italic script, 'Deepest Sympathy'. Inside I read, 'Dear Mike, Our thoughts are with you after this terrible tragedy. Do please call us if there is anything at all we can do for you. With all our hearts, Alan and Stacy'. I dropped the card as the repressed memories began to overwhelm me. I half expected to hear the clunking sound of the rocking horse in the lounge but I did not. Everything was quiet.

THE PEDAGOGUE, OR, THEY MUTTERED

There was a time that he would have spent the entirety of 'Learning and Teaching Committee' replying to emails or working on a book proposal, now though, chairing it, he had to maintain some discipline. He knew that behind the array of laptops there weren't diligent notes being made on the agenda of the meeting; some would be messaging on social media, others watching the cricket; one or two might even be doing some work, but not the work of the committee. Occasionally an agenda item might provoke a little debate, especially where workload was concerned, but most were content to nod everything through like a line of plastic dogs on the parcel-shelf of a tatty car. He had been Head of Department for four years now, and during that time his management style had deteriorated from the convivial and collegiate to the passive-aggressive and now to the downright confrontational. What he despised more than anything was the constant whingeing from those who were unwilling to take on roles themselves. Indeed this was why he was now having to chair this meeting; everyone had stepped backwards hastily when a new Learning and Teaching Co-ordinator was required—the previous incumbent now off sick with stress. So it fell to him to either impose his will upon another victim or do it himself; his position had become increasingly problematic though—all of his closer circle of supporters having suffered at the whims of his relentless demand for perfection—he would find it difficult, from such a weak base, to force anyone to take on the role, and besides, he'd do a much better job of it than any of them could anyway. So he added that administrative responsibility to his others and his days were governed by the length of agendas and the bullets of action points.

The meeting finally ended, late as ever, with his upbeat summation of the plans ahead and the wonderful reports of student satisfaction with teaching—it did not transform the glum faces around the room into beaming smiles, but did rouse a chorus of enthusiastic comments from a small coterie of syco-phants who would not have been out of place with bright cheerleading pom-poms and air horns. Back down the familiar corridor he had a few minutes to make himself a cup of tea before heading off to Senate for the last meeting of the day. At his office door, fumbling with his keys, he noticed at the far end of the corridor some of the more junior members of staff, gath-ered around the water cooler, chatting. They were jovial, keen and full of a love of research and teaching. He liked to encour-age them—he hoped they would not become as cynical and bitter as many of his colleagues had; they were the future of the department that he had worked in for over thirty years. Whilst other colleagues had used this institution as a stepping stone to other places, and more powerful positions, he had stayed, constructing for himself an idea of duty that would have been more at home in the armed forces than academia.

As he put the key in the door he looked up at his name plate, 'Prof. Cook', which slotted into a groove below his role, 'Head of Department'. Someone had put a strip of white tape over the side of the second 'o', so that it now read, 'Prof. Cock', and had finished the graffiti with a penis and hairy balls ejaculating through the first 'o'. That was the second time this week it had happened. He took the name plate out of its slot—he had a box of alcohol wipes to remove marker pen. Then he heard laughter from the water cooler group, and was sure he heard one say, 'Oh, he's had his time now . . .' A sudden rage overcame him and he stormed down the corridor and confronted them.

'I suggest you get on with your work, rather than frittering your time away here, *muttering* and *gossiping*,' he said, furiously.

The three faces looked up at him in shock. He turned and was gone.

Back in his office he wiped away the abuse from the name plate. It was probably the three of them, he thought—whilst he was in the meeting. He was quick to blame his colleagues for such misdemeanours; the students were beyond reproach in his eyes. He sought to cultivate an infantilised environment where the students looked to him more as a father figure than a teacher. It was a tactic he had perfected over many years and, despite its reprehensibility and dubious ethical implications, pats on the head and sweeties in the last class of term had done wonders for his module feedback scores, and gained him a reputation as the kindest tutor in the department.

A knock on the door.

'Come in,' he said.

It was Dr Farnham, one of the water cooler mutterers. He was a specialist in twentieth-century literary theory, an area of work that Professor Cook found entirely pointless, unless it was of a Marxist persuasion—Dr Farnham's certainly was not.

'Look, Steve,' Dr Farnham said. 'I don't know what caused that outburst but it really isn't on to storm into a conversation like that, especially in front of one of my PhD students. It's very uncollegiate. I don't know what had just happened, but there's no need to take it out on us.'

'Dr Farnham,' he said, sternly. 'I don't really think that advice from you on how to conduct myself is required. If you recall, despite my reservations about your area of work, I recog-nised the Department's need for someone like you, and argued the case at the appointment board for your employment. May I remind you that you are still on the probationary phase of your appointment and, given my years of experience, I might be better placed to understand the requirements of leadership in a role such as this—a role that, if you are lucky enough, you might one day grapple with.'

'Look Steve,' Dr Farnham said, stuttering against the veiled threats. 'You always said that we're on first name terms here. I thought I could just talk to you about how that made me feel. It was very threatening; I just thought you should know that.'

'Ok, then, *Mark*,' he said, taking a seat at his computer and turning his back on his colleague. 'Thank you for letting me know. Now, if you don't mind, I have a Senate meeting in a few minutes and need to prepare for that.'

Dr Farnham stood in the doorway for a moment, not really knowing how to take the issue forward. He closed the door quietly.

A few emails and then he'd go to Senate; a request for study leave from a professor who had repeatedly blocked his own promotions when Head of Department—permission denied; two students worried about referencing—copious copied and pasted explanations of the two optional referencing systems and their peculiar idiosyncrasies; a request for research funding to visit a special collection of Victorian ephemera from someone who had written a particularly scathing review of Cook's last book before joining the department months before Cook's reign began—funding denied. He sat back smugly.

Bing! Another email popped in.

The subject line read, 'Whispers!'

Opening it he read, '. . . mutter, mutter, mutter . . .'

He could feel the anger rising in him.

The sender: fancypants231@gmail.com.

He deleted it. It was Farnham, or one of the others. He'd find a way to get back at them. Off to Senate now.

The meeting went on for quite some time. There was a new ethics policy being introduced and one of the lay committee members, who ran the local museum, was a dog with a bone on all of the elements of it. It was gone six o'clock when Professor

Cook got back to his office. The corridors were empty, most of the staff tried to get away well before rush hour, and whatever teaching was still going on would be on one of the other campuses, this being primarily an administrative and support services campus.

He sank into his tutorial chair and sighed. He felt weary. He felt old. Everything had become a battle now. He had thought that he would take the Department forward to great things; all of his predecessors had been so feeble, unimaginative or just plain lazy. His whole career had been plotted to this point and yet, even after four years, he had been able to do little to turn its fate around; higher committees scrutinised admissions figures; higher committees scrutinised grant capture; higher committees scrutinised research output quality—all of them found the Department wanting and it was by default, his problem. He reasoned that most of the issues were to do with internal politics; almost half of the staff had not wanted him appointed as Head and positioned themselves to cause him maximum hindrance.

Suddenly his mental grumblings were disturbed by a flurry of small pieces of paper that burst into the room from underneath his door. They fluttered about by the doorway, stirred by some breeze he could not feel, and then settled to the floor. They were torn shreds from a book and on each was written, in black marker-pen, 'MUTTER'. He pulled the door open quickly and looked up and down the long corridor to catch the culprit. There was nobody to be seen. He raced towards the foyer by the main entrance—that was the most likely escape route they would have taken; and from there it was the expanse of car park at the front of the building where he would still be able to catch sight of them.

Again there was nobody.

A scampering of feet on the stairs leading up to the first floor offices, and a giggle, alerted him to where they were hiding. The corridor ran for the length of the building and they could not escape being spotted. He bounded up the stairs and called out after them, 'I'm warning you, this is a very serious matter and will involve disciplinary proceedings.'

As he entered it the corridor illuminated with the automatic sensor lighting that flicked its way down its length like a wormhole opening in space. Nobody. He walked slowly down the corridor, listening at the door of each office, checking for an occupant. As he approached the last office he could hear voices. The office belonged to Dr Moussa, a visiting fellow, working on poetics. As he got to the door he heard a younger, female voice proclaim, conspiratorially, '*Of course he's one of the old school; he's had his day.*' Dr Moussa was in his late fifties with a deep melodic voice.

He cleared his throat and knocked on the door, 'Dr Moussa, could I have a word with you please?' There was no answer. He knocked again, more forcefully. 'I know you're in there, now please open this door.' Perhaps he was engaged in an affair with a student. Well, this would serve him right, to be caught like this. It had seemed like a good idea to support his fellowship application but a few weeks previously he had dared to question the Department's commitment to a diverse programme of international literatures.

A thickly accented Eastern European voice from behind him roused him from his anticipation of vengeance, 'Can I help you, Professor?'

It was Natalia, the cleaner. She stood there with her vacuum cleaner trailing behind her like a plastic dog.

'Oh, er, good evening,' he said, awkwardly. 'I just needed to see Dr Moussa.'

'I saw him going away about an hour ago,' she said. 'The place is empty now. Only you and myself are remaining here; like most of the nights. We are the hard workers, aren't we, Professor.' She laughed.

210

He laughed too and was about to go when an idea occurred to him. There was somebody in there, he knew that for certain, and that person must have stuffed the torn pages under his door. Natalia had a master key to clean every room; she could let him in.

'Well, it's just that Dr Moussa was going to lend me a book earlier and I forgot to take it with me when I left his office,' he lied. 'I need it rather urgently for a paper I am writing this evening. You couldn't let me in to get it could you?'

'Of course I can, Professor Cook,' she said, flipping through a great bunch of keys. 'Although you really should get some rest yourself too, you know. Each day I am here I find you here, first thing in the morning, or last thing at the end of day. You must take a break at some time or you will become an ill man. I admire you very much. I admire hard working people, but you also must have a little time for yourself.'

He was getting irritated by her lecture, but also felt flattered by it. He prided himself on his staff knowing he was there before them, and that he stayed after them. It contributed to the sense of benevolent omnipresence he sought to foster.

'There you are, Professor,' she said, opening the door wide.

He strode in to confront them. The office was empty.

She looked at him expectantly. He looked back at her.

'Your book, Professor, do you know where it is?' she looked about the office as though it might float off a shelf.

'Oh, er, yes, *my book* . . .' he said, peering around. He grabbed one from the desk and left the room.

'I do admire you so much, Professor,' Natalia said as she locked the door. 'You are so clever.'

'Oh, thank you very much,' he said, thinking more how baffling it was that there was nobody in the room.

'I mean, with all of the work you produce anyway, to know Arabic too, that is a great achievement,' she said.

'Arabic, what are you talking about?' he said.

211

'The book,' she pointed. 'I didn't know you read Arabic.'

He looked down to see the flowing script of a title—a complete mystery.

'Oh, er, yes. Arabic . . . indeed . . . a great passion of mine! Now I must get on,' he flustered. 'I shall see you in the morning, Natalia, many thanks for your help.'

Back in his office he was puzzled. He was certain he had heard a voice in Moussa's office, and footsteps at the top of the stairs—maybe more than one person. He looked down at the floor and saw all of the torn strips of book, that was evidence of a more tangible kind. He gathered them together and took out an envelope to keep them in. As he was placing them inside he noticed something familiar about the torn pages—they were from his own books, even more of an insult. He scribbled the date and time on the envelope so that, should he need it, he would be certain of what had happened, and when.

A few more emails and it would be time to go home.

Turning on the computer he had the usual dispiriting feeling when he looked at the number of unread emails in his inbox— forty-six—and that was just in the space of three hours! He scanned down them, most of them seemed straightforward enough but then he came to a block of eight that had been sent in the last few minutes. Two of them were from 'fancypants231' and others looked to be from equally dubious spam accounts. Each had the same subject line, 'Rumours!'

He opened the first one from fancypants231. The message read, 'Mutter, flutter, stutter, butter, gutter, shutter, clutter, putter, nutter.' He deleted it. He opened a few of the others, most just read as the earlier one had, '. . .mutter, mutter, mutter . . .'—delete, delete, delete. It then occurred to him that he should not be deleting them; as with the envelope of the torn book pages, they were also evidence. A new folder, 'Mutter', was created in his Inbox and the emails retrieved from the Deleted Items. They'll soon regret this, he thought.

He opened another,

MUTTER
mutter
Mutter Mutter

Mutter 1
Mutter mutter mutter, mutter mutter

Mutter mutter mutter, mutter mutter mutter mutter mutter mutter. Mutter mutter mutter mutter mutter, mutter mutter mutter—mutter mutter mutter mutter, mutter mutter mutter mutter mutter. Mutter mutter mutter mutter mutter mutter mutter. Mutter mutter mutter mutter mutter; mutter mutter mutter mutter mutter mutter mutter mutter mutter mutter mutter mutter mutter mutter.

Mutter mutter mutter mutter mutter mutter mutter; mutter mutter mutter mutter. Mutter mutter mutter mutter mutter mutter mutter mutter mutter, mutter mutter mutter mutter mutter mutter, mutter mutter. Mutter mutter mutter mutter mutter mutter.

'Mutter mutter mutter, mutter,' Mutter mutter. 'Mutter mutter mutter mutter mutter mutter mutter mutter!'

Mutter mutter mutter mutter.

'Mutter mutter mutter mutter, mutter mutter mutter mutter,' mutter mutter mutter mutter mutter. 'Mutter mutter mutter mutter mutter mutter. Mutter mutter mutter mutter mutter.'

Mutter mutter.

Mutter mutter mutter mutter mutter, mutter mutter, mutter mutter mutter mutter mutter mutter. Mutter mutter mutter mutter mutter; mutter mutter mutter

mutter mutter—mutter mutter mutter. Mutter mutter mutter mutter mutter mutter mutter.

'Mutter mutter mutter, mutter mutter mutter mutter?' Mutter mutter, mutter mutter. 'Mutter mutter, mutter.'

'Mutter!' mutter mutter.

Mutter. Mutter.

Mutter mutter mutter mutter mutter mutter mutter mutter, mutter mutter mutter, mutter mutter mutter; mutter, mutter mutter mutter, mutter mutter mutter mutter, mutter mutter mutter mutter mutter mutter. Mutter mutter mutter, mutter mutter mutter mutter mutter mutter mutter. Mutter mutter, mutter mutter mutter mutter mutter. Mutter mutter mutter mutter mutter mutter mutter. Mutter, mutter mutter mutter, mutter mutter—mutter mutter mutter mutter mutter mutter. Mutter mutter mutter. Mutter mutter mutter. Mutter mutter mutter; mutter mutter mutter. Mutter? Mutter mutter mutter mutter, mutter mutter mutter mutter; mutter mutter mutter mutter. Mutter mutter mutter mutter mutter mutter, mutter, mutter mutter mutter mutter mutter—mutter mutter.

Mutter mutter mutter mutter mutter mutter mutter mutter mutter mutter mutter.

'. . . mutter, mutter, mutter . . .' mutter mutter.

Mutter mutter mutter mutter, mutter mutter. Mutter mutter mutter mutter . . .

He scrolled down through the email. There were pages and pages of it. This was frightening. It reminded him of a scene in *The Shining* where Jack Nicholson's wife discovers the writing he has been working on for months. At least that had a variety of words in it, 'All work and no play makes Jack a dull boy'. The endless repetition of the word 'mutter' made his eyes ache—let alone the disturbing implications for the fragile mental state of someone prepared to spend the time writing this out, punctuating it, and laying out the text as though it were a work of fiction. He converted the email into a Word document. It was eighty-five thousand words. It really was insane.

Professor Cook turned off the computer, packed his bag and decided to head home for the evening. He heard the hum of Natalia's vacuum cleaner upstairs and thought that she was probably right, he needed a break. Since becoming Head he had only taken a few days off here and there, trusting so few in the Department to deputise for him. Whoever was doing this ridiculous mutter-nonsense was doing it in response to his own pedantry and recent aggressive attitude in meetings. He needed to calm down and treat people with more respect. He would look into booking a proper holiday and, in the meantime, report the incident to HR in the morning.

∞

Over the next couple of weeks the number of emails increased each day. First there were ten or so but by the end of the first week there were fifty. He looked at a few of them. They ranged from the standard few words to great long screeds; some even had attachments where the letters were arranged into intricate patterns, or artwork—all using only the word, 'mutter'. HR were concerned—in their distant, non-committal fashion—and asked him to keep a record of everything. By the end of the second week the emails had reached over a hundred a day. It had started to absorb all his thoughts. It was approaching the end of the semester, and the students would soon be going on their holidays—then there would be the exam boards and graduation. Then he could look at having a holiday. He'd try somewhere in the sun, for a change—a beach, swimming in the sea. He'd read for pleasure, for once. He'd drink wine and

215

dance in nightclubs. He took a few moments to search the internet for possible destinations.

As he typed in the search engine he had a feeling of being watched. He turned; there was nobody. He tapped away at the keyboard . . . *clatter, clatter, clatter* . . . the noise became stranger, less plastic, less real. The noise softened until it became a whisper . . . *mutter, mutter, mutter* . . . He sank his head into his hands. He was going mad. He looked up at the computer screen and then down at the keyboard. He didn't want to touch it. There was something alien about it, something wrong about what it did; how it converted speech and thought into digital marks that were stored in electric circuit boards and wiring. His mind started to race. He imagined all the future technologies, as swollen with hope as his own pointless world, and as weary with desire. One day they would be able to unlock all of the past just through the residual sounds in the walls of buildings—he'd heard that such things were already being experimented with. There were all those possible 'ghosts' they would unearth: the conversations in secret, the endless gossip and prattle—the senseless glue of our everyday encounters. Who knows, perhaps one day they would listen to the echoes of his own keyboard; tapped out through space and time, resonating through the void into a reconstructed future hologram of now. What then? What would they hear? What would they see? They would note, through the flicker of the reconstruction, his fingers hovering upon the keyboard and perhaps they would comment on how smooth—almost sensuously—they caressed the keys; whispering, no *muttering*, their secrets. What primitive technologies, they would laugh; what quaint iterations of the human project.

The phone rang.

'Hello, Stephen?' a voice said. 'It's Alan here, Alan Garrett.' It was the Deputy Vice-Chancellor. 'We've got a few issues we need to discuss. I wonder if you're free later this afternoon, say three o'clock?'

It wasn't really a question. Whatever he might have on at that time would have to be postponed, or cancelled entirely. This was something serious.

'Yes, certainly, Alan . . .' he stuttered. 'Anything I should do before hand, or bring with me?'

'No, Stephen, no, nothing at all,' he replied, in a serious tone. 'Just bring your good self and we can discuss it later.'

He had his secretary check his diary. There was a meeting with the Internationalisation Office at three and then he was due to give a lecture to the dissertation students at four. Internationalisation could wait. He was disappointed about the lecture though. He did so enjoy, in the little teaching he could do given his other responsibilities, guiding the students through their final year projects. He liked to think he had a hand in each of their successes—the ones who failed normally had poor supervisors, or had started from a weak choice of subject-matter. He would try to reschedule the lecture. He did not see why his students should suffer because of the whims of senior management.

The meeting proved to be quite a surprise though. He thought it would be another telling off for various targets unmet—a slap on the wrist and more warnings. It was not, it was the beginning of a disciplinary procedure, in a most informal way; testing the water before the Union and HR were involved. He had done it a dozen times before, sitting on the other side of the desk.

Alan Garner had a heap of brown folders beside him—complaints apparently, complaints again *him*. They were all open cases and, as yet, unresolved. Garner probed the issues surrounding them, constantly asking him if he wanted to delay the meeting and have a Union advisor with him. He did not; he wanted to know more before he made his next move. With the opening of each folder Stephen Cook tried to peer over to see if he could glimpse any names, or read any further detail. He could not, all he saw on page after page, in folder after folder, was a single word, repeated on every line—*mutter*.

He accepted everything that Garner proposed. He was to step down as Head of Department immediately, to allow enough time to appoint a replacement in the next few months, before the new academic year began. He would be granted a year's research leave after which he would take early retirement—he had, after all, only a few years before he would retire anyway. During the leave he was to have only limited contact with his colleagues, restricted simply to the research he was working on. After that an emeritus post would be granted him to use the library and contribute to the general academic life of the Department, but any further bullying or other unacceptable behaviour would result in immediate dismissal.

During the final minutes of the meeting all that Cook could hear of Garner's word was the idiocy of, '. . . mutter, mutter, mutter . . .' On his walk back he overheard students, '. . . mutter, mutter, mutter . . .', colleagues, '. . . mutter, mutter, mutter . . .' In the bistro he ordered a coffee, '. . . mutter, mutter, mutter . . .'

Over the next few months he packed up his office. The advertisement was circulated for his replacement. It read, '. . . mutter, mutter, mutter . . .'

His holiday did him some good. Only occasionally did he hear the muttering, or see text crumble into the hateful oddness of that word. September came and he had the last boxes to pack before his year's research began. Few of his colleagues had been around in the Department, probably for fear of running into him—the place had a tense emptiness.

He closed the office door for the last time, feeling the pang of weary years unfolding like a dusty sheet behind him. Before him stretched the uncertain span of retirement, filled with the marginal addenda of the emeritus. One long last whisper came to him, along with an echo of light, youthful laughter.

'It was never yours . . .' the breathy voice gasped.

218

THE PEDAGOGUE, OR, THEY MUTTERED

He walked slowly to the foyer and looked out across the car-park—dotted with the various metallic emblems of success; Reserved for 'Head of Department', 'Dean of School', 'Director of Research'; all nameless posts filled for months or years, before being handed on, rebranded, restrategised. A lonely groundsman was sweeping up and tidying plant beds. They were preparing for autumn; making the place look good for the new intake of eager students, just starting out on their journey.

As he watched this perennial scene he saw the space transform; erupting with a proliferation of roots that probed the tarmacked ground for weakness. A swath of unkempt grasses unfurled across the immaculate institutional grounds, and the rhythm of years contracted into a rupturing revelation of eternity. In the end only ruins remained, as the mighty feet of incredible molluscs, and the fronds of garish corals, tried the last remaining bricks of the institution now sunk beneath unthought of seas. And these gentle, timeless creatures fed on ancient pulses of joy from vibrant ancient voices by means undreamt by earlier beings; slowly, through intricate mechanisms that synchronised the workings of incredible internal organs, the mutterings they craved were rendered corporeal, cellular and strange.

OUR SECOND HOME

It was the most gorgeous house you've ever seen. We fell in love with it straight away. From the moment we drove up to it we knew. I could feel Gill's excitement before we'd even taken off our seatbelts. It looked out across the sea, on the South side of Coverack, where fewer of the tourists enter the village. It had a wonderful, but manageable, garden. It was big enough to enjoy, and to entertain in, without being too large for a couple of our age. Yes, as a property to retire to, and probably our last home, it was nothing less than perfect. We'd come into a bit of money from Gill's mother a few years previously and had been on the hunt ever since for somewhere to begin a new life. Her parents had inherited their house, in some up and coming suburb in London, from another relative and we were quite astounded by the price it eventually went for. The move from Cumbria to Cornwall seemed a bit daunting but something in the project gave us vitality and I was sure we'd finally find some happiness. My God we deserved some. All of our parents had passed away within three years of each other and then, a week after my father's funeral, our lovely daughter, Carole-Ann, died in a crash. She was only twenty-two. She was a keen biker and she'd been on the old country road to Edinburgh with a few friends from her motorcycle club. It happened on the way back. A logging truck was coming around a bend too far on her side of the road. It clipped the bike's front wheel and sent her spinning into a ravine. By then the house in Cornwall had all but completed and we weren't sure whether to pull out of the whole thing. I persuaded Gill that it was probably best to start again; to make a new life in a new place. So the removal trucks appeared one morning and packed up our old house and we began the long journey to our second home.

Nothing can prepare you for the loss of your child. Even though you've already been over every horrific scenario in your mind; worrying about them on the climbing frame, by fast-running streams and by the sea; wondering if they're too cold, or too hot—taking temperatures endlessly; ringing them to check they're alright; picking them up late when they have spent their taxi money; and aside from all the banal anxieties there's the nightmarish visions, especially when they're away from home. Gill and I both had our concerns when she first started getting into bikes when she was around eighteen. I'd been through every crash you could imagine, even the kind she died in. Her death released me from perpetual fear and bound me to an aching melancholy that nothing could assuage. With Gill it was different; in the first few weeks we talked often about Carole-Ann, but I don't think she ever really told me what she was feeling. After a couple of months she never mentioned her again. I think she locked the memories away somewhere inside and just ploughed on with sorting out the new house, in the hope that the grief would one day wither—grief does not wither it merely transforms.

Carole-Ann died in September 2016. In early December we moved into the house in Coverack and spent our first Christmas there, watching the wind-battered wintery seas, locked inside with memories of our daughter. I suppose the strangeness of the new house took the edge off of the first Christmas without her. It was certainly strange for me. I'd lived in our old house in Penrith for so many years. We'd moved there when I was only five from a small village near Ambleside. My father was a stonemason and he'd done work on some new council houses in Penrith, the Scaws Estate, and was so impressed with them we moved into a caravan and went on a waiting list for one. That took two years. But once we were in it we loved it. In the eighties Mum and Dad purchased the house in the Right to Buy scheme but soon they got quite frail and decided a bungalow would be best for them. We bought the house off them and we were all happy. Carole-Ann came along very late, at the point Gill and I had really given up on the thought of having children. We were happy in Penrith. It was a good town. It gave us a good life. Our house was a good home.

We were in a lucky position, having two places, but we'd both decided that we needed to sell up in Penrith. Even with the money Gill had inherited it wouldn't last forever and didn't really stretch to keeping another house on, even if we rented it out, or did it up as a holiday home. Once we were a bit straighter in January I said I'd go up for a few days and get it in order to put on the market.

When we'd holidayed in Cornwall we always stopped off in Gloucester for one night, with Gill's cousin Sheila. It was almost exactly halfway from Coverack to Penrith and was certainly a welcome break in the driving. This time though I decided to do it in one hit. It was nearly eight hours, even if there wasn't a hold up on the motorway, and with a few stops for drinks and breaks you could add on another hour or more. I was keen to get on with it. I set off at 6 am one Saturday morning and hoped for the best. It took ten hours in total and I was shattered.

I turned the key in the familiar lock and dropped my bag in the hall. I felt a bit dizzy from the hours of driving—that sense of still travelling making me a bit nauseous. Maybe it was that that made me overly sensitive to the empty house. What struck me most was the feeling of not belonging there anymore. It had only been a couple of months and I'd already left this life behind. I walked into the lounge and looked at myself in the mantelpiece mirror that we'd left there because it didn't quite go in the new property. I looked washed out, thin and drained. My pale skin was further emphasised by the late afternoon sun bursting from behind a cloud and shining through the slats in the blinds. It sort of chopped me into segments that seemed to slide apart from each other, making a hideous image. I must be hallucinating. I blinked a few times and turned back to the hall. It was then that I had an awful feeling. It was as though I were a ghost in my own home. I could sense that I was standing beside myself in the most eerie and unnerving way; as though I had split in two, doubled; another *other* me. My eyes struggled with competing perspectives of the room. I wasn't sure which me was me; who stood in the rightful place; which of us occupied the true reality. I rubbed my eyes and my vision returned to normal. I hadn't thought that the long drive would do that to me. I resolved to stop off at Sheila's on the way back to Cornwall. I went through and put the kettle on and went to unload the car with all the bits I'd brought with me to tidy the place up.

I stayed there for three days. My mate, Gary, helped me with some of the things that needed doing, including emptying out the shed, which we'd not got round to before we moved. We had a couple of nice evenings out too, going over old times. I'd certainly miss my friends here, but we'd make new ones soon enough. Everyone down there was very friendly.

It was the night before I was due to come home that another strange sensation seized me. I'd got back from a curry with Gary and we'd also finished off a couple more cans sitting in the empty lounge. We joked that it was like being teenagers in some squat. I guess I'd had rather more to drink than I thought I had so maybe it was a slightly tipsy mind imagining things, but I'm not sure; it felt so real. After I'd seen Gary out I decided to head up to sleep. When I was halfway up the stairs I heard a key in the lock and then a quick, quiet relatching of the door. I turned around and then experienced the most peculiar thing. I can only describe it as being 'walked through'. And then I smelt it; Carole-Ann's perfume. I forget what it was called. She used to get it from one of those expensive soap shops that seem to stink out whatever shopping arcade they're in. It was completely unmistakable. I felt tears in my eyes—it is strange how something like scent can be a more powerful short cut to emotions than a photograph or even the memory of an event. I had to sit down on the stairs to compose myself. I slept very badly that night and had my first serious doubts whether we had done the right thing. Perhaps the house was our only real connection to her still.

In the morning I packed the car up and headed off. I'd called Gill to arrange the stop at Sheila's. I didn't mention my odd experiences to either of them. At Sheila's I kept things upbeat about how much we were loving it down south and that she must come and visit us soon.

I was glad to get back to Coverack though; driving down towards our house I saw the sea, it filled me with joy and a kind of relief. I felt the exact opposite to what I had on the last night in Penrith—this was the right thing to do, the right place to be; it was our new home on the coast. I contacted an estate agent later that week and got them to go round and put our house in Penrith on the market. Gary held a key and said he'd help out with anything we needed doing, and check in on the place every now and then. It seemed as though things were coming together very nicely.

Spring was gorgeous and I spent most mornings on a slow walk across the beach. Gill came occasionally, but when she did she would stop frequently, just gazing out at the waves; rather forlornly, I thought. Whilst the weather was wonderful and the views from the house spectacular, especially of the gorse that fell in yellow waves down the steep cliffs, things were not so agreeable between Gill and I. We began to argue regularly until one late May weekend, when we'd just returned from a fish supper down at the hotel on the front, Gill confessed to how unhappy she was.

'How can you be unhappy looking out on that?' I said, pointing to the beautiful sunset on the still sea that was the view from our lounge window. 'I really don't know what more you could want from a place.'

'I don't know either, Jack,' she said, pouring herself a large gin and tonic. 'Do you want one?'

I shook my head and just sat on the sofa staring at the sea.

'I never thought it would be this hard,' she said, sitting beside me. 'I never thought I was that attached to home. It was *your* home after all and, if I'm honest, I rather resented it. I thought we'd look for our own place together, rather than buy your parents'. But I got used to it and gradually it became *our* home, you know—just for us, and for . . . for . . .'

She went quiet.

The room was darkening as the last pinkish rays of sun faded.

'You can say her name, Gill,' I said. 'It might do you good to say her name.'

She didn't say anything.

'So what do you want to do then?' I asked. 'Do you want to sell here and move back?'

Another silence.

'I see her in the waves,' she said quietly. 'I see lots of faces in the waves . . . old friends . . . family . . . you know, people that are *gone*.'

I got up and turned the lights on and poured a large scotch.

'Do you think I'm going mad, Jack?' she said, almost in tears.

'God, no,' I said, taking her hands and kneeling beside her. 'We've been through the mill these last few years, love. We've really been through it. They say that moving house is one of the most distressing things you can do. And how can we get over Carole-Ann if we don't talk about her?'

'I don't want to get over her, Jack,' she sobbed. 'How can you *get over* your only child's death? I want to know she's ok. I want to know she's not unhappy.'

225

I didn't know what to say. What can you say? She wasn't ok—she was dead. She was neither happy, nor *unhappy*; one could only assume, or one could only *hope*. My heart was as broken as Gill's; my life just the same drag of senseless days. I had buried the torment, in a way, somewhere deep inside. When it burrowed out of me God only knew how it would show itself. Poor Gill was struggling with that monstrous grief and I had nothing to say to her.

'I think I'll go to bed, Jack,' she said, draining the last of her drink. 'I'm so sorry. I'm so sorry to still be like this. I can't help it.'

'I know, it'll get better soon, I promise,' I said, flatly.

She nodded unconvincingly and went upstairs.

I stood by the window, swallowing whisky after whisky, watching the silvery, wild crests of night waves collapse into the dark blackness beneath them, until I could barely stand. Then I went to bed in the hope that my brain was sufficiently sedated to allow some sleep.

I woke sometime after noon, my head throbbing. There was a note on the pillow beside me. I hurriedly read it, fearing the worst,

Dear Jack,
I'm going home for a week or two. I know what you'll think, but please don't. This isn't about us. I still love you dearly. We're not breaking up! Please believe me. I just need to sort myself out. Being up there is the only place I can do it. All I ask is that you don't call me. I will call you, I promise, when I'm ready to.
All my love,
G.

At least it wasn't 'the worst', but nearly. How had I made such a balls of the previous evening? I should have been able to get her to talk it through with me. Perhaps we needed counselling.

Thus began a terrible week. I was determined not to call. I was adamant I wouldn't. Each evening I tried my best to keep my mind occupied with other things; television, books, even a few games on the mobile phone, but all I returned to was an image of Gill in the old house, roughing it on the mattress we'd left behind, crying her eyes out.

I managed to make it a couple of days into the second week. Still there was no call. I couldn't take it any longer. I called. It went to answerphone, as I'd expected. I just left a quick message to ask her to let me know she was ok. Another day went by— nothing. I sent a text saying the same thing as I'd said in the message. I added that I wasn't putting any pressure on her; I just wanted to know she was safe—again, nothing. Two days later I packed some things in a bag and headed up to see her.

I stopped at a motorway hotel near Gloucester. I didn't want to go to Sheila's; she'd probably been talking it all over with Gill and I didn't want her knowing I was coming. Equally I didn't want to arrive at the old house in the same state I'd ended up in before. I left the hotel as early as possible and didn't bother with breakfast.

Pulling into our old street was rather depressing; all the memories came back, but on top of them was the weight of the situation with Gill. I had to convince her to come back home. There was no sign of her car though. I pulled up on the drive, grabbed my bag from the boot and headed in.

I opened the door as quietly as I could and called out to her. It felt odd, as though it were her house and not mine; or even, as though it were a house I had never even lived in—entirely alien to me, a mystery. The small hallway was, of course, empty. The walls showed the scars of where we once had a mirror, and there were scuff marks near the door, where we had kept a shoe rack; all of these traces of our past seemed more prominent now than when I was here last. Again, there was that particular silence of an uninhabited house; the gentle solidity of bricks and timber, occasionally groaning and creaking with their burden of sanctuary.

I went through to the lounge, knocking the door before I entered—I didn't want to scare her. A thought flashed through my mind that she may be there with someone else. Of course I'd already considered the fact that she might be having an affair, but it wasn't until then, like some stranger in my own living room, that I thought it might be a reality. The room was strikingly empty, so different to when we had lived there in such clutter. It hit me so suddenly this time that we were leaving this all behind; the dark laminate flooring echoed my footsteps around the space with a haunting hollowness.

Through in the kitchen diner the sun was shining brightly through the blinds in brilliant contrast to the darkness of the lounge. There were dirty coffee cups, plates and knives in the sink. We'd left a few bits and pieces there as we knew we'd be up a few times before the place sold. These were quite old though, a couple having developed a purple mould on the surface of the drinks. I looked in the fridge—a dribble of skimmed milk, some low fat soft cheese and a block of butter. Half a loaf of stale bread on the side completed the picture. She clearly hadn't been here in days. Where the hell could she have gone? I looked over at where our small dining table and chairs had been. It looked very odd with nothing there—a kind of expectant space, calling for something to fill it. The home needed new owners to make it live again.

I called up the stairs, not expecting an answer. I didn't get one.

I went into each bedroom in turn. All of them were empty still, other than the smallest one, where we'd left a mattress to camp out on, if we needed to. The duvet was dishevelled and there was a small bag with a few of her clothes in. A carrier bag beside it contained dirty laundry. In the bathroom an opened washbag contained a few toiletries. Her toothbrush and toothpaste were in a cup by the sink.

I stood on the landing and half-heartedly called out, 'Gill, *Gill*, are you here?'

A bang came from downstairs and I hurried down—the lounge, empty; kitchen, empty. I went to the back hall and found the back door ajar. Out in the garden there was nobody. I stuck to my useless calling, 'Gill, Gill, is that you?'

Then I noticed a cushion on one of the old garden chairs that we'd decided to leave behind and on the grass beside it a mug. I walked over and picked it up. It was half full of tea, but it was still warm. On the other side of the chair was a Danielle Steel book, opened out on the ground. Gill loved Danielle Steel and had read everything she'd ever written; ordering each new one as soon as it was published. I looked around the garden, holding the book limply in my hands as though it might somehow lead me to her, like a papery divining rod. After searching every corner of the garden and finding myself absurdly peering round the edge of the water butt by the side of the shed I'd had enough.

'Come on, Gill, this is stupid,' I shouted. 'Where the hell are you? I know you're here . . .'

Drizzle began to fall.

I picked the mug and cushion up and headed back in with the book.

The back door had shut and I leant down to nudge the handle with my elbow. It wouldn't open. Frustrated I put all of the things down and tried again. No, the handle just wouldn't budge. It was the kind of door that you needed to lock with a key from the inside, so no latch could have flicked down. Gill must have slipped back inside while I was out and locked it. But, if so, she would have known I was there. She would have seen me in the garden. She would, at the very least, have heard me. I was getting angry now, the rain was coming down heavier and she was obviously just being plain awkward. I knocked loudly on the door and shouted at the upstairs windows.

Nothing.

Then an irritatingly memorable voice called to me from over the fence.

'Hello, Jack, haven't seen you in a while now.' It was our old neighbour, Terry, under a large golf umbrella. 'I heard your voice and all the banging so I thought I'd pop my head over and see what all the fuss was about,' he said, grinning.

'Er, hello, Terry, I just popped up with some things for Gill and she seems to have accidentally locked me out,' I said awkwardly, knowing how peculiar that would all sound.

'That's a long way to come, just to pop some things in, Jack,' he said, puzzled. 'And besides, I saw your Gill a few days ago. I saw the car parked out the front, you know. But she hasn't been back in a while, certainly not today at any rate.'

'Really?' I said, wondering what I should do next.

'They said on the forecast it would be sunny today,' Terry blathered. 'Just shows you don't it. Bloody useless these weather folk, bloody useless. Anyway, you take care now, see you soon.'

His annoying little head bobbed back down and the umbrella disappeared. I sighed with relief and then suddenly realised that I was getting drenched, with no way back into the house. I shouted for him to come back, and explained that I'd be grateful to be able to just nip through his house to get back through our front door. He made his usual meal of things, offering to fetch me a step ladder to climb the fence, and even tea and cake when I got inside. I declined both and easily shunted myself over the wall on a fence post and dashed through the house, waving a nervous 'hello!' to his wife as I went through to the street.

Thankfully Gill hadn't locked the front door on me and I was soon back inside. Again, I did a circuit of the house but found nobody. I was fuming by this point but thought it best to dry

myself off first before calling her. As I did so my phone rang—
an unknown number. It could just be a sales call but somehow I
knew it was Gill.

'Hello,' I answered tentatively.

'Jack, Jack, it's me,' Gill said, the line fuzzy and her voice
distant and stern. 'You have to leave, Jack. You really do. It's
best for both of us. It's best you just go now.'

'What the hell are you talking about, Gill,' I said, trying my
best to keep calm. 'Where the bloody hell are you, for a start?'

There was a long silence. 'I'm upstairs,' she said, so quietly I
could barely hear it over the crackling line.

'You're having a laugh, aren't you,' I said, racing up the stairs
two at a time. 'Why the bloody hell are you calling me then.'

I switched the phone off and looked in all the bedrooms.
Nothing.

'Oh, now come on, love, this is getting ridiculous!' I yelled.

My phone rang again.

'Now stop playing these stupid games,' I said. 'Where the hell
are you?'

There was another long silence, with just the awful crackling
noise.

'Don't get upset, Jack,' Gill said slowly. 'Just calm down and
listen to me. Don't be shocked, and don't fly into a temper.'

'I'm not going to get in any temper,' I said. 'Just tell me
where you are and I'll come and meet you. We've really got to
talk.'

'Yes, we have,' she said. 'But you don't need to go anywhere.
I'm right beside you.'

'What!' I shouted. 'This stupidity has gone on long enough,
Gill. Stop winding me up.'

Silence.

'I *am* right beside you, Jack,' she continued calmly. 'I can see
you right now, pacing about in our bedroom in the usual way
that you do when we're having an argument. Do you want me

to describe what you're wearing? Do you want me to tell you what you have done since you arrived? I've been with you the whole time.'

I didn't know what to say. She'd gone quite mad. I went to the window and looked out in the street to see if her car had appeared, or if she was even in the street with some binoculars.

'I told you, Jack, I'm here in the room with you, not out there. I just wanted to tell you that I want to stay. I want to stay in the old house. This is my home,' she said, her voice breaking up a little.

'What are you talking about, Gill, you just locked me *out* of the bloody house. You just left me in the garden to have to talk with Terry the Twat and go through his house to get back in here,' I said, reaching the end of my tether. 'Now just quit mucking about and let's talk.'

'I didn't shut the door on you, Jack,' she said, the line really starting to break up. 'It's one of the effects . . . not quite there . . . sometimes things happen . . .'

'Look, Gill, you were sitting in the garden, having a tea and then you slipped back in and now you're making me look a prick . . .'

'Just *shut up*, Jack . . . must listen to . . .' she said, barely audible now. 'The tea was from days ago . . . just one of the effects . . . you'll hear soon enough . . . I'll try to call . . . wanted . . . say . . . love . . .'

The line went dead.

I didn't know what to do. There was no recorded number, so I couldn't ring back. I wandered about for an hour or so and then decided to go and check into a cheap hotel for the night. It was there, as I was picking at some dinner, mulling over the bizarre day I'd had, that the police called me. It had showed up as another unknown number, so I assumed it was Gill. They wanted to know where to find me—they'd tried the house in Cornwall and the one up here and needed to speak to me urgently. An officer would be with me at the hotel within the hour.

It reminded me of when Carole-Ann was killed; we'd been away for a long weekend in Whitby and they rang us there, just as we were getting ready to go home. They wouldn't tell us anything; they needed to meet in person. That journey back was agony. So, I knew what they were going to tell me. Gill's body had been found the previous evening in Haweswater reservoir, a few hundred yards from her car. There was a note. It all seemed fairly straightforward but they needed to make some further enquiries and would need to know my whereabouts for the next few weeks. I would have to identify the body. They asked me if I needed a support officer. I declined; I had to make arrangements.

The evening after the funeral the phone rang. It was Gill; or the noise that sounded like Gill. I couldn't make much out for all the background static; there was something about 'thanks' and 'feel so settled at home' and 'lovely to be with her again'. I'm not a religious person but I sort of believe in ghosts—in that more scientific fashion, I suppose; like a kind of residue of the person, an echo of them. I can't explain the phone calls though. I had one or two a week for the next few months, especially when I headed up to Penrith to sort odd bits with the house. I had a prospective buyer then and I think Gill said she liked them; a young couple who were settling down to have a family. I liked them too. By the end I could barely hear what she was saying, the background noise was so deafening. I had to hold the phone at a distance and could just pick out the occasional word here and there. The last time I was at the house, the day before it completed, I stood in our old bedroom and I'm sure I felt a hand in mine, and a gentle squeeze. I called out her name, the blinds rattled a little, as though stirred by some breeze. There was no wind. I stood a while longer, talking to her through the subtle manifestations of the house; a creak here, a rustle there.

The light flickered momentarily and then nothing more; it was time to go.

As I drove away for the last time it was a late spring evening. I'm sure I saw in the car mirror my lovely Gill waving goodbye and just behind her another silhouette, a very familiar one—one I would never forget. I headed back to Cornwall the following morning—to make the best of it all, to make the best of our second home.

A SPECIES OF THE DEAD

She ran the blade down the back, to the base of the tail. Her knife was old, thin and worn from many years of sharpening. She slid the tail bone out carefully and made another incision along the length of the tail. She continued with the little legs, and feet, making sure the claws were still attached to the hide. She folded the skin back out and moved on to the head, carefully peeling over the skull with gentle prods of the knife to loosen stubborn, clinging threads of flesh. She set the skull aside in water for later cleaning and lit a cigarette.

The squirrel's hide lay on the table, half inside out, tufts of grey fur poking from a wallet of skin, flecked with bloody clumps. The carcass itself looked sadly foetal; a marvel of sinews and purple veins, the majestic skeleton beneath holding the entire masterpiece together. She folded it carefully inside newspaper and wrapped it in bright red crêpe paper, tying the whole together with a strand of purple ribbon and carried it through to the garden with solemnity and ritual. The open fire pit was already lit. As she knelt by the flames she whispered words of thanks and words of love and placed the package upon its pyre.

Back in her workshop she sewed the mouth together and cleaned the skin of the last flecks of flesh. She rinsed it well and then placed it into methylated spirits to soak for a couple of hours. She also prepared the skull to bleach and went back through to the main house for some lunch and to watch the news. She also flicked through that morning's post as a further procrastination—that afternoon required her to finish two mounts for a client and she was not looking forward to them; an awkward pair of pigeons dancing together, a quirky gift for a wedding.

There was a rare thing—a handwritten letter—in amongst the colourful marketing leaflets and superfast broadband offers. She opened it eagerly.

Folding Gallery
13 The Mount
Shrewsbury

9th August 2018

Dear Alison,

I hope all is well with you. I was so sad to hear of Michael's passing. He was a great artist and he will be sorely missed. Claire and I still walk past his 'Horse in Winter' every morning on our way to the gallery. Do come over to Shrewsbury any time you'd like, we'd be very happy to see you.

I am writing to ask the schedule for your piece, 'Flight from the Divine', and whether it might be possible to get its manoeuvres to coincide with an exhibition on The Animated Object *we are hoping to arrange around February 2020. Might this be possible at all? I believe it is currently in Warsaw but am not sure what other destinations are planned between there and when we are thinking. If it was back in the UK by then that would be a great help with our budget, but let me know what you think, and if it's a possibility then send me a cost breakdown for it (I know it is difficult to install, but fingers crossed we have the funding for it!).*

I know you don't like email so am happy to do things through letter if you'd prefer. If you've started to get on with the computer better now obviously that would make things easier at our end—we have two good interns at the moment who'll do a 'social media blast' on it, or something!

Take care,
Benjamin

It was from Benjamin Meyer, who ran a gallery on the outskirts of Shrewsbury, with his mother. He only contacted Alison when he needed something and was usually unreliable on the financial side of things. Whatever they might agree would probably end up being halved due to 'unforeseen expenses' and other excuses. Still, it was important that 'Flight from the Divine' continue doing the rounds, it was one of her few almost permanently exhibited pieces and now with her husband gone she needed to maintain a decent income from gigs like this. It was a very complicated piece and she really doubted that Benjamin had the resources to display it properly. It consisted of over four hundred birds erupting from a darkened space, through a stained glass window that hung in over fifty shards. It was a beautiful piece and she'd been approached to sell it a number of times; no doubt the time would come when she would have to. She'd get the costs together and then hear nothing from him for months, no doubt.

Mention of her husband's sculpture, 'The Horse in Winter', upset her though and a wave of grief came over her. It had only been six months since he had died, quite suddenly, and each day something would bring him back to her and force her to sit down and remember, in tears or laughter. The relentless extremes of emotion were shattering. The sculpture had been dedicated to her and was the first he had completed after they married. It consisted of four great vertical timbers, blackened by fire, with a metallic cage above, from which shards of iron came down, like cracks of lightning. It was commissioned by

Shrewsbury council to celebrate some civic event that she had entirely forgotten the purpose of now. She was one of the few that knew that under its base there was a plaque that read, 'I dedicate this beast to my darling Ali, may he charge through the years carrying our love forever, Michael'.

Thinking of it now brought back how lonely she was and how uncertain she was about the future. She'd had a number of exhibitions back in the late 1990s, with some unusual works; five eagles carrying a musket between them, rats at a conference on poison resistance, two dogs doing a drug exchange, a Siamese cat in a shop doorway with a sign that read, 'Homeless and Hungry, please help!' They were well produced pieces, with a facile social critique. Looking back on that period of her work she was embarrassed by them. The few interviews she now had focused on them to the exclusion of the more recent work, which was more mature, she thought. The works were tragic and grand now, with a kind of sympathy; she had managed to combine the materials with a proper response to the world. But few were interested in the subtlety it had taken her twenty-five years to perfect. It hadn't helped that she'd had to also maintain a more commercial aspect to the work, so alongside the more artistic pieces she'd also had to churn out the carol-singing mice, the toads on surfboards, and those damned wedding pigeons. And now that Michael was gone she wasn't sure she wanted to do any of it anymore.

They had met at university. He was a tutor and she was his student—twenty years had separated them. They had lived for many years beneath the shadow of others' assumptions about the origins of their relationship. Even those they considered good friends would make occasional remarks—good hearted enough, but painful nonetheless. Michael's colleagues were the worst, some of whom had taught her. It was, if their assumptions had been true, a betrayal of the ethical relationship between a teacher and their student. But none of their innuendo and fantasy was true. Ali had courted him; rather than the predatory man in power, grooming her and bending her mind to his desires, she had pursued him. Once she had her mind set on something little could stop her. He had been married before, but they were estranged. His work fascinated her; he sculpted animal figures, but his style was more to capture the essence of the creature in stylised movement—a hare became a jagged zig-zag of brass and dried grasses; an owl was a swathe of dark cloth swooping between two poles of grey driftwood; a badger a round stone that rolled gently through a circular groove in a slab of granite; that stone came to her regularly in dreams since he had died, just rolling and rolling and rolling, on and on through the tormented synapses of her sleeping brain.

∞

She was introduced to Dr Jozsef Szarka at her lowest ebb. It was a conspiracy of well-meaning friends that had arranged for them to meet, at an exhibition launch party she'd been nagged into attending. He was a nutritionist and lived up in Yorkshire, but he seemed to work most of the time in Somerset, for various health centres and spas. He was charming, witty, kind and quaintly gentlemanly. He invited her out to the races and for dinner. They went to the theatre a couple of times together. She felt awkward and guilty being out with another man so soon, it seemed to her, after Michael's death. Her friends assured her that it was not unreasonable to start thinking of another relationship by now, and she really did need some company. It seemed that there could be more between them but he never pressed the matter and Alison was reticent.

As she struggled on through her sorrow he suggested pills to help her sleep. He recommended vitamins and supplements that gave her energy and helped her focus. Everything about him exuded vitality and confidence. She even met his mother and father when they came over from Hungary. They spoke excellent English but seemed quiet and withdrawn. They commented on what a lovely woman she was and hoped she would be happy again soon after her loss. Jozsef stayed at her house frequently, talking long into the night about politics, books and philosophy. He reminded her so much of Michael; the passion of his earlier years, and the creative energy. He offered her pills and powders to improve her mood, to help her move on. At first he simply gave them to her but, after a few months, he said he couldn't afford to keep providing them to her free—it was a reasonable demand, they must be costly, after all; and they really seemed to be working. She felt quite elated now, most of the time. Occasionally though, when she was running low on her medication, and had to start to ration it, she began to dwell on darker things.

She thought of Michael rotting in the ground; the crawling, sliding creatures that would have penetrated his cardboard eco-coffin, devouring him, transforming him back to soil and sludge. What a waste of a fine carcass; his skin pale and rotten, his soft hair matted and patchy. Then she thought how fine he would have looked, mounted—the kind of insane idea that comes to one in the depths of grief. She laughed, imagining him stuffed in his workshop, a couple of tools in his hand; at work on another sculpture, frozen like it forever. The arts they had practiced were not so different really, both attempting to lock the world into a permanent record—hers was more literal, no doubt; the preservation of things that had existed. His was more abstract— a reflection upon the thing, rather than its actual representation. And, if the preservation of people's pets was considered morally acceptable, why not the preservation of one's loved ones? Why was it that Gunter von Hagens could exhibit his anatomical bodies around the world yet it was illegal to keep the ones most precious to you? There were societies that had made the veneration, and preservation, of ancestors and family the foundation of their civilisation. Not everyone was as squeamish about skin and bone as modern, supposedly civilised, humanity—it was the barbarity of a sterilising social amnesia. Such things were considered primitive. In an evolved world of shiny metal and garish plastic, who wanted great-aunt Maud's skull looking down on them from a shelf in the corner of the room—everything is life, life, life; forget the dead. The dead called to be remembered.

Jozsef arrived, with light and laughter, with flowers and prescriptions. The days were illuminated with walks and conversation, with wine and forgetting. He was full of the energy of enthusiasm; a new business venture, his sister's new daughter, a recent film he had watched—everything was flow and force. He needed a little more money to get him through it all. She sold some older works, and one of Michael's lesser pieces. They visited Venice. She had always wanted to visit Venice.

She was living again. Michael would have wanted her to be like this. He'd have wanted her to be happy—he'd probably have wanted her to begin a proper relationship with Jozsef and start a new life. Or would he? Perhaps that is our greatest misunderstanding, she thought. Maybe the dead lay there in permanent envy of the living, craving that they join them, sooner rather than later. Six feet under, across the planet, lay tonnes of putrid flesh festering with resentment and hatred. Why us? Why do you still live? Your time is coming, we will see you eventually! But she did not believe that consciousness of any kind continued beyond death. She had seen too many dead things; she had worked with their remains and knew the empty eyes; the nothing that lay within. But human beings might be different; she might glimpse a soul.

She called Jozsef. She was low on pills. He came, late one night and briefly. He gave her a package. She gave him some money. He would call soon; he promised he would call her soon. They would go out—she needed to go out.

Months of morbid meditation took her thoughts to the darkest of places. What were bodies, after all, but intricate contraptions forged through others' flesh and chemicals, atoms upon atoms that were all once other things? Everything she touched might once have been a being, or would become one at some point in time. Her house fizzed with fecundity—even the most basic of household chores set her pondering the bacteria in the plughole of the sink; the microbes multiplying in the washing machine; and behind them all that growing mound of what once was, reforming itself for another time. What did they say, two-thirds of a human body is water, and each body supports millions of life forms, from the mouth to the anus—all exchanging substances, all busy with the exigency of existence. She stared at her fingers, at her toes. She wriggled them and imagined they were different creatures. The musculature of her arms, her thighs—tight sinews that belonged to some other entity that flexed and contorted itself around a being made of bone; and somewhere within their struggling forms there resided her—a pair of eyes peering from the darkness, hovering on the edges of non-being.

Joszef sent her a package; she paid into his account.

The question was not what the secrets were beyond death but what differentiated anything from anything else. If, in time, all became everything else, then who was anyone? The quest was not what lay beyond but what lay within. She was resolved. It would take some considerable effort, if it were achievable at all. It would take much planning. She began her research immediately.

Jozsef would be able to acquire what she needed—what could see her through her task.

&

When he was led through the house he knew it was going to be a tough one. He'd already had the outline of what had happened from his colleague and that was bad enough but the house itself gave him the shivers. Everywhere there were stuffed animals and birds, reptiles and insects in cases. The high walls were crammed with shelves supporting glass cases and domes with endless rows of glassy eyes that watched as he made his way carefully between the clutter of books and drawings, sketches and notepads that were strewn everywhere about the place. It hadn't been ransacked or vandalised, but rather than a home it had been transformed into a site of urgent endeavour—all leading to what he was about to witness.

He vomited three times before he was able to stay in the room for any length of time. He'd worked for many years on gang crime and thought he had seen most things. He believed he had become immune to the sight of a tortured, ruined body, but this was different. He'd seen a flaying once before; a dealer who hadn't paid up and ended up without the skin of his upper body. But, from the report he'd had, she had done this to *herself*.

The skin was hanging on a large wooden hanger that was suspended from the ceiling light. The face hung limply over the right shoulder, no features were discernible. It looked like a thin hood on an old coat. Sitting in a white plastic garden chair opposite the horrific skin was something worse. A flayed corpse, but one that had clearly lived for some time beyond the flaying; all about it were dozens of used syringes, pills and white powder, blue disposable gloves, scalpels and thin blades of varying lengths. There was a lot of blood, but not as much as he might have expected. And strangely, there was a glass of red wine, half drunk, and an ashtray with three cigarette ends in it.

A voice beside him said, 'Yes, She seems to have had a drink while she was doing it, and a few fags too. She left a note, for what it's worth. Do you want to see it, sir?'

He nodded.

PETALS AND VIOLINS

He was handed a sheet of thin blue airmail paper with a few shakily written words, smeared with dried blood.

I have seen the place where I once was. I have looked into those endless mirrors and my empty eyes; on through eternity into the space where I became an illusion. All of this world's varied garments—leaves, feathers, shells or skin—are thin shrouds draped over reality; everything is anything.

GOLDEN IN THE MERCY OF HIS MEANS

I
Old Friends

'So, I'm still curious—why Dinan, Michael? Was it some romantic haunt for you both back in the day?' David asked, settling into the rather tatty leather sofa in his friend's lounge.

'Something like that,' Michael said, pouring them a couple of glasses of Scotch. 'It started way before then though, in the late 1990s, when we were both kids.'

'Wow! The 90s, we really are a couple of old farts aren't we,' David laughed.

'Certainly feels like it,' Michael said, sighing himself into the sofa next to David. 'We remembered Dinan years later, when we met again in London. We'd actually been on holiday together with our parents, who had been friends for a time. It was just a week but I remember her so vividly—what a little pest she was! I was eight and she was seven and she wouldn't leave me alone for a minute—even stood outside the toilet waiting for me to come out. We came back here for our honeymoon just after we'd left the EU. God, that was a nightmare; the baggage checks, over-zealous security guards, and the bloody passport issues. Sara almost got refused entry. It was such a petty revenge by the French. Things could have been so different, we just wanted our bloody country back from those pigs in Brussels.'

There was a silence.

'Sorry, David,' Michael said. 'Probably best not to bring all that up again.'

'*Quite,*' David said, 'Let's leave the politics out of it, especially after all these years. We are where we are, now.'

'Yes, I suppose we are,' Michael replied. 'Well, to get back to Dinan, we thought about it for ages and when Clara was ten we said—sod it! It's now, or never. Then up popped this place for sale, straight opposite the Château; gorgeous views, five minutes from the town centre, and a lovely walk down to the port—it couldn't have been more perfect. I won't go into the hassle of residency visas, and now since the RFN bombings, and then this third freedom war, they really have cracked down on us. We have to go to the town hall each week to show our papers and outline our plans for the coming week. But it's the beauty of the place I love so much. For my money you can keep the food, I will tip my hat to the wine-making skills though.'

'Well, I'll have the wine *and the food*, thanks,' David laughed; Michael didn't. 'Sorry it's just going to be a flying, one night visit, but I thought it would be mad to pass up the opportunity to catch up as I was in the area.'

'Yes, yes, I understand, and am so pleased you made the time to pop round,' Michael said. 'But, God, how long has it been now?'

'Well, it must be nearly twenty years,' David said. 'I came down to see you in Shrewsbury for a week or so just after Jack was born... now that was, erm, 2026, wow! . . . and I think we also came down a year or so later, didn't we; without the boys?'

'Oh, God, yes, that flat in Shrewsbury,' Michael laughed. 'I ordered in those vintage Burgundies and they got detained by customs. I had to drive to Liverpool to collect them, and pay the surcharge . . . over a hundred quid, robbing bastards!'

'Hmm, but this one's nice,' David said, sipping his whisky. 'What is it?'

'It's actually Japanese,' Michael said. 'To bring the proper Scottish stuff over is too expensive these days. I find this one hits the spot though.'

There was another long silence.

'So . . .' they both started at once.

'You go on,' David said. 'Please.'

'I was just going to ask about Sally and the boys,' Michael said, gathering their glasses to top them up.

'Oh, well, you know Sally and I just drift along; she does her thing, I do mine,' David said, sadly. 'But the boys are doing well. Liam is back from his second tour. He was part of the battalion that retook Haskovo last month . . .'

'God, I heard about that, bloody savage wasn't it?' Michael said.

'Yes, from what I can gather . . . he doesn't talk about it much,' David said. 'Jack is still doing his training back in England, thankfully, at the moment. I hope they don't get deployed together—they're in the same regiment. I wish they could have chosen another profession.'

'You should be proud, David,' Michael said, settling back into his seat. 'You've got two strapping lads, they do you great credit. They do *England* great credit. They'll be fine.'

'I hope you're right,' Michael sighed. 'I really hope you're right.'

The evening wore on in a tedious fashion, both carefully avoiding issues that might ignite the arguments that so nearly drove them to blows all those years before. The kids were grown up now but that didn't mean they could revive their own younger days. The whisky flowed, various nostalgias bloomed momentarily and then withered into uncomfortable silences. And still the whisky flowed, edging each of them towards the brink of disagreements and the fragile politics of a disintegrating Europe that had engulfed Liam and Jack into very real danger. And inevitably the whisky flowed, until the hours had finally consumed themselves and tiredness overwhelmed each of them enough to justify sleep; any earlier and whoever had suggested it would have appeared not to value the attempt to resurrect the friendship. Now, thankfully, each of them could retreat to bed knowing that they had done their best.

'Well, it's been a great evening,' David said, rising from the sofa with a long stretch. 'I'd better get to sleep though. Do you have a spare room, or shall I kip on the sofa?'

'Yes, it's on the first floor, first on the right, next to ours,' Michael said. 'Clara's room is on the top floor, but we turned the playroom opposite into a store room, as Sara seems intent on buying every piece of furniture ever made in France over the last two hundred years.'

'Right, I'll head up then,' David said.

'Yes, I'll just get some water and then follow you up,' Michael said, tidying away the bottles of whisky and the glasses.

Michael took a few minutes to busy himself in the kitchen in the hope that David would have settled into his room and that they could get the evening behind them and then have some brief goodbyes in the morning.

As he sauntered slowly up the stairs he saw David standing at the large mezzanine window looking out across the back garden. It was still dark but there were slight glimmers of dawn gathering on the horizon.

Michael stood a moment beside him, seeing how intent his gaze was, 'Everything ok, David?'

'Yes, yes, fine,' David said, stirring from his intense thoughts. 'What's that house through the trees there, backing on to your garden; the one with the lights on in the top floor?'

'Well, I tried years ago to find out about that place,' Michael said, peering through the trees at the faint lights in the top windows of the great mansion whose vast gardens backed onto his own. 'I became rather obsessed with it actually. I asked all the locals about it, and nobody seemed to know much, most of them saying it had been abandoned for years. The most sensible, or perhaps incredible, answer I got was from an old lady who said she had been a pupil at the place in the 1970s when it was a boarding school. I couldn't find anything in the local records about that though, and nobody else could recall it.

'If you turn left outside our house and then go round the corner, as though you were going down to the port, you'll see big iron gates a few hundred yards down the road. They lead up to the place, but all you can see beyond is weeds now, and the rusted chain and padlock on the gates can't have been opened in decades. But the lights are often on, all through the night too.'

'How odd,' David whispered.

'Yes, it is, especially in these troubled times,' Michael said. 'You'd have thought the authorities would have done some digging. It could hold insurgents, or an RFN cell.'

His bad joke went unnoticed. More light was now appearing in the sky and through the trees they could just make out the brown stone of the walls and the bright white bay windows on the upper floor with hatched leading.

Chup, chup, tseep, tseep—a bird began to sing nearby.

'I mean it's odd because there's something about it that's so familiar; those small, high windows,' David said. 'And even that bright red wall at the bottom of the garden. I'm sure I've seen somewhere similar recently.'

They looked out in silence.

Chup, chup, tseep, tseep. Silence.

'. . . *that time allows, in all his tuneful turning, so few and such morning songs . . .*' David said, quietly.

Both men continued to look out of the window, trying to peer through the thick branches, heavy with foliage, to make out further details of the house. The bird sang again—chup, chup, chup, tseep, tseeep.

'What . . . what was that you said?' Michael asked, as though stirring from a daydream.

David sighed, 'I just said that time allows so few morning songs.'

'Oh, right,' Michael nodded. 'Where's that from?'

'It's from a poem,' David said, still staring sadly at the trees. 'It's a poem by Dylan Thomas, called "Fern Hill". It's very poignant.'

'I didn't take you for a poetry sort of guy, David,' Michael said with a vague chuckle. He wasn't sure where this was heading and wanted to get to bed as soon as possible.

'I'm not, really,' David said. 'It's just that one came back to me, seeing that house just brought it back for some reason. We learnt it at school and I didn't have a clue about it then. I read it again a few years back, after Welsh Independence Day and it really spoke to me. I can't describe it really . . . I must be getting sentimental in my old age.'

Both men sighed the hollow laughter of those lost years.

'Well, anyway, not much point in going to bed really, not with that early flight to catch, but I may as well get a couple of hours kip,' David said, turning to go up the stairs.

'Yes, I need at least a few hours too,' Michael agreed.

'I'll call for a taxi in the morning and I'll pop the key back through the letterbox, eh? Save waking you and Sara?' David said.

'Yes, yes, that's probably best,' Michael agreed. He stood there nervously, uncertain what to do. The disagreements of the past still hung heavily about them. He held out his hand.

David looked down at it, and shook hands with him gently. He smiled and looked up with unhappy eyes, 'Thanks for the evening, Michael. Give Sara my regards. No doubt we'll see each other again sooner next time.'

'Yes, yes, we will. No doubt we will . . . *of course we will,*' Michael said, knowing he would probably never see David again.

II
The Letter

It wasn't a premonition of David's suicide that he had that evening, rather the knowledge that the divide had become too great, the experiences of the more recent past too overwhelming to allow the power of the deeper, but more aged, experiences of their youth to hold them together. It was that natural moment of acceptance that you cannot step into those same waters again, they have been carried far out to sea, and the carefree joys of those times must be replaced by other pleasures, other responsibilities, and indeed, more simply, by other people.

But the emails that arrived a few months later had shocked Michael and he had sunk into a gloomy despondency. David had written to tell him that Liam had been killed in a Turkish helicopter gunship raid on their base at Svilengrad. Most of the casualties had been European defence volunteers that were being trained by Liam's unit before they returned back to England at the end of their tour the following month. The email was very matter of fact and Michael did not know how to respond initially. He thought he'd leave it a few days to mull over the best way of phrasing his reply. Then the second email arrived the following day. Jack had been killed too, in his first firefight, against a Greek unit pushing into Kirkovo.

Sara had tried to keep him motivated but he just became more depressed, even after she'd sat him down to compose the message of condolences to David and Sally. He drank more; he stayed up even later, and slept very poorly. Just as things seemed to have turned a bit of a corner, and he was speaking brightly about Clara's return from her studies in Edinburgh, the letter arrived from Sally.

It had been sent nearly a month before, but with post only delivered weekly in most places, and the further customs checks made on any correspondence entering from England it normally took over three weeks. And besides, hardly anyone wrote letters or sent cards any more, it was all electronic.

The letter explained that David had committed suicide a few days after Jack had been killed. It didn't go into any detail. She just said that she didn't know how to carry on herself, but that to even try she would have to leave the country. She'd never liked the mood of the place anyway over the past decade and wanted to move on and begin again. She had family in Canada and would be going there once everything had been finalised. She said she'd send through her new address once she was settled.

Michael left the house without saying a word to Sara. She thought it best to leave him. They could talk later. He wandered over to the château walls opposite their house, idling along like some sulky teenager; without real destination, absorbed in his own darkness. He looked out across the meandering Rance, heavy with lush trees along its banks. A few small boats pottered back and forth across it but it was mostly still. The tourist boats were all moored up, their blue and yellow, and red and green canopies making them look like a packet of discarded sweets. Few people came to see the town these days. The threat of bombings had turned everywhere into a fortress and every home into its own castle. Visiting and travelling about had become both a task but also a suspicious activity; having the wrong documentation, or a missing pass or ID card could result in a very difficult situation and normally arrest.

Michael sighed. David! Was it somehow his fault? He remembered his flippancy about the boys being ok. Why couldn't he just keep his mouth shut? He couldn't help thinking about what David had done, and *how* he must have done it; *when* and *where*. He felt guilty that this must be some ridiculous morbid interest, but he felt he needed something more concrete, something that would still tie David's body to the world, if not his soul.

Michael walked into town somewhat aimlessly, uncertain what to do next. The winding ancient streets, with their crouching antiquated buildings reminded him of his own past—of happier days; of times with Sara, of times with his parents, of fun and freedom. Years before he had rather resented the hubbub of tourists, their silly shorts and holiday attire, their cameras and guidebooks, cluttering the beautiful church with their sweaty bodies and polluting the air with their oohs and ahhs. Now, with an armed policeman on every corner, and hardly a soul to be seen; most of the crêperies closed and every other shop boarded up, he wished them all back again in an instant.

He meandered around and stopped off for a few glasses of wine along the way, going on a roundabout walk back down to the port, where he stood on the old bridge, watching the gentle waters of the river flowing their relentless way on to the sea. He decided to have some food, the wines were getting to him and he still felt agitated and strange. After a leisurely seafood platter he decided to head back home; early evening was coming on, Sara would be worried.

On his way back up the steep hill from the port he paused by the gates to the house that had so fascinated him years before, and had been one of the last things he had talked with David about. The gates were much the same; unused. The weeds were thicker and taller on the driveway beyond. The rusted chain and padlock still in place, untouched. He noticed a plaque on the crumbling stone pillar to the left of the gates. He had not seen it before. It was of cracked ceramic, and in a blue italic script it read, *La Maison Anglaise*. Beneath the plaque there was a push button bell.

Michael pushed it. A burst of blackbirds broke from the trees above him, cawing and cackling. He heard nothing else, and nobody came. He waited.

Suddenly he came to, it was dark. He was still standing by the gates. In the distance the church bells chimed eleven. It had been just after seven that he had stopped by the driveway, he was sure. He couldn't have been standing here for nearly four hours could he? He felt very cold; he had left the house in a thin shirt and trousers and the evening chill was quite severe. He rushed home, trying to warm himself with the vigour of the short walk.

As he turned the key in the door he heard spirited bird song from the direction of the château. He remembered some of those last words of David's, *so few and such morning songs . . .*

Well, it wasn't morning! He was just being melancholy.

Once inside he poured a large whisky and started flicking through the news on his phone. Sara was no doubt long in bed, he saw there were four missed calls from her. They could talk about it in the morning. David was dead, there was nothing to be done about that. He had been a friend once. But other friends had come and gone too.

Another whisky and he started to think about the house again. He went up to the first floor landing with the lights off and peered out into the still darkness. Through the trees he could see the upstairs lights on again. The bell clearly wasn't working. Perhaps tomorrow he'd take some bolt cutters and cut through the chains and go right up to the door and find out, once and for all, who lived there. Yes, he damn well would!

For now though he'd just pop up to Clara's room, on the top floor, to get a better view of the place.

It felt odd going into her room alone, and in the dark. He wished he had some binoculars, but he pressed his face almost up to the window and squinted out through the canopy of higher branches. The view from here was excellent and he could make out the silhouettes of figures moving back and forth against the yellow light of the windows.

He felt calmer now, watching the waltz of dark against light; to and fro they went, to and fro, inside The House; that curious, wondrous House.

III

The Dream

Michael was suddenly brought to consciousness by Sara squeezing his arm, quite tightly, and calling his name loudly. He was still stood there by the window in Clara's room, dressed in his clothes from the night before. His mouth felt dry and his teeth dirty. His legs ached and he felt disoriented and strange.

'What on earth are you doing here?' Sara said. 'I heard you come in but you didn't come to bed last night. I thought you'd fallen asleep on the sofa *again*.'

'I don't really know . . .' he muttered, feeling his legs begin to buckle a little. 'I don't know what happened at all. I think I need to sit down and have some coffee.'

He was very unsteady on his feet and Sara helped him down the two flights of stairs and sat him down at the dining table as she boiled a kettle and got out the cafetière.

Michael just sat there staring at her, or beyond her, more precisely, at the kitchen window, to the bank of grass heading up into their garden. He noticed her looking over at him occasionally with a very concerned expression.

'I think I was there all night,' he said as she put the steaming black coffee on the table in front of him and sat opposite with a half-scowl.

'Where?' she said, abruptly.

'In Clara's room,' he said as a shaky hand spooned two heaped teaspoons of sugar into the coffee. 'I think I stood there all night, looking out of her window.'

Sara looked as surprised as he felt. She sipped her coffee, waiting for him to continue. He didn't.

'Okay then, *why were you standing in Clara's room all night, looking out of the window?*' she said, exasperatedly.

'Oh, look, Sara, there's no need to say it like that,' he said. 'I'm as perplexed by it as you.'

She knew he was serious; he only called her Sara when he was serious, or when they argued.

'Alright then, I'm sorry, but why, Michael,' she said. 'No-one can stand up all night staring out of a window. What on earth were you looking at?'

'I started out looking at that old house behind ours, the one you can just see from the first floor landing, through the trees,' he said, draining the last of his coffee and sighing. 'You can see it so much better from Clara's room on the top floor and I thought I had seen lights on in there.'

'I know, Clara often talked about it,' Sara said, quietly.

'And as I watched I think I must have drifted off to sleep because . . .' he said, turning to look at her with a pleading look that seemed both embarrassed and worried.

'Go on, Michael,' she urged. 'What happened?'

'I dreamt,' he said, flatly.

'And what did you *dream of*, Michael?' she said, the exasperation returning.

There was a long silence. He stared out of the kitchen window. She waited.

'How about another coffee?' she said. 'Then you can tell me all about *your dream*.'

'Yes, please,' he said, distantly.

She hurried about, making another pot. Somewhere, as though in another room, he could hear the chiming of the crockery and the tinkling of the spoons, the gurgle of water frothing around the ground coffee. All the sounds seemed distant and faded, as though sunk below a deep, still lake; beyond them he detected the mumbling melody of her voice but no words were discernible. As he looked up even her face seemed blurred and the room's colours pale and misty.

Then he felt himself speaking, as though his voice were not his own.

'I found the silent soldier at the east door. He had been waiting for me. His uniform was red, as it was the evening of his beloved's ball. He wore the medals of honour passed to him by his father, and his grandfather before him, and those he had earned for himself upon the Fields of the Fallen, when the war was still winnable and our brave men still had fight and valour.

'He showed me to the robing room where I took up the attire that I had so yearned to wear again. I had a golden gown and a red flowing cape. In one hand an attendant gave me a branch of mistletoe and in the other a long silver needle. I walked through into the ballroom and all about me there were people drinking and celebrating, all dressed in different coloured gowns, exactly like mine and each with two objects to offer to the betrothed.

'Then his betrothed was brought in to a fanfare of trumpets and a long red veil, carried by six handmaidens walking slowly before her; behind her a white headdress, carried by six more. The silent soldier then met her in the middle of the ballroom and knelt before her. As she reached down for his hand the twelve maidens became like banshees and pursued us all from the room, through huge doors that opened to the garden. Everyone was screaming with delight and I did not feel afraid; it was all part of an elaborate ritual. They all went running into the darkness of the gardens and I was left alone.

'I walked through a maze of pergolas with a canopy of wisteria threading its thick branches above me like a sky of entwined, writhing limbs. Its pale purple flowers hung in

257

bunches about me like grapes and I drifted and wandered, sometimes skipping and dancing through the thick carpet of petals, until I came to the south door. This was of solid oak, with sturdy metal trusses, yet it was open and a pale orange light illuminated the worn stone steps up to it. Enticing smells wafted to me on bursts of warm air; meats, herbs, wine and rich spices. As I entered I was greeted by a grinning cook, mixing a thick brown pudding in a bowl and he danced about a large kitchen with a dozen other of his kind, all dressed in white and each with a task that they were busying themselves about; each with a great wide smile, or laughter, as they joined in a chorus of welcome to me. All about there were open fires upon which were roasting every kind of poultry, game and meat one could think of. On huge ranges there bubbled stews and pans of vegetables, all being attended to, stirred, drained or added to, by the dancing company of chefs. As I wandered about watching their happy work, they skipped and dodged about me, with platters of fish, garnished with fruits, and great wobbling blancmanges of every colour. The whole kitchen seemed to be a waltz of preparation for a vast banquet.

'The great gong sounded from the hall beyond and we all fell silent, and solemn. There were seven strikes of a piercing bell and double doors were opened to allow a score of young maids into the kitchen. They filled the place like a cloud of black butterflies, gathering plates and trays of food, carrying teetering piles of them that looked at any moment to collapse under their slight frames.

'I was ushered through into the great hall where long tables were laid for a hundred or more. Besides the maids—busying themselves with the food back and forth, and the cooks, who had lined up against the opposite wall, their heads bowed—the only occupant of the hall, besides myself, was a gloomy man, sitting upon a huge silver throne, his head sunk in his hands, a golden crown sitting askance upon his head, thick with curls of grey hair. He stared at the proceedings almost with despair. I approached him. He did not acknowledge me. One by one, the maids brought before him each of the wonderful creations and he nodded his tired assent before they placed them upon the tables. Beside him a smaller throne, of the same design, in the same bright silver, sat empty, beside that, again, another smaller one, identical in all details—again, empty.

'Then, other doors opposite were opened and an army of children flooded into the room, like a great flock of excited gulls. The man jumped up to welcome them, with delight, and they fell upon the food in waves of joy and abandon. I could not help but share in his delight as he watched them all finish off the banquet. The cooks were also smiling with happiness, congratulating each other and applauding as platters were finished and further offerings were brought out by the diligent maids, who sang songs with the children as they scurried about each other.

'Soon I felt the urge to move on and walked through the doors where the children had come from and I was soon outside again by a side door near to the one I had just entered from. I continued round to the west of the house and saw a set of huge steps leading up to the main entrance to The House. All about the steps were animals, standing, or lying, sleeping and cleaning themselves; all mixing happily together in the calmest of ways; squirrels nuzzled against wildebeest; cats lay sprawled up the backs of cattle; a leopard licked the fur of an arctic fox. Birds of every kind flew in and out of the wide open doors and I walked inside hesitantly; the animals lifted their heads to watch me pass, but none stirred to attack me.

'Within, a great staircase led to a huge landing, where many people were gathered, talking and laughing. All about them the birds swooped and played; owls and tits; ravens and humming birds; doves and kestrels—the air was alive with colour and the chatter of their song.

'To my right there was an open doorway to a room lit with what must have been a thousand candles. On a throne of wax there sat a man dressed in a yellow robe. Beside him were two attendants, dressed in black suits, each held a copper plate on a long black rod, near to his face; each plate half of a mask. From behind it I heard him speak, "You are welcome to this place, you must reside with us a while until we come to know you, and soon you shall know the manner in which you can remain. Now go upstairs and become acquainted with our people."

'I followed his instructions and found many rooms, each having the windows I had seen through the trees from our house. Within each there was a tree growing from the floor, at the roots of which people sat and talked, played games and joked with each other. Each room had hundreds of birds in it, but mostly of one kind; and beyond each room there seemed to be further rooms, so that entering each led one further and further on into spaces that multiplied far beyond the possible size of The House. I did not speak to anyone; I wish I had. I was so mesmerised by the birds that I followed them about as though they were speaking to me. A little brown wren alighted on my shoulder and I followed it back down the stairs to the main door, where it jumped onto the back of a camel and trilled at me loudly.

'I left again, treading carefully over a slumbering tiger and walked through an avenue of pink and yellow roses, their petals lifting lightly into the air about me on eddies of wind. I reached the north door. It was small, no more than four feet high, and down a small flight of stone steps, covered in slippery green algae. It was blackened, as though from a large fire lit before it. I tried the handle, but it was locked. My heart sank. The House was resisting me. I knew I was not welcome there.'

Then he stopped speaking and turned to look at Sara, rubbing his eyes as though rousing from sleep.

Sara sat there staring at him. She was ashen, her mouth hung open.

'What's wrong?' said Michael, feeling more himself now; his legs no longer weak, his eyes more focused, his hearing normal again.

She still sat there staring.

'Sara, *what's wrong*,' he said, standing to come over to her.

'I think you'd better come with me,' she said, raising herself slowly with the support of the table. 'There's something I should show you; something in Clara's room.'

'What . . . what is it?' he said, following her like a nagging child. Everything seemed to have suddenly taken on a weight of meaning, a portent that made him shake excitedly but also shudder with fear. 'Please, Sara, *tell me*, what is it, tell me now!'

'You'll understand when you see it,' she said, turning to him, her eyes filled with the same terror and wonder that he felt surging through him.

She held his hand as she led him up the stairs to their daughter's room.

IV

The Diary

Sara reached under Clara's bed and pulled out a box, filled with old magazines and satirical political papers. She pushed them aside and reached further in, drawing out dusty jackets and old clothes.

'Here it is,' she said, with a grunt, 'Clara's ballet case.'

Michael looked down at a battered white suitcase that he vaguely recalled from years ago. Sara was fiddling with the rusted clasp. When finally it gave way she opened it and a musty smell filled the room. Worn ballet shoes and flimsy leotards were pulled out, along with bundled tights that seemed more like thick black string. Michael didn't understand what Sara could be doing with this stuff but it felt like some kind of betrayal, watching her go through Clara's things like this, especially such personal belongings, her clothes—memories of driving her to dance classes began to come back to him. Clara had been a wonderful, joyous child.

At the bottom of the case there was a faded pink towel that Sara placed on the floor and began unwrapping. Within there was a black leather book, on the front in faded silver lettering it read: *Diary, 2033*. Sara handed it to him.

'What . . . ? We can't . . . ? Why . . . ?' he stuttered.

'Just open it wherever you want and you'll see what I mean,' Sara said, her voice choked and hoarse. 'It actually covers over three years, there are multiple entries on certain dates. Just read some of it . . .'

Michael stared at the cover. Eventually he opened it, about halfway through.

23rd June, 2033

Dear Diary, I think I have become a professional dreamer and I have made myself a new home to get out of the dullness of this one. The bird rooms are the most enchanting, each with their throng of people chatting at the roots of the trees. They welcome you so easily and talk of all the places they travelled and the people they'd seen. There are stories of spice traders and warriors, polar explorers and desert nomads. All time seems to be mixed up together there. What a House! And the animals, I've never seen so many animals, all mixing together and dozing around the upper floor. One minute you're stepping over a leopard in the hall and the next you are walking side by side with a badger into a room alive with humming birds and laughter.

And just below it, on the same page:

23rd June, 2034
I waited with the others in the Hall of Welcome. I have only seen so many children together at school, but there are no teachers there, and no parents. There were all sorts of ages, from about eight to lots of children my age. *I will be thirteen in a month!!!!* Everyone was very well behaved, and excited. Some were carrying posies of wild flowers. Then big doors were opened and we were taken into a huge room, like it was in a castle, or something. There was a man on a big silver throne and when he saw us all come in he got up and shouted to us to eat as much as we wanted and to enjoy ourselves. He had a big crown on his head, and so I knew he must be the King. But still there was something sad about him as he watched us eat all of the wonderful food his cooks had made. When we had finished all the boys and girls with flowers took them over and laid them at his feet.

Mum woke me up then and said I would be late for school. I get so sick of her disturbing me . . . I don't get a moment of peace from either of them. Next time I go there I will take flowers to *The King*.

Below that:

23rd June, 2035
I don't know, after I went into The Garden and met the beautiful horse, for the last few nights The House seems to be empty. The lights are off and when I go there I can't get in at any of the doors. There is snow on the ground all around it and there are no leaves on all the lovely bushes and plants anywhere near it. But tonight when I got to the main door there was an old lady in a blue shawl. She had a

263

wicker basket and she offered it to me. There was a big key inside it, and she pointed to the door.

I don't know why but I shook my head and ran away until I woke up.

In my room I heard her voice. She said, 'If you ever want to return then you will always find me here.'

Michael flicked back nearly to the beginning of the diary:

5th February, 2034
Cecile Dubois wasn't in school today, her dad had been killed in the war. He had been shot down in Lithuania somewhere while his plane was bombing something. I couldn't really follow it all but when dad found out he started on about it all. Mum and I got bored of hearing his voice, as usual, so I went off to my room for a nap, so I could go to The House.

I was with the man with the masks and he told me *my bird*. He said, 'You, my pretty creature, are the wren, and your presence here will multiply them in this house until a tree shall grow at the root of which you all shall live for ever more.' Then a little bird fluttered down the chimney and burst into the room from the fireplace. The masked man's attendants all cheered and I went upstairs with my little bird flying about me.

He flicked forward again:

14th April, 2035
I don't know how to describe it. The House has no place. It is not *a* place. It is like a place *of belief*; a sort of thought-place; a space that opens because of my wishes, desires, emotions. I think it was made by me, for me. It really *is* me. It's more me than I am here. I don't know

how to tell you, Diary, how stifled I've been for years, how I've been locked up, like I was in a cupboard while Europe falls apart, and dad looked away into old books as though he were in some English Empire, with the Raj and Earl Grey tea, and newspapers in the evening; and mum just seemed to ignore it all and want me to be all the things she could never be . . . but all sorts of old useless things . . . a teacher, an artist, a writer, an accountant (I mean, for f's sake . . . an accountant!). I told her, they've got apps for these things now, they've got algorithms for all these things! I let it slip a couple of weeks ago, about The House . . . to her . . . by mistake. I told her of a visit there, but told it like a dream. She said she's seen somewhere like it too when she was growing up. But she never really understood. She never took the time to know *me*, to find out about *me*—how I couldn't grow *into me*! Dad is always on at me about being a 'lefty', and mum is always on at me that I'm not 'making enough of myself'—whatever that means!—but then when I get dressed up to go out and have a good time then I'm 'attracting the wrong attention' . . . I can't f'ing win!

No, The House is *my* place . . . the only place I'm happy in these days. I want to be with the quiet soldier, he is to be my husband. I want to eat again from the table with the children—why was I kept away! What had I done wrong? I want to be a child again! I want to see green skies and blue grass. I want to imagine pirates flying through the clouds on galleons powered by the breath of fairies. Why is this world such a dead place, a *dead place* full of *death*, and *death* and never-ending *death*! I want to live again in that other place, in the fullest sense—in the freest way. I want to live again in a place that has no place *here*.

He closed the diary, 'I think I've seen enough. I don't know what it all means, Sara, I really don't. I've never seen any of that in my life before.'

She took the diary from him and wrapped it up again carefully. She placed it back in the case, and that back under the bed. Her face was blank, emotionless.

'Well, if you don't know, then I sure as hell don't know either,' she said flatly, and went back downstairs.

For the rest of the day they drifted about the house, avoiding each other as much as possible. They had a light evening meal, in silence, and then separated, she upstairs to her bed and he to the lounge with his drink.

He tried to think back to anything Clara might have said to him that would have provoked these correlations in their thoughts and dreams. But every way he tried to explain it failed and he returned to the power of his own dream and the intensity of the emotions it had conjured in him. Rather the worse for wear he headed up to bed sometime after midnight.

V

The Garden

By 3 am he couldn't take any more. He had lain there for over two hours, wishing himself to sleep. But his mind raced with all the possible implications of what they had read, and what he had recalled of his dream the previous night. It couldn't have been a dream though, could it? Somehow he had tapped into something that Clara had also seen, dreamt, or sensed. He wanted to ring her and tell her; he wanted to find out so much more. It would be a way back to her too; a way to become friends again after all the arguments. Perhaps they were both psychic, or maybe it was astral projection—he'd briefly been interested in that and had bought a book on it years before . . . *where could that be now*, he thought.

Sara snored softly, and laughed a little.

Oh, for God's sake, Michael, he thought. *What's the point of all this silly speculation? Get some sleep and make sense of it tomorrow.*

He clenched his eyes shut and tried again.

But rather than darkness all he could see were the tall red brick walls of the garden and the beautiful trailing flowers draped over the pergolas beyond. The large brown stones of The House raised themselves like towers in his mind, dotted with those small bay windows and their white surrounds. The great wooden doors imposed upon him like spectres, chasing his thoughts back to The House, back to the myriad personalities and games that were at play there. *Come and play with us,* he could hear them calling, *come and laugh with us; you must learn to laugh again—run with us through the dewy morning grasses, dance with us as the moon's silver embers give way to the morning sun. You are not alone any more. Come back to us, come back.*

He threw the bedclothes off and dragged on his shirt and trousers as he headed up the stairs to Clara's room.

He pulled out the white suitcase and pushed aside the ballet shoes and leotards. His previous awkwardness was now gone. In many ways he felt that the diary belonged to him. It was the key to understanding this yearning for somewhere he was not even sure he had actually seen.

He opened it randomly, trusting that he would find what was necessary. He did.

20th June, 2035
I can't believe how much this f'ing world sucks! Got back from school today and hadn't even been in the house an hour before dad started on one of his stupid lectures about

how the government should do this or that, and besides it's all the fault of the Turks this time. He didn't even know anything about the US bombing of Gebze. I don't know what to say any more, he doesn't listen to me, or mum, just talks over us with his old ideas—it's as though the 22-24 war never happened. I walked off with my sandwich—I bet he never even noticed, just kept yacking away to himself.

Now I'm up here I have decided to go over the wall—for real this time. Maybe I can get into The House and live there forever. Anywhere's better than here! I don't even care if I fall down a disused mineshaft and am never found again—honestly, I don't f'ing care—I've got to get out of this place!

!!!!!!! Whoa! I am back. That was so f'ing amazing! I cannot believe that place! It is so incredible! I want to live there! I so do! I wish I could . . . I wish I could find a way to be there forever!

I went up to the fence and those four panels still haven't been fixed—thank god!—and I was soon through them and up at the red wall. There's no way through at that point, because of all the brambles, but if you follow it a bit further to the right you can find a little opening in another fence that leads through into next door's back garden. It's a bit higher there and they never go down there, same as we don't. I climbed up a bit of a tree and then hung down from a branch and that got me onto the top of the wall.

Dawn was just coming up over on our side of the wall but on *their* side—on *The House* side—it was dark! So dark! I could see all sorts of bushes and shrubs, their leaves glinting as though they were in moonlight. I could feel my heart racing but I just went for it and jumped down. It was like landing on a duvet. There was springy, wet moss all over the ground, on top of an old stone pathway. In the distance I could see The House, but it seemed miles away. The lights were twinkling brightly in the upstairs rooms and so I headed towards them, following the path.

But I must have walked for hours. I didn't get any nearer. The path always seemed to veer away, taking me into deeper shrubs and undergrowth. It was hard to keep the lights in my sight. Everything seemed to get darker, and the further I went the stronger the smell of the trees and blossom became. It got so sickly that I began to choke and I thought I would pass out with the power of it. I could almost taste the pollen. My eyes were streaming. But then I sensed IT near to me.

It was big! I wasn't afraid though! I've never felt something so powerful! By then I could barely see a few inches before me. I could hear it breathing near me. It was as loud as thunder—like it was taking in all the air around us at once and then filling the space again with each exhalation. I felt my hair flying all around me with each breath. It must have been looking right into my face! I knew what it was—a great horse! But no ordinary horse—twice the size of a normal horse, maybe bigger!

I reached out and felt its skin—it was soft and rough at the same time, like thick handcrafted paper. I felt its warmth. I felt its love. I could have stayed there until my body turned to dust, it was like seeing a miracle and I cried with such overwhelming joy. I could feel its whiteness, there in the darkness; as though it had come to find me and take me to where I belonged—to carry me up to The House like some triumphant bride! I followed it but we got no closer to the lights from The House. Then suddenly we were back at the wall again. I still couldn't see the horse, just sense its presence. I cried again, as I knew what it wished of me. I wailed and pleaded not to be forced to depart from it, and rushed to embrace its vast neck, my tears streaming down into its thick mane. It lowered its neck and I climbed as best I could upon it as it helped to raise me onto its back. From there I could simply step up onto the wall and then it was gone. How long I sat there crying I have no idea. I want so much to go back there. I want so much to dwell there—with IT, with all of them! I want so much to go to my *real* home, which is *their* home—Their House!

Michael threw the diary into the case and ran down the stairs two at a time. He rushed to put on his walking boots and nearly toppled over by the back door in the rush. He strode down the garden and was soon pushing through the thick weeds at the bottom of the garden and up against the even more dilapidated fence; some of the posts were now so rotten it was in danger of falling over completely. He soon discovered the broken panels that Clara had mentioned and he pushed them aside. Beyond there were even taller weeds and dense patches of nettles. He pushed through them all though, desperate to find the wall. He soon did—bright red bricks, as fresh as though it had been built the week before. He followed the instructions and edged along it until he came to the neighbour's boundary, where the fence had collapsed entirely. After a steep clamber up a wooded slope he found the tree that Clara must have used and was up it in a moment, moving from hand to hand along a low branch like an excited monkey. He was on top of the wall, looking into the garden. It was exactly as she had described, dark on that side and light on this. He jumped down.

His landing was not into the soft mosses that Clara had described but into a cloying, thick mulch of rot. The stench that rose up from it was foul. He slid over in it and felt all about him wet ferns and sharp brambles. He stumbled forward, peering through the leaves to discern the house and its lights. He could see them faintly through the thick branches above him, like distant stars. He stumbled on, each step like breaking away from grasping quicksand. Eventually he was onto firmer ground but the stink of rotten leaves, and something more animal, persisted. His feet found the stone paving that Clara had described and he moved forward cautiously, step by step. His eyes had not become accustomed to the darkness; it seemed to be a kind of fog of gloom, rather than a lack of light, as though the darkness had formed a kind of cloud about him. He could feel his keys pressing on his legs through his muddy trousers and remembered that he had a small torch on the key ring. As he fumbled to get the keys out he just prayed that the battery hadn't run out—it had been years since he'd used it.

Light!

What the small beam illuminated was indeed thick swirls of dark mist that hung all about him, like smoky layers, blocking out the thin sunlight that had managed to break through the trees above him. The ground was a black carpet of slimy leaves and decaying materials; it seemed to undulate and writhe though, and as he crouched down he noticed large millipedes and beetles swarming and squirming through the fetid mass— the ground was as much their bodies as it was the vegetation. His skin crawled.

The light flickered on and off, as the swirls of blackness blocked the stuttering beam. In one of the brief glimmers of illumination Michael picked out the stones forming the path beneath the decay. They were great thick chunks of flat stone; brown, black and white, some seemed quite polished and others holed with age and covered in grey and green lichen. He caught sight of a name etched into one; Catherine Dever . . . the rest was broken off, but below it read, Born 17th October 197 . . .

They were broken gravestones. Michael gasped and felt himself begin to shake with fear.

The torch began to flicker further. He shook it, but there were only moments left.

Behind him a great snort sounded and he whirled around. The last second of the torchlight showed a huge, repulsive creature—reptilian, or amphibian, its black skin glinting with moisture. Its vast pink maw opened and a croaking, rasping screech erupted around him, the branches above him shook and a shower of leaves burst around them.

The light was out. Michael began to run.

It was behind him, its great legs breaking through the undergrowth with thunderous crunches, sending showers of the filthy sludge into the air with every stride. The roars continued, but with the blood pounding in his ears Michael barely heard them. In a few seconds that seemed like hours he was at the red wall, scrambling up at it trying to find some foot, or hand holds that he could pull himself up with. His fingernails were splintering and his fingertips ran with blood. The thing was upon him and he felt the air about him heat with its putrid breath. With a flick of its immense nose it had propelled him up and over the wall. He landed with a crunch on a mound of brown pine needles, but nothing was broken. In an instant he was on his feet again and running. A triumphant snort rose up from The Garden as he tore through the fence and sprinted to their house.

Michael ran inside and locked the door behind him; he also shot the top and bottom bolts, which he hadn't done in years. He was hyperventilating and had to get back some control or he knew he would faint. He could feel scratches across his chest and arms and the blood welling at them. Once he had regained a little composure he charged upstairs to continue reading the diary.

Opening the door he saw Sara silhouetted against the bright light of Clara's bedroom window. She turned to him slowly, smiling a smile that he remembered from the early days of their relationship, 'I've been *there*, Michael; to that beautiful place, The House. I've been there *too*.'

VI

A Homecoming

Clara got back home three days later. It was getting later in the afternoon now, and she was supposed to be back early in the morning. She had been surprised that her mum hadn't been endlessly calling her to check on her progress. She was shattered, especially as she'd been held up in immigration for four hours because her agreed residency return date did not match her planned return date that was registered on 'the system', so had had to fill in an application all over again and go through the 'scheduled activities' interview for the three weeks she was going to be there. Thankfully it was with Gendarme Simone Avril, with whom she'd been at school, so it was just a formality, but it still took nearly two hours.

She turned the key in the door and dropped her rucksack on the kitchen floor. She knew there was something wrong then. Dad's whisky was out on the kitchen table, with a half-drunk glass beside it. *There's no way mum would have left that there all day*, she thought, *she hates the smell of it*.

She started calling for them, going from room to room. As she climbed the stairs she looked out across the garden to see if they were out there. The plants were really starting to overtake the place, and the grass clearly hadn't been cut in weeks.

'Mum, Mum, Dad, are you home?'

Their bedroom was a mess; clothes strewn about on the floor and the bed unmade. The guestroom was empty.

She looked up the next flight of stairs towards her own room but thought it unlikely they'd be up there. *They must be out somewhere*, she thought. *But why leave the place in such a state?*

But what if they are up there, rummaging through my stuff!

She bounded up the stairs, two at a time, to her floor. 'Mum, Mum, Dad, are you up here?'

Clara opened the door of her room tentatively. She saw her mother and father there by the window staring out, hand in hand. He wasn't wearing a shirt and was covered in mud, bruises and great long scratches all across his back and arms. Her mum was standing there in her nightgown. They didn't turn around, or seem to even notice her come in. She looked about the room and saw a sprawl of clothes and papers from under her bed; then her old ballet case, its contents emptied into the middle of the floor. She gasped as she noticed her old diary lying open on top of her old homework desk.

She rushed over to look at her parents' faces.

They were ragged with delight, their eyes ringed with dark circles of enchantment; their mouths set in grimaces of wonder. Clara knew where they were, and she had been desperate to go back there too. She held her mother's hand and stared out of the window—through the trees, swaying with a gentle afternoon breeze as though to beckon on a journey—at The House.

'I'm home, mum,' Clara said, with a contented sigh. 'I'm home with you now. And now I'm home it's time for us all to go *home.*'

The three of them stood looking out on the golden, dying light of the afternoon; bathed in bliss, cradled in the mercy of time without time, sheltered in a place without place.

FOUR WINDOWS AND A DOOR

He had given the usual edicts—no laptops, no tablets, no texting endlessly on the phone, no this, no that. *We're going on a nice, relaxing family holiday,* he'd said, *where we can spend time together; walking, swimming, playing, picnics and beaches and the like.* It didn't quite happen like that. It never does.

The first day had gone quite well. The kids were thrilled enough by the strangeness of Polperro. They enjoyed having to lug all their bags through the streets that were too narrow to get a car down. They liked their quaint cottage with views out across the harbour. They looked over at a small promontory and could see a little beach where some other children were playing. David was the first to get irritated though, when his tablet wouldn't connect to the Wi-Fi. Emily followed suit in the morning, when she couldn't play some online game on her mother's phone due to a poor signal.

Tom thought he'd need to be very proactive right from the off if he was to rescue the week from moaning and grumbling about computers and phones, so he planned a packed schedule of walks and visits to nearby attractions to keep them amused. Over a glass of wine he chatted with Sarah about how he couldn't understand it; when he was David's age he'd have adored a place like this, if his parents could have afforded to have taken them there.

Yes, but when you were ten, they'd just got the electric light in hadn't they, and a light bulb was entertainment for the whole family, Sarah joked with him. She was twelve years younger than him and his age, and grumpiness, had become a family joke. They had a lovely evening together. It really felt as though the holiday might bring them all back together.

Tom had been spending a lot of time away recently, especially at conferences. He had been a computer programmer in the early 1990s and had worked his way from company to company, with a bit of freelancing here and there, and had made quite a bit of money—enough to purchase most of the expensive house they lived in now in rural Oxfordshire. He certainly wouldn't be able to afford it now. He'd settled into a more stable job in the early part of the new century, and then David had come along, and then Emily. He now worked for a large accountancy firm, maintaining databases and servers, and it frequently took him to London for long periods, and up to Glasgow where there were other company offices. One of its directors was an old university friend of Sarah's and he'd jumped at the job that now made him feel rather inadequate, as younger people arrived, more skilled and knowledgeable in a rapidly changing industry. To even keep up to date he'd had to start on the conference circuit, and even go to extra training sessions during some of his holiday periods. It had all become rather a bind now. But he had to keep up with it, for the sake of Sarah and the kids. It made him feel dull and uncreative—the responsible adult he'd always abhorred.

Sarah seemed quite the opposite—a real bundle of joy. She'd worked as a teaching assistant for years, at the local primary school, and loved every minute of it, even though the hours were long and the pay poor. Tom couldn't remember a time she'd ever moaned about work to him. She'd given it up when David was born but was intending to apply again as soon as Emily was at school. She was four now and in September she'd be going. Tom was torn by the sadness of another milestone in her childhood, but also relieved that the intensity of those toddler and nursery years would soon be behind them. She was that perfect age and Tom was desperate that this be the perfect family holiday.

On the second day they visited The Eden Project; David moped about complaining about the heat and that it was 'just a load of flowers'. Emily loved it. The Lost Gardens of Heligan were more popular with David as he pretended to be on the moon of Endor, racing about on a hover bike. Emily got very tired there though and had to be carried around most of it. Tom reflected that it had probably been a mistake to do two gardens on two consecutive days. The Wednesday was marked out to see The Minack Theatre and Lizard Point. That was quite a trek though and he had told everyone that they needed to be up very early and away with no messing about. Emily woke up with a tummy ache though and most of the morning was spent looking after her and trying to get a decent signal on the television before David had a meltdown. At around 11 am Emily suddenly declared herself better and wanted a walk around Polperro and to play sandcastles on the beach. Tom bristled that his agenda had been thrown out entirely and they'd be lucky to fit Minack and the Lizard into the rest of the week with the other things he had planned.

At the beach there was a long stone wall that offered further protection for the small vessels moored inside and there, on a large billboard chained to the jetty railings, was advertised a boating trip. Immediately Emily and David were grabbing at their Dad's sleeves begging to go on the trip, which went over to Fowey and claimed to 'almost guarantee' seeing some dolphins.

'Well, I don't know how you can have an "*almost* guarantee", either it's a guarantee, or it isn't. Sounds a bit dodgy to me,' Tom said. 'And it's £15 each; I mean how long is the trip? It'd need to be a good length to be worth that.'

'Oh, come on, grumpy,' Sarah whispered to him. 'At least they want to do something like this for once. Look, the next trip is at 1 pm. I'll ring them and book it—my treat!'

277

It was duly booked and rather than go back to the cottage for lunch they decided to eat in a packed pub at the edge of the harbour, The Blue Peter Inn. Despite the long wait it was worth it and they all enjoyed fish and chips, and Tom and Sarah had a couple of the ales from the vast selection. The kids enjoyed playing with the pub dog, Timmy, and Tom was beginning to feel it wasn't so bad that his plans had been scuppered for the day.

At one o'clock they jumped on a small boat with about ten other people and chugged out of Polperro as the sun got brighter and brighter. There were a few other children and David was enjoying talking with another boy; it was nice to see him being a bit more sociable, Tom thought.

The boat hugged the coast for a good ten minutes and then headed out into deeper waters, to avoid the perilous rocks near the shore the captain told them—many a smuggling boat had been sunk there in years gone by, apparently, one skippered by one of the captain's own ancestors, a Mr John Creedy, the scourge of the King's Excise Men. Other tall tales came across the Tannoy at regular intervals. The kids loved it.

'See, not so bad, eh?' Sarah said, huddling up to Tom on one of the padded seats for, despite the sun, it was quite cold out on the waves and none of them had brought particularly thick coats.

'Yeah, not so bad at all,' Tom said, smiling.

'Look, Dad,' shouted David. 'It's a haunted house.'

Tom looked over at the cliff, where David was pointing, and saw a large house, almost silhouetted against the climbing sun. It was very imposing, not in a grand way, quite the opposite. Its plainness and size combined to force it upon the landscape in a way that seemed crude and vulgar. The windows and door had been bricked up with grey breezeblocks. It was oppressive.

'It's where the pirate ghosts go at night, Emily,' David said, teasing his sister. 'And then, when they've drunk all their ghost rum they go out looking for little girls to eat! Ha! Ha!'

'Don't say things like that, David,' Sarah said. 'You'll scare her.'

Tom looked over at Emily, who was sitting on the middle row of seats opposite them. She didn't look scared. She didn't look like anything at all. Her face was blank. Her eyes fixed on the building David was pointing at.

'Are you ok, dear?' Tom said, reaching out and putting his hand on hers. It was very cold.

'It's just a house, David,' she said, quietly. 'It's just a house like any house . . . like *every* house.'

'Come here and cuddle up with Daddy, you're cold,' Tom said, lifting her over onto his lap and rubbing her hands.

As she sat there she turned and watched the cliff house intently, disappearing from view as the boat swung round and made its way into Fowey.

They had a good afternoon, browsing round the gift shops and enjoying an ice cream in the town square. Tom found a little bookshop, that specialised in Daphne Du Maurier and got chatting with the owner. She had discovered a lost story of Du Maurier's from the 1930s, 'The Doll' and had helped get it republished recently. Tom bought a copy of the collection and had the proprietor sign it to him. He didn't get much time to read these days but hoped he might be able to enjoy the story that evening. He turned to leave to find the children at the window, making faces at him to hurry up, pointing over the road to a toyshop, with a window full of wooden boats. After purchasing a small sailing boat for each of them, blue for David and red for Emily, there was just time to look around the church and its beautiful grounds before catching the boat at 5 pm.

On the way back the waters got a bit choppier and just as they came out of the shelter of Fowey they really began to get quite rough. Tom felt queasy—the kids loved it, as the spray washed over them. A dolphin joined them and followed the boat, diving in and out of the water just ahead of the bow. It was covered in long grey scars and had notches across its fin and flippers from numerous battles.

As they came past the abandoned house Emily stopped her excited calling to the dolphin—now named 'Dolly'—and stood staring up at it as though it were a stern headmaster admonishing her for minor misdeeds. Tom nudged Sarah to look at her and they both cast worried glances back at each other.

The rest of the trip back—twenty minutes, or so—Emily seemed self-absorbed and didn't acknowledge 'Dolly' at all, and barely spoke to her parents, or brother. As soon as she stepped off the boat she returned to her old self again and wanted a knickerbocker glory in the teashop on the way back to the cottage. They indulged her, relieved to see her strange reaction to the cliff house disappear.

The Thursday was spent in Looe, round the shops and amusement arcades. Despite it being rather less edifying than he'd hoped Tom was pleased to see the kids enjoying themselves. Emily was delighted to have found a boxed set of Mr Men stories in a remainder bookshop, and a bumper pack of crayons and A3 sketchpad, that she bought with her pocket money.

As was their tradition their last full day of a holiday was always spent relaxing in their holiday home, reading, dozing and playing games. Emily made up Mr Men stories about Mr Dolly, the dolphin man and got into an argument with David who said that the Mr Men weren't animals. Tom retreated to the kitchen and not having got to the Du Maurier tale on the Wednesday evening he read it that afternoon.

'Any good?' Sarah asked, after he'd put the book down.

'Er, well . . . it's certainly not what I was expecting,' Tom said, feeling rather unnerved by the oddness of the short tale. 'I think I'll stick to the novels.'

After a few minutes of reflection he decided to prepare dinner to take his mind off the image of the weird doll, Julio, in the story.

On their final morning, as everyone busied themselves with packing, Emily just wanted to sit at the breakfast table and do some drawing. So they left her to it as the bags piled up in the hallway and rooms were checked, and rechecked, for stray belongings. It came time to leave and Tom went over to get Emily to tidy the crayons and paper away.

She seemed sad, and oddly contemplative; precociously thoughtful and troubled.

She had drawn a picture of the sea, with a small cliff and a large distorted building atop it. Four windows, of the childish cross-frame variety, looked out from it. It was more a symbol of a house than a depiction of a real one. But it was clearly meant to be the place they had seen from the boat.

'Well that's a really good picture, darling,' he said. 'But, with four windows and no door how on earth are people meant to get in?'

She thought for a moment and nodded her head solemnly.

'Yes, Daddy, I see what you mean,' she said, slowly. 'But the real question is . . . how do you *get out?*'

Tom couldn't get those words out of his head for the whole journey home.

⁊

It was later that year, in October, when it happened. And, *when it happened*, Tom was in Hull listening to poster presentations and participating in a 'working group' on archive resilience and backup retrieval. During the late afternoon coffee break he looked at his phone and saw a list of missed calls from Sarah, and five answerphone messages.

He rang back, wondering what on earth the problem could be. It was 5 pm.

'Where the bloody hell are you?' Sarah yelled at him. 'And where's Emily?'

'What do you mean?' he replied. 'I'm at this conference in Hull.'

'What? But you were meant to pick her up from school this afternoon,' Sarah said.

'No . . . I wasn't . . .' Tom stuttered. 'Wait, I'll come home now. I'll be there in three hours.'

They talked for most of the journey back, Tom weaving in and out of the traffic, two speed cameras flashing him on the M1.

Sarah had gone round to the school and checked and Miss Hargreaves (her best friend, Susan) had said that Tom had collected Emily at around three o'clock. Arguments ensued and finally Tom put the phone down on Sarah in case he had an accident.

He finally got in at about 9 pm to find two police officers, and Susan Hargreaves, in their front room.

Susan seemed to need more calming down than Sarah. She was distraught and kept breaking down in tears. Questions came from all possible angles and the police were making many notes.

Something terrible struck Tom as Susan explained Emily's behaviour as though it had been waiting for him somehow.

'Well, she seemed so preoccupied throughout the whole morning,' she said, cautiously. 'I asked her what was wrong and she said she hoped the new windows and door would be fixed in time for her to play later.

'I asked if you were having new double glazing fitted and she said no. She said that Mr Mann was putting in new windows and a door to your seaside house so you could all look out at the waves. I assumed you'd bought a holiday cottage and was going to ask Sarah about it when we were going to the concert on Friday.'

Tom looked at Sarah but she did not look back, she just stared straight at the empty blackness of the television screen and hugged Susan as she began another round of sobbing.

Everything began to fall apart.

Lines of enquiry were begun. Alibis were checked. Hours and hours of questioning and requestioning as the investigating officers tried to trip them up and find any weakness in their statements. Amidst it all Sarah and Tom were increasingly perplexed. Sarah blamed Tom for never telling her he was going away, and for forgetting it was his turn to pick Emily up.

The real horror began early the following week when Tom was called into the police station to watch the CCTV footage. Sarah had also been asked to come along but they were asked to view it separately.

The officer assigned to the case, Detective Sergeant Lyle, asked Tom to look at the footage and see whether he could notice anyone on the edges of the film that he recognised, or seemed even vaguely familiar.

Tom watched the black and white silent footage. Miss Hargreaves tidied her classroom and the last few children waited in the reading area for their parents. Emily played happily with them and seemed to chat on occasion with Susan, who turned then and greeted someone slightly off camera. Emily turned and ran to whoever it was. The detective was watching Tom carefully.

After a short exchange they were gone. The view changed to a camera in the main corridor. Emily was alone and heading for the doors. There was nobody else to be seen. As Emily walked excitedly to the doors she seemed, to Tom, to be talking to someone, turning her head up and nodding in the way she would normally, pouring out the excitement of the day to her mother or father. But there was nobody there. Nobody at all.

The scene cut to the playground, and then the front gates. Other parents were milling around, doing up coats, packing up bags—the usual scene. Emily walked along, arm in the air, and then she was gone from shot.

Tom asked to view it all again. The detective played it again; and again; and again.

'Do you see how she's walking,' Tom said. 'She's holding someone's hand.'

The detective played the tape again and looked puzzled.

'Do you recognise *anyone else*, Mr Flanagan?' he asked. 'Or do you see *anyone* you do not recognise as a member of school staff, or another parent?'

'It looks as though she's holding someone's hand as she leaves the building,' Tom muttered to himself.

'Look, I know the footage is poor . . .' the detective said.

'Have you been looking into this *Mr Mann*, and the things that Susan said about?' Tom asked, urgently.

'We've been looking at everything, Mr Flanagan, *everything*,' he said. 'It's difficult because we have a sworn statement from Miss Hargreaves that you picked Emily up—corroborated by the children in the classroom, and two parents in the playground. But we have statements from all those you were working with at this conference in Hull that you were nearly two hundred miles away at the time. That leaves us in a very tricky position, especially with no other leads at the moment.'

'Can I go now?' Tom asked.

The detective nodded.

On the drive home Tom kept on about how Emily seemed to be talking to someone, and holding their hand. Sarah said she hadn't really noticed Emily's hand raised in the footage; all she could think of was what she must have been thinking of and where on earth she was now—but she kept that to herself, and it would haunt her.

As the desperate days crawled by into weeks, and the weeks crumbled into months, Tom and Sarah saw less of each other at home, and when they were there together they seldom spoke.

Susan Hargreaves had a nervous breakdown as the guilt and remorse overwhelmed her. Sarah saw her often, they seemed to offer each other some strange consolation.

The divorce came through about a year later, among the hollow grief of the anniversary of Emily's disappearance. The house was sold by Christmas and Sarah and David moved in with her parents in Manchester.

Tom stumbled on for six months, going through the motions of his job, renting a little flat in Aylesbury. But his thoughts returned constantly to Susan's words; to Mr Mann, the abandoned house, Emily's drawings, the boat trip and her sad, serious expression, and a terrible sense that without being there—in Polperro, without searching *there*, he would never feel that he had done all he could to solve the mystery of her vanishing.

With his share of the money from the house, and the few investments remaining to him he managed to secure a bedsit in Looe, from where he could try to set his mind to rest.

⁊

This place is strange; the craggy coasts and windy roads; the little, half-deserted villages and lonely houses that grow, fungus-like from the sides of hills. The daylight is so bright and vivid, as though it actually shed colour into things rather than simply illuminated what lay within. And the nights are so dark, as though it sucked the daytime bounty back out in some unending cosmic trade.

The stars—the billions and billions and billions of galaxies, each with their billions and billions of suns, planets and moons

—sparkle with a brightness you cannot find anywhere else in the country. They mock us with their flickering hope of life—that somewhere out *there*, there are *others*, billions and billions of *others*; all dying; all losing; all crying; all laughing at the pointless madness of the universe.

Just before Tom moved here they pulled the old cliff house down. It was hazardous, apparently. Some local boys had tried to get in and one broke his arm on the back door they'd jemmied open after smashing out some of the bricks in front of it. It was a practical response to a practical problem; it would have collapsed into the sea anyway, eventually. For Tom, and for Tom alone, it answered a question—a terrible, unbearable question—with another question.

I see him walk by this crumbling cliff every morning, and every evening, searching for his answer, wandering by the place I have lingered in for what seems like an eternity; as I too search—for other homes, and other people, that I might dwell within.

Every house has a door and *every* door has a key; *every* key unlocks another secret, and once you are *in* be very sure you can get *out*.

AFTERWORD

AFTERWORD
Helen Marshall

'I must see! Tonight the moon begins to wane. I have a spade and shall shortly make another visit to Dieter to see what final teachings he has for me. Soon I shall know the truth of paradise or abide forever in hell.'

One pound of the flesh of the departed, saltpetre, herbs and spices, enough grave clothes to wrap the flesh to cure. What shall we see when we look beyond the threshold? Memories, joys, sorrows, love gone by, and perhaps, hatred too—and then something further, unseen in the text: the truth of paradise.

This is the domain of the weird. 'The oldest and strongest emotion of mankind is fear,' wrote H.P. Lovecraft in his seminal essay, *Supernatural Horror in Literature,* 'and the oldest and strongest kind of fear is fear of the unknown.' Yet it isn't the fear of the unknown which drives the stories within the book we're holding. The characters are enticed and besotted, lured, attracted, enchanted, captivated—but they are seldom afraid. Perhaps we fear for them, but don't we also wonder what we will find? The answer tantalises. We turn the page and there is another story, another set of yearnings. If we're honest we're a touch disappointed. How much do we wish we could share that forbidden knowledge?

Blood

We put down the book and stare at our hands. We find it strange to see them now, the knuckles bulging beneath the skin.

Perhaps they are older than we remembered them to be. Often when we see our hands we remember them as they were when we were children. Soft hands, newly formed. Bitten fingernails, fewer lines—the paleness (or darkness) of the hairs.

We wonder what our hands will look like when we are dead. What burial clothes would our bodies be wrapped in? How much would it take for our own bodies to cure? Who would eat of us, if only to see paradise? Or to remember the things we saw and loved and forgot?

We turn to our loved ones. They are reading next to us, as they often do. We get tired sooner than we used to while they seem indefatigable. We close our eyes for a moment but their light is too bright. We roll away. Then their hand touches our shoulder and we smile, grateful for their presence. We don't look at their hand. We know their hand better than we know our own: the nails, the skin, the scarring and callouses.

Do we know what lies beneath their skin? We dream it. But perhaps nothing at all is there.

Smoke

We are wondering now about where we'll go when we close our eyes. We aren't accustomed to dreaming anymore. When we were younger our dreams were very vivid. Our loved ones dream better than us. They sleep easily and in the morning they have nonsensical stories. We can see the logic of them, once so urgent, draining away as they are related. They never tell us their full dreams. They never can.

We wonder who we are when they dream about us. They often tell us we're present, in their dreams. But whenever we dream and they appear, they are not *them*. It's a trick of the sleeping mind. We feel a vivid sense of recognition but if we were to assemble the parts we know they wouldn't correlate. Our loved ones have brown hair, or blond, are fatter, shorter, better looking, lacking that cleft jaw or the dimple in the cheek.

But in the moment of dreaming we believe it is *them* and we speak to *them* and sometimes we kiss *them*. Sometimes we are happy when we're dreaming. Why? Our dreams are terrible! There's always some murder going on, some attempt at escape. The most vivid dream we recall is the knowledge that we can fly if we want to—if we need to. But we can only fly as high as a man stands, which isn't high at all, and only if we tell no one about our power. We never want to fly. We are happier knowing we *could* fly.

But why is it so disappointing then when we wake up? Our loved ones are beside us. So is the book, as we left it—dog-eared, a habit our loved ones hate. Nothing here would we wish to escape. We've made a life that keeps us happy, or happy enough. We love it when we wake five minutes before the alarm clock, and it's still dark—blue light through the window and our loved ones sleeping beside us. We can see their faces as they sleep, soft-edged, when they are them but not *them*—the people they will be later in the day.

There shouldn't be any disappointment, should there?

Vinegar

We don't always like hearing their dreams. Dreams are supposed to be expressions of wild inner desire and it's slightly off-putting in a relationship such as ours to have such elaborate fantasies. When we hear their stories we don't know how to respond. We can't unmake gravity or melt solid objects or freeze hearing, speaking, or cause one's teeth to fall out. We have only our hands and what our hands can do, which is largely what any set of hands can do. So why do they look at us like that? Like they want to ask us a question?

We think it would be easier if we could assemble the ingredients and make them a meal of ourselves in answer. Venison loin and brine, coriander seed, the sweat of our body. We've given them sweat enough, haven't we? If they can't answer their questions of us now, on their own, will they ever be able to? Do we want them to? They'd ask us, perhaps, if we could fly—and we would be bound to tell them. We've made a promise not to lie to one another. If they asked we would answer, and in answering the answer would change and we would give up our power forever. We are afraid of this. We make contingencies plans, prepare answers that are diversions rather than lies. We'd tell them we have no wish to fly so it doesn't even matter if we could or not. We'd tell them they don't need to worry. Gravity is still as strong, here, as it ever was.

And they might look relieved at this. They might take our hand in theirs and bring it to their lips. They might clip our nails with their teeth and swallow the fragments whole. The fingernail continues to grow when you're dead. We have read that. We would let our loved ones do this. It's another kind of asking but this would cost us nothing. We could tell them with our body, but not with our words. And the body isn't ours anyway, is it? We can't control our bodies perfectly. They bleed and secrete and breathe and we allow it to happen, because we must, but they are autonomous. As we are autonomous. Our bodies do all sorts of things we aren't privy to.

But our loved ones would never ask us for a secret we were not prepared to give them. Which is why we love them.

Ashes

The day passes. We settle in again for the night. Old rituals: the locking of the door, stripping down, climbing under the covers and taking the book in hand. We begin at the next page and we stumble over it at first because the words aren't what we expected them to be. We're very tired, as we always are this time of night. So tired we can't remember properly what came before. We flick back through the preceding chapter and find ourselves confused because the book is finished. We have read its entirety. When? We aren't sure, only everything before is familiar and there is nothing after. The back of the book.

Our loved ones are sleeping beside us, and so we must have been reading for a long time. Look, there are streaks of white in the hair, a stern bit of silver. Delicate wrinkles. They twitch for a moment and make a sound. Apples, plums, a large stem of ginger, a lock freshly cut, larva and ashes. We remember the recipe. We wish it were as easy as that to traverse their dreams. That is the danger of looking, isn't it? We know that our loved ones are strangers in their own ways, just as we are strangers to them. We could hold the pillow over their mouths if we wanted to. Or we could gently slip a plastic bag around their heads. When their eyes flashed open we expect we would see a different person.

We imagine for a moment their flesh unbundled from their spirit. Ours to traverse and ransack as we wish, like rummaging through a neighbour's house when they've given us the key. We take their hand in ours and stare at the fingernails which are carefully maintained, a touch too long perhaps. In need of trimming.

But we will not do it. We take up the book again. How long have we been reading? We don't remember starting it. We don't remember how it came to us. It must have been a gift from our loved ones who like to give us presents like this. We turn to the first story, 'Blood and Smoke, Vinegar and Ashes'. There are other preserves than these, we know.

We begin again.

> 'There are many curious routes to insight; and as many, often more banal, routes to ruin . . .'

Publication History

'Our Second Home', 'The Magician, or, Crab Lines', 'The Rocking Horse', 'The Pedagogue, or, They Muttered', 'Ophelia', 'Mizpah', and 'A Species of the Dead' are original to this publication

'But They Withered All' in *The Book of Flowers*, ed. Mark Beech, Egaeus Press, 2019

'Blood and Smoke, Vinegar and Ashes' in *The Silent Garden: A Journal of Esoteric Fabulism, Volume 1*, 2018

'Doreen' in *The Scarlet Soul: Stories for Dorian Gray*, ed. Mark Valentine, Swan River Press, 2017

'Golden in the Mercy of His Means' originally appeared as 'The English House' in *Darkly Haunting*, ed. Robert Morgan, Sarob Press, 2017

'Four Windows and a Door' in *Terror Tales of Cornwall*, ed. Paul Finch, Telos Publishing, 2017

Conflagration, Ex Occidente Press, 2016

'We Don't Want for Company' in *The Ghosts & Scholars Book of Shadows Volume Three*, ed. Rosemary Pardoe, Sarob Press, 2016

'Oh, Pretty Polly' originally appeared in 'Memorabilia' in *The Transfiguration of Mister Punch: A Triptych*, Egaeus Press, 2013

295

Acknowledgements

Thanks to Ray and Rosalie at Tartarus Press for their interest in my work, and the courage to include 'Conflagration'. Peter Holman, with the Introduction, and Helen Marshall, with the Afterword, have produced creative and thoughtful works, so in keeping with the mood of the collection—I am deeply grateful to them both.

Thanks to the many friends who have offered advice, critical comment and good company over recent years, including Adam Nevill, Tim Jarvis, Paul Finch, Gary Budden, Marian Womack, Al Diniz, Nick and Erin Bullard, Jon Padgett, Mike Kelly, Richard Gavin, Catriona Shattuck, Acep Hale, Damian Murphy, Dan Ghetu, Robert Morgan, Rosemary Pardoe, Douglas Thompson, Jonas Plöger, Brian Showers, John Pelan, Nick Freeman, Samantha Beckett, Tom Newport, Adam Cantwell, Victoria Nelson, Eugene Thacker, Martin Ruf, Tobias Reckermann, Mark Beech and Mark Valentine. Please accept my apologies for any unintentional omissions.

To Peter Watt for his constant support over many years, and especially to Jen for putting up with me for so long, and for listening to all of the nonsense that plays around in my head. Finally, and far from least, to Sam and Alfie who gave me the keys to unlock wondrous playrooms, overflowing with playful pirates, fairy castles, and infinite, incredible imaginings.

17118041R00185